Mac knew that Washington was right. If he didn't get rid of Johnny right now, he was going to be stuck with him forever. But as he looked across the room at Johnny sitting quietly watching television, Mac knew that there was no way he could leave him. Johnny needed him. And maybe, Mac realized, he needed Johnny just as much.

Then Simon was forced into the picture. Together, the three men form the

TRIANGLE

TRIANGLE

TERI WHITE

CHARTER
NEW YORK

A Division of Charter Communications Inc.
A GROSSET & DUNLAP COMPANY
51 Madison Avenue
New York, New York 10010

An Ace Charter Original

First Ace Charter Printing May, 1982
Published simultaneously in Canada
Manufactured in the United States of America

2 4 6 8 0 9 7 5 3 1

THIS BOOK IS FOR "MOM"
AND ALL THE BELIEVERS

And how am I to face the odds
Of man's bedevilment and God's
I, a stranger and afraid
In a world I never made.

A.E. HOUSEMAN

TRIANGLE

-PROLOGUE-

The baby blue BMW glided almost silently through the alley, stopping finally behind a modest brick apartment building. A moment later the car door opened and Johnny slid out of the passenger seat. He pushed the door gently and it closed with a muffled thud. The man behind the wheel lit a cigarette and slid down in the seat a little.

Johnny walked with long strides toward the building, his soft-soled shoes making no sound against the brick surface. The morning felt clean, somehow filled with newness after last night's rain. It was Johnny's favorite kind of day, and he took a couple of deep, satisfying breaths, smiling with quiet pleasure as he moved.

When he reached the back door of the apartment building, he paused, taking a narrow length of steel from his pocket. It took exactly five point six seconds for the lock to click open beneath his slender fingers. Without turning, he lifted one hand in a V-for-Victory gesture over his shoulder.

The door opened at his touch and he slipped into the dim coolness of the hallway. As expected, it was quiet. Sunday was the best time to work. Somehow, no one ever seemed to anticipate anything unpleasant happening as he digested his eggs and comic papers.

Johnny knew exactly where he was going. Nothing was ever left to chance during these operations, and he had complete faith in the plan as it had been explained to him. Apartment eleven was at the far end of the hallway and Johnny didn't even pause until he was standing directly in front of the door. He knocked firmly with his left hand, at the same time reaching his right inside the worn corduroy sport coat to grasp the gun that hung at his side. The eight-inch barreled piece of blue steel rested easily in his grip as he waited patiently for a response to his knock.

The door opened finally and Papagallos stood there smiling, a plump grey-haired man wearing a red silk robe and black patent slippers. The smile lost a little of its brightness as he realized that this visitor was not whom he had expected to find on his threshold this particular Sabbath morning. His expression, however, remained genial. Johnny often noticed that same reaction on other faces. People just seemed to trust him on sight, even people like Papagallos, who had reason to fear every stranger at the door.

One day, after Johnny had given a great deal of thought to the whole matter, but was still unable to figure out why everyone seemed to trust him so implicitly, he went to Mac for an explanation. Mac, who usually had all the answers, only shrugged. "You just have a nice face," he said absently. That wasn't much of an answer, but Mac seemed satisfied, so Johnny accepted it.

Papagallos obviously felt no fear, no sudden pang of apprehension. No premonition. His apparently somewhat near-sighted gaze swept over the tall blond man in the doorway, seeing the battered running shoes, the much-faded, too-tight Levis, the bright yellow T-shirt topped by the brown cord jacket. And then he noticed the gun, but by then it was too late, because the bullet was already on its way toward him.

The jacketed hollow point slug collided with Papagallos' forehead. Blood, fragments of bone, and lumpy pieces of grey brain matter splattered against the seagreen brocaded wallpaper of the foyer as Papagallos, still smiling, slid to the floor.

It was not until then that Johnny saw the other man inside the room and the sight momentarily confused him. Papagallos was supposed to have been alone for at least another hour. The confusion didn't last long, however. His instructions had been drilled into him time after time. No witnesses. A finger pressed against the trigger once more, the silenced gun popped, and the gangly redhead flew back against the chair, blood gushing from his chest.

Carefully avoiding Papagallos' body, Johnny reached in to pull the door closed, wiping the polished brass knob with the sleeve of his jacket. He tucked the gun back into his holster before walking swiftly, but calmly, back down the hall.

Emerging into the sunshine and fresh air again, he paused, giving a sigh as light as the gentle spring breeze, then moved briskly back to the car. Mac already had the engine purring softly. "Everything go okay?" he asked, as always.

Johnny ignored the question, resting back against the seat, his eyes closed. The car pulled out of the alley, slipping neatly into the flow of traffic.

For nearly five minutes, the two men rode in silence. Finally Johnny straightened. He took off his tinted aviator glasses and began to clean them with a crumpled tissue. "Do you know what I'd like?" he asked dreamily.

Mac's grip on the steering wheel relaxed. "What?"

"A strawberry ice cream cone." Johnny put the glasses back on, settling them precisely on his nose, and peered at Mac. "Could I get one, please?"

"Sure, if we can find a place open this early."

Johnny smiled.

It took a little searching, but they managed finally to locate a small dairy store with an OPEN sign stuck in the front window. Mac pulled the car into the parking lot and stopped. "Strawberry, you said, right?"

"Yeah. Two scoops."

"Coming right up." Mac got out of the car and walked into the grimy little store, his hand-tooled western boots making sharp clicking noises on the linoleum floor.

There was no one in the place except a pimple-faced teenage clerk, who gave Mac a look of complete boredom. "Yeah?" he said around a wad of gum.

"Double dip of strawberry."

"Cup cone or sugar?"

"Ah, sugar," Mac said absently, never able to remember which kind Johnny preferred. He turned around to stare through the dirt-streaked window. Sunlight reflected off the hand-polished finish of the BMW. Johnny sat slumped in the seat, his glasses catching rays of the golden light, making it look as if he had a bright halo around his head.

The sight bemused Mac and the clerk spoke twice before he really heard him. "Huh?"

"Sixty cents, mister," the kid repeated wearily.

He tossed some coins down onto the sticky counter and took the cone carefully, grabbing a couple of napkins from the dispenser at the same time.

Johnny greeted his return with another smile, reaching out to take the cone. "Thank you," he said.

Mac only grunted a reply as he got behind the wheel again and headed the car back toward the motel. Johnny was quiet during the ride, eating the ice cream with studied concentration.

It took only fifteen minutes for them to reach the Welcome Inn. Their room was undoubtedly a depressing place to inhabit, with walls that were painted an indeterminate color somewhere between brown and grey, and painfully utilitarian furnishings, but the type was so familiar that neither one of them even noticed the quality of their surroundings anymore.

Mac stood at the window, watching the traffic on the busy street just beyond, and listening to the crescendo of the shower running in the bathroom. Behind him, the fuzzy black-and-white TV flickered soundlessly as a white-haired video preacher exhorted the masses to spiritual awakening. Mac smoked three cigarettes in a row as he waited for the shower to go off.

Johnny came out finally, barefooted and shirtless, his Levis sporting damp patches, his face flushed. "Someday you're going to boil yourself alive," Mac said sourly. Johnny only shrugged, turning up the volume on the TV.

". . . and Jesus Christ wants you to accept His offer of eternal life."

Mac turned to stare at the screen. "Why do you listen to that crap?"

"*Bonanza* comes on after," Johnny replied. "Little Joe might get hung." He sat down on the edge of the bed and moved his shoulders slightly. Mac crushed out his just-lit fourth cigarette and came over. Using both hands, he began to massage the tense muscles in Johnny's neck and shoulders. "So?" he said shortly. "What's the matter?"

"There was somebody with him," Johnny said after a moment.

Mac's hands paused briefly in their movements, then resumed the massage. "Yeah?"

Johnny nodded. "A skinny redheaded guy. You told me Papagallos would be by himself." It was an accusation.

"Sorry." Mac never wasted much time regretting what couldn't be helped. "So?"

"I shot him."

Mac's fingers moved efficiently through still-damp blond curls clinging to the back of Johnny's neck. "Well, you had to."

"Yeah, I know. I know." Johnny's voice sounded old and very tired. He moved away from the massage abruptly and stretched out on the chenille bedspread, covering his eyes with one arm.

Mac watched him for a moment, then picked up a faded green windbreaker and pulled it on. "I'm going out," he said. "I probably won't be gone long." He waited for a response, but when there was none, he left the room, shutting the door carefully behind himself.

BOOK

I

-ONE-

They had been humping through the bush for three days now, and nobody really knew why. In fact, no one was even sure just where the hell they were. Mac just kept them moving, following a map that must have been drawn by an idiot with one thumb up his ass. He figured that the simple momentum of their journey would sooner or later provide a motive for the trip.

Needing to piss, Mac stepped off the path and let the line of men continue to move past him. As he sprayed the nearby plants, his mind was trying to dredge up the title of an old song made famous by Nat King Cole. Something he used to play all the time on the jukebox in the Hi-Time Cafe back in Okie City. Years ago. Must have played that damned song two thousand times, he thought, zipping his trousers. Why can't I remember the fucking title? He wiped his hand on the seat of his trousers. Wonder if maybe I'm losing my mind?

It wasn't the first time that question had presented itself.

The last man had gone by him. What would happen, he mused, if he just started walking the other way? Maybe it was time he just checked out of this whole fucking mess. Nobody told him there was going to be a war when he joined the goddamned army. It wasn't fair. Somebody had changed the rules on him.

He stepped back onto the trail and found himself walking next to Crazy George. George was an old man of nineteen. His eyes looked at least a hundred years old, though he hadn't yet been able to raise a moustache. The soft line of down across his upper lip just made him look as if he'd been drinking chocolate milk. "Hey, Lieutenant," he said, "where we going anyway?"

"Beats the hell out of me, George," he said lightly.

"Shit. Well, I hope we get there soon."

"Why?"

" 'Cause I like to know where the hell I'm at."

Crazy George made him nervous, ever since the night they'd caught him trying to rig a grenade to the door of the officers' latrine. Mac nodded and smiled, moving a little faster until he caught up with Washington, his sergeant. Washington was a good man, and he even seemed almost sane.

The smell hit them first.

The acrid, too-familiar odor of gunfire and smoke floated across the heavy humid air, making their noses itch. Everybody tensed. Mac rubbed his burning eyes with the back of one hand, trying to ignore the creepy, crawly sensation beginning to flicker across his groin.

There was a small rise edging the city of Tan Pret, and they moved over it cautiously, staring down into what had to be a corner of hell. "Jeesus," someone said aloud.

Even from where they stood, the bodies were clearly visible—women, children, old men, the fallen figures making little patches of color against the smoldering brown earth.

The only signs of life in the devastated village came from the American troops walking through the remains. As Mac and his men moved down the rise toward them, one of the soldiers looked up. His face was red; his eyes glittered. "Spies," he said loudly enough for them to hear. "All of them were spies. Had to root them out . . . had to. . . ." His voice trailed off.

Mac could only stare.

It came to him suddenly. *Mona Lisa.* That was the name of the goddamned song.

He didn't know what the hell he was supposed to do, so he decided not to do anything at all, at least for the moment. Leaving Wash to deploy some men around the perimeter of the village, Mac just walked away from it all. He walked as far as a large boulder that rested on the eastern edge of Tan Pret. Resting his automatic on the ground, he perched on the rock and closed his eyes.

. . . .*Mona Lisa, Mona Lisa, men have named you. . . .*

Now he couldn't get the damned song out of his mind. Made him think about the apple pie they used to serve at the old Hi-Time. With homemade vanilla ice cream plunked on top. Crust real crisp, with cinnamon sprinkled on.

But that was before he joined the army and how was he to know that fifteen years later he'd be sitting in the middle of a frigging jungle gagging from the stink of death. The recruiter promised him he could become an auto mechanic.

. . . .*or is this the way you hide a broken heart*. . . .

This was a helluva fucked-up mess. How come it all had to fall into his lap anyway? And what the devil should he do now?

"What a helluva fucked-up mess." He said the words aloud that time. It was then that he opened his eyes and realized that he wasn't alone. He turned wearily, not ready yet to give an order, to take charge.

The unwelcome intruder was a stranger. Tall and slender, he had shaggy blond hair that stuck out from beneath his helmet and blue eyes that were as dead as Tan Pret itself. "Yeah?" Mac grunted, thinking that the kid looked like a choirboy in search of a congregation. Except for the empty eyes. "What?"

There was no answer. The man kept staring at him.

"What's your name, Sergeant?" When there was still no reply, Mac reached out and took hold of the guy's dogtags. The stranger flinched away, as if he expected to be struck. "Take it easy, buddy. I only want to find out who you are. Griffith, John Paul." He released the tags.

Griffith suddenly opened his hands, letting the M-16 fall to the ground. He stared at the weapon for a long time, as if he'd never seen it before, as if it had nothing at all to do with him.

"Griffith?" Belatedly, Mac realized that the man was suffering from some kind of shock. Shit, it was no wonder. He slid from the boulder and stood in front of the blank gaze. "Hey, man, can you hear me?" There wasn't even a flicker of response. Mac sighed. Great. A real whacko. Just what they

needed at a time like this. Maybe he should go find
Crazy George; the two of them could probably
have a great conversation.

He turned away, looking back across the village.
There must be something to be done here, although
only God knew what it was. He felt a light but ur-
gent tugging at his sleeve and glanced around.
Griffith was holding on to him. "It's all right,"
Mac said absently. "I'm not going anywhere."
There was no change in Griffith's expression, but
his hand slipped away from Mac's arm.

Washington appeared. "Some bitchin' thing,
massa."

"Yeah. And I don't know what the hell I'm supposed to do about it."

"Better you than me." Washington gestured.
"Who's the zombie?"

Mac shrugged. "One of them, I guess. A real
spaceman." He sighed, rubbing a hand across his
face. "Well, we better get something going here,
right? See if you can find the bastard in charge."

Washington gave a mock salute and walked
away.

Mac sat on the rock again. "You a Nat King
Cole fan, by any chance?" he asked. "No, guess
not. Probably too young, right? Hell, when I joined
this man's army you were—" He did a little mental
calculation from the birthdate on the dogtags.
"—twelve. Christ, this is a frigging children's
crusade." Griffith wasn't a child, of course. He was
twenty-seven. Mac shrugged. "I could listen to that
man sing for hours." He leaned forward a little.
"Hey, John? Anything getting through to you? Are
you in there?"

Nothing.

"Hell. Sit down, dummy." Surprisingly, Griffith

sank down onto the rock. Mac figured that was a step in the right direction. "Hi. Welcome to my rock. You may not talk much, but you take orders real fine, don't you? That's an outstanding quality in a soldier." Mac had the fleeting thought that it didn't say much for his own mental state that he would sit and talk to a zombie, but what the hell. "How do you feel about apple pie, John?"

The lieutenant in charge, a hard-faced man named Delgado, managed to be both belligerent and non-communicative when he finally appeared. They talked about what had happened, or what Delgado claimed had happened, or maybe what he'd dreamed had happened, but it all added up to nothing. Finally, in disgust, he sent Delgado off to organize his men to dig some trenches into which the late citizens of Tan Pret could be dumped. Mustn't litter up the country, Mac thought.

He turned back to Griffith, who sat very still, both hands folded neatly in his lap, his young face guileless. "I have to go talk to Wash," Mac said slowly and distinctly, as if he were speaking to a backward child. "You just sit tight, okay? I'll be right back." Griffith didn't acknowledge his words, but neither did he try to keep him from going.

Washington was supervising the digging of a shallow trench. "Tote that barge, lift that bale," he murmured as Mac joined him.

"How long is this gonna take?"

"Couple hours, I guess." They watched the digging for several moments. "What happens after that?"

"I don't know." Mac rubbed the bridge of his nose. "Shit." He kicked at a lump of brown earth, sending it flying through the air.

A moment later, almost as if in perverse response to his action, the world began to explode around them. From somewhere beyond the trees an artillery barrage descended upon the already dead village. The grave diggers scattered, some heading for the trees and the rest leaping into the unfinished trench in a desperate search for cover.

Mac turned quickly and peered through the smoke and mass confusion. Griffith was sitting where he'd left him, his hands still folded, his apparently unseeing eyes fixed on Mac. He seemed unaware of the flaming apocalypse around him. "Jesus H. Christ," Mac whispered, beginning a broken field run across the space between them.

The shelling ended as suddenly as it had begun.

He reached the boulder, aware that dark figures were entering the village. The Americans were still scattering in all directions. He knew that he should have done something, given an order, taken charge, but all he wanted to do was run. He grabbed his rifle with one hand and Griffith's arm with the other. "Move it, dummy!" he shouted.

Mac didn't know or care what was happening behind them. He only knew that they had to get away. It wasn't only the enemy he was scared of; it was the village of Tan Pret and all its horrifying implications.

So they ran.

-TWO-

For years after, Mac would dream about the days following Tan Pret. He would never be able to forget wandering through that damned jungle, sweating, stinking, tired to the point of tears, his every step through that purgatory dogged by a mute shadow.

He didn't know where they were, didn't know which way they should go; he didn't know a god-damned thing, except that he was going to lose whatever little bit of his sanity remained unless something happened soon. He was heartily sick of the sound of his own voice and sick of playing nursemaid to Griffith.

As night approached on the third day of their odyssey, they both collapsed beneath the vines and branches of a fallen tree. "Looks like home for the night, John. Okay with you?"

Griffith smiled. It was the same smile he used when Mac grunted a morning greeting, or when they shared a melted chocolate bar from Mac's pack. He smiled and he smiled, but he never said a word.

Mac dug into his pack and found the last can of fruit cocktail. He opened it and wiped the spoon on

16

the edge of his shirt. "Better enjoy, buddy-boy," he said. "Might be the last food we see for a while. Maybe you'd like to feed yourself this time?"

But Griffith just sat there. Mac sighed and lifted some fruit onto the spoon. "Open your mouth," he said flatly. "Or I'll stick the fucking garbage in your ear."

The blond's mouth opened obediently, and the spoon slippd in. They alternated bites until nothing was left in the can except the sweet syrup, which he irritably fed to Griffith. After only three days, his already slender face was etched into sharp lines. Beneath the foggy blue eyes, his cheekbones were painfully prominent.

Mac reached into the pack again and took out the bottle of cheap scotch. It was almost empty. He dumped the rest of the pale amber liquid into his canteen and pressed it into Griffith's hand. "Drink some," he ordered absently. Griffith drank and, without prompting, handed the cup back. Mac rewarded that unexpected burst of initiative with the weary imitation of a smile. "Good boy. Maybe I can teach you some more tricks. You could probably roll over and play dead real good."

Mac downed the rest of the scotch in one gulp. "So who do you like in the World Series, kid?" he said.

Griffith smiled.

It was like being trapped with a recalcitrant child, and Mac often felt like a parent driven to the end of his patience, wanting to slap the cheerfully blank face into some kind of realization. But he fought for self-control. "We better get some sleep," he said.

Mac spent some time trying to figure out how

many new insect bites his body had acquired, but
then realized that he didn't give a damn anymore.
He finally fell asleep listening to the soft sound of
Griffith's breathing.

It was very dark when he woke up. The pale
moonlight seemed much too fragile to penetrate
the blackness in which they were enveloped. Griffith slept like a child, curled on one side, his hand
stretched toward Mac, almost touching him.

Mac needed to piss. He got up slowly and moved
out of their hiding place, trying to stretch his
cramped muscles. His flesh stank of sweat and Tan
Pret. Of death.

He peed, then lit a cigarette and walked a few
more feet away, not ready yet to try sleeping again.
The situation they had here was going to get
critical before much longer. At least, by the time he
got back he'd have some money waiting. This time,
he wasn't going to blow it all in one of Wash's
damned poker games. Hell, no, he'd go into Saigon
and treat himself to a steak, some booze, a good
screw. Yeah.

"Mac!"

A cry of naked, nearly animalistic terror rang
through the heavy humid night, and Mac jumped,
burning his cupped hand against the glowing
cigarette. "Shit," he swore in startled reaction to
both the cry and the burn.

"Mac!"

It was Griffith, of course, but the sudden sound
of another human voice was as frightening as the
previous silence had been. Mac dropped the rest of
the cigarette, crushing it under his heel, then stumbled back through the tall grass to the place where

Griffith had been sleeping peacefully a few minutes earlier.

He was unmistakably awake now, crouching like a caged animal, both arms wrapped around his legs. Even in the washed-out moonlight the terror on his face was clearly visible. His head jerked around as Mac crashed into their refuge. "Mac," he said again, this time the word a hoarse sob. He scrabbled across the distance between them, grabbing Mac's legs. "I thought you were gone. You said if I couldn't keep up, you'd leave me and I thought you did; I thought you left me." The words came in a rush, as if he'd had them bottled up for a long time and somebody had just pulled out the cork. He stopped finally, taking deep gulps of air.

Mac sank down, gripping the trembling man by both arms. "Hey, you're talking. That's good, kid, real good."

"I woke up and you weren't here, Mac."

"I just went to taking a fucking leak, Johnny, that's all. Hell, you think I'd just *go*?"

Johnny seemed to be calming a little, but his hands still clutched convulsively at Mac, shaking fingers seeking a firm hold. "I'm sorry," he said. "I'm sorry. I didn't mean to be bad. Please, don't be mad."

Mac didn't know what to do. He wrapped both arms around Griffith and just held on. "It's okay, Johnny," he said. "Don't worry."

"Something terrible happened, but I don't remember what it was. I can't remember, Mac. I just remember you and me running."

"It doesn't matter. Go to sleep, kid."

"Okay." Johnny twisted his fingers in Mac's

shirt. "But you won't go away, will you?" The eyes were intense, unrelenting.

"No, I'm not going anywhere," Mac promised.

They didn't talk anymore. Mac just sat there, rocking back and forth, humming *Mona Lisa*. After a long time, the tense body relaxed against him and the ragged breathing steadied. Mac shifted slightly, untangling the slender fingers from their death grip, and rested the sleeping man on the ground. Stretching out next to him, Mac spent the rest of the night staring through the branches at the sky.

-THREE-

It was two days later when they stumbled across the Marine patrol. Mac was so worn out by then, so exhausted physically and mentally, that he just let someone else take over. Johnny, who'd spent the time since he'd started talking rambling on in great detail about his life, seemed to creep back into a shell of silence with others around.

With no time lost, they were shuffled from the Marine camp onto a truck for Saigon. It was a long, hot, bumpy ride. Johnny spent most of the time huddled in one corner, staring with disconcerting intensity at Mac.

"Hey," he said at last.

Mac lowered the beer he was drinking and looked at him.

"What's going to happen when we get to Saigon?" Johnny's words echoed hollowly in the truck.

"Nothing. What the hell do you think is going to happen?" Mac felt angry, without knowing why, and he saw Johnny flinch away at the sharp tone. He took a deep breath. "Don't worry," he said more quietly, not even sure what the hell he meant. "Just don't worry about it, okay?"

21

Empty as the words were, they seemed to be accepted at face value. Johnny closed his eyes and in a few minutes was asleep.

Mac sighed and lit another cigarette.

What happened when they got to Saigon was a fast shuffle. Everyone wanted to keep Tan Pret and what had happened there quiet. *In the interest of national security.* Mac swallowed the bad taste it was leaving in his mouth, and agreed to abide by the official line. Johnny took no interest at all in the proceedings, apparently content to just sit back and let Mac handle it.

He managed to talk headquarters into a three-day pass for each of them, trying not to think of it as a payoff for his silence. At last, they escaped the major's office and relaxed in the hall.

Johnny wiped both palms on the front of his shirt. "Thanks," he said, the first word he'd uttered in several hours.

"What?"

"For the pass."

"Oh, hell. I just figured we could both use a little time to get our heads on straight." There was a moment of silence. Mac stared down the hall and out through the glass door, watching the people walking by in the sunshine. "Well," he said finally, "guess I better see about finding someplace to crash. Until I can collect my pay, I'm flat. Why don't we have a drink or something later, huh?"

Johnny didn't say anything.

Mac grinned and held out his hand, taking care not to meet the other man's eyes. "Quite a time we had, huh, kid?"

They shook. Johnny's hand felt cold to the

touch, but he returned the pressure of Mac's grip firmly. Mac broke the contact and turned, walking swiftly toward the door. Behind him there was silence.

He reached the door and put both hands on it to push. He paused. Damn, he thought, I'm not responsible for him. I saved his fucking ass out there and got him a pass on top of it. What the hell more can I do? It's not my business. I don't want it to be. The guy's a nutcase. Besides, I have enough trouble just looking out for myself.

Alexander McCarthy had spent thirty-five years avoiding involvement. If he'd learned nothing else growing up at Our Lady of Mercy Orphanage, he had learned that it didn't pay to get close to other people. If you made a friend, he'd get adopted and leave. The couple who took you home and offered the chance of a real family decided after three months that what they wanted was a baby, not a gangly eleven-year-old who swore like a sailor and played cards with deadly intensity. After things like that happened too often, he learned. Even with women he didn't like to take chances. Maybe that was why he never found the right girl to marry and make all his fantasies of a home and family real. If he paid for what he got, there was no chance of being disappointed. Of being hurt.

He had the army and he had his poker. That was all he needed. Goddamn, he especially didn't need this. Didn't want it.

He pushed the door open with a vicious shove, then let it swing closed again. Oh, hell. A couple days. What could it hurt? "Johnny?" he said without turning around.

"Yes, Mac?"

He turned then. John Paul Griffith was still standing where he'd left him, arms at his sides, his expression reminding Mac of the look he'd seen on the faces of gook refugees leaving bombed-out villages. "You want to come with me? We could hang around together for a day or two, I guess. If you want."

Johnny took a deep breath. "I-I—" He shrugged helplessly. "Yes. I'd like that."

"You have any money?" Mac asked, wondering glumly just what the hell he was getting into.

Johnny moved toward him, making Mac think of a kid on his way into a circus tent. "Yeah, sure, I have money," he said eagerly. "Plenty of money."

Somehow that figured.

They stepped out onto the sun-dappled sidewalk. Johnny was grinning now and there was something infectious about his mood. "Shit," Mac said generously. "Who the hell knows? We might even have a good time."

-FOUR-

The apartment was stifling hot. A small ceiling fan managed only to stir the heavy air around a little. The only sounds were the soft slap of card against card and the low murmur of an occasional comment by one of the players.

The game itself was a total mystery to Johnny—even Old Maid and Authors had been frowned upon in the strict fundamentalist household where he'd grown up. In the years since, it had not been the supposed evils of cards he had avoided, but the enforced society of others entailed in the games. He sat in one corner of the couch, drinking the cold beer someone had handed him, and watched as Mac played poker. The six men had been playing for hours, but Johnny wasn't bored. He was watching Mac, bemused and a little frightened by the changes that had come over him when he sat down to play. The differences were visible in the way Mac handled the deck, with quick, familiar fingers, and even more so in the eager, intense expression on his face. The jade eyes seemed to glow.

Johnny was glad he'd given Mac the stake money to get into the game. Mac had been reluctant, at first, to accept, but Johnny had convinced him. It

made Mac happy to be here and that pleased Johnny.

If he was also a little frightened by the intensity
on Mac's face, the almost ferocious determination
with which he seemed to approach each hand,
Johnny chose to ignore the fear.

As if aware of the scrutiny, Mac looked up from
his deal and met Johnny's gaze. Nothing in his face
changed, no hint of emotion that might be in-
tercepted by the other players. Despite that, Johnny felt sure that Mac was glad to have him there.
He shoved away his own apprehensions and took a
gulp of beer as he watched Mac finish the deal.

Mac came out of the game a winner. Not a big
winner, but at least not a loser, and that put him in
a good mood. He grinned at Johnny as they walked
back onto the street. "Let's celebrate my luck," he
suggested, shoving the small wad of bills away.

Johnny forgot to ask for his stake money back.

They went into a bar, where Mac ordered a bottle of cheap wine so they could toast his win. Johnny wasn't used to drinking and he didn't much like
the taste, but he didn't want to disappoint Mac, so
he drank whatever was poured. As the level of wine
in the bottle began to drop, the evening started to
grow fuzzy around the edges for Johnny. He was
never quite sure just when the two women joined
their party, or why. All he really knew was that a
small redhead had slipped into the booth next to
him, and that the conversation was all too hazy for
him to understand. He talked very little, never
quite sure what he was saying, and listened without
knowing what he was hearing.

Sometime later, he found himself walking along

the sidewalk with the redhead. Mac and the other girl were several feet ahead of them, and Johnny could see that they were talking, but the words were too soft for him to hear. The redhead had her hand in his and she was telling him about her job at the embassy. None of it made any sense.

When they reached the girls' apartment, someone opened more wine and someone else turned on the stereo. Mathis began to sing in soft, intimate tones. Johnny felt as if he were on a runaway roller coaster, speeding toward some dangerous place he didn't want to go.

Before very long Mac and the other girl disappeared through a door, and he was alone with Kathi. "With an 'i'," she'd said, giggling. Johnny wondered what the joke was. She brought her glass of wine and curled on the couch next to him. Beneath the thin cotton blouse she wore, he could see the dark circles of her nipples. When he moved away slightly, she laughed. "You're very shy, aren't you? Well, that's okay, because so am I. It's just that over here things seem to move so much faster. I guess we sort of live for today, because who knows about tomorrow?"

He thought her words sounded familiar, like lines out of The Late Show. Her hand undid the buttons on his shirt, then slid in across his chest. He shivered at the cool touch and her breath quickened in response. Without any conscious thought on his part, they were both suddenly stretched out on the sofa. He kissed her tentatively, without opening his mouth. She poked and probed with her tongue, until his lips parted. He could taste salt and wine and raspberry-flavored lip gloss.

"Oh, boy," she sighed. Her hand slipped down

to the zipper on his fly, and a moment later he could feel her fingers twisting in the soft hairs on his groin. "You wanna do it, John?" she breathed into his ear.

His hand was on her thigh; he felt the slender body turn, shifting, so that his fingers nestled in warm dampness. He started to shake, a black terror beginning deep inside, rushing headlong toward the surface, threatening to drown him in its waves. She was suddenly all over him, her mouth and her hands trying to devour him. She whispered as she moved, but the words were swallowed up by another voice, the echo of his father's words coming down the years to attack him again. Condemning him. Damning him. The heat that had built up inside him turned icy, and he was afraid. He looked toward the bedroom, praying for help, but the door stayed closed.

Her lips touched him again, possessing him. His arms stiffened abruptly and he pushed her away. She fell to the floor with a thud. "Hey," she said, shocked, "what the hell—?"

Without answering, he lurched up from the sofa and tried to find the door. He knocked over a table, sending a lamp crashing against the wall as he tried desperately to escape, fighting back the nausea rising in his throat.

"What's the matter with you? Are you crazy?" She was screaming at him.

He ignored her. Finally, blindly, his fingers found the knob and he plunged out into the hallway. The door slammed shut behind him and he felt safe at last. Wearily, he leaned against the wall, sliding to the floor.

He had no idea how much time passed before he

heard the door open again. Heavy footsteps came toward him, then Mac crouched down. "Johnny?"

He couldn't look up, afraid of what he might see in the other man's face.

"Hey, Johnny, you okay?"

He nodded.

"What's wrong?"

"Nothing," he said, his voice muffled against his arm.

"Kid, if nothing's wrong, why'd you run out like that? You scared Kathi half to death."

"I'm sorry." He lifted his head finally, looking up at the other man. Mac's shirt was on, but un-buttoned, and his craggy face was bewildered. "Tell her . . . I'm sorry."

Mac relaxed on the floor next to him. He lit two cigarettes and handed one to Johnny. "Can I ask you something, kid?" he said, a hand resting on Johnny's leg.

"Sure."

"Haven't you ever made it with a broad?"

He shook his head.

"You a fag?" There was no change in the voice, or in the grip of Mac's hand on his leg. " 'Cause if you are, Johnny, that's okay. I mean, to each his own, you know?"

"No," Johnny said wearily, "I'm not a fag, either. I just never did. Not with anybody."

"Hell." Mac glanced at the closed apartment door. "She was hot to trot, that's for damned sure. Probably all over you, huh?"

Johnny nodded again. "She was on top of me and I felt like . . . like I was suffocating. Like I was gonna disappear." He could feel himself trembling. "One time I knew this girl, can't remember her name, but she and I were kissing, that's all, I swear, just kissing, and my father caught us. He made me stand up in front of the whole church and tell everybody what I'd been doing. He was the minister. I had to tell them all." He gagged slightly. "My father said I could go to hell for that." He fought to hold back the tears that threatened to spill out. "I don't want to go to hell, Mac."

"You won't. That was a long time ago, Johnny. Your father can't do anything to you now. They're long dead and gone, right?" Mac grinned a little. "Hell, boy, I've been screwing around for years. You think I'm going to hell?"

"No."

"Well, then?" Mac sobered. "Hey, look, I know the first time is a little scary, but it'll be okay."

"You don't understand." Johnny wiped his sweaty face against one sleeve.

"So explain it to me."

Johnny stared into the green eyes, wanting to gauge the reaction to his words. "I don't want to do it. Why do I have to?"

Mac blinked twice. "Hey," he said finally, "you *don't* have to. It doesn't matter."

Johnny took a long drag on the unaccustomed cigarette, then coughed. "I must be some kind of freak." It was not quite a question.

"Hell, no, you're not. Some people just aren't interested. It's your business." Mac smiled again. "Shit, half the time fucking's overrated anyhow."

Johnny kept looking at him. "Can we still be friends?" He'd never called anybody friend before. The word felt a little strange on his lips.

But Mac didn't laugh. He just gave Johnny's leg a squeeze. "Of course. Whether or not you screw that broad has nothing to do with us."

Johnny sighed in relief. He lowered his eyes. "I would have tried, Mac, if you wanted me to," he said very, very softly.

Mac didn't say anything.

Johnny rested his head back against the wall. "My father always used to tell me that I was a burden," he said almost dreamily. "Like the Lord sent me just to test them, and see if their faith could carry them through. They were stuck with me because they were my parents." He rubbed at the floor with the heel of his hand.

"Yeah?" Mac crushed out his cigarette.

"You ever wonder why you were born, Mac?"

He snorted. "Hell, kid, I know why I was born."

Johnny stared at him. "Really? Why?"

"Because, asshole, otherwise you'd be sitting in this hallway talking to yourself."

Johnny laughed aloud. It didn't last long, though. "I just meant . . . well, you don't have to feel responsible for me or anything."

"I know that."

Johnny felt a sudden chill course through him. He wrapped both arms around himself, trying to get warm. "I didn't mean to screw up your pass, Mac."

"Why do you keep apologizing all the time? It doesn't matter."

The tears wouldn't stay back any longer; they flowed down Johnny's face. "I'm scared, Mac. I just get so scared."

"I know." Mac put one hand on his shoulder and gripped. "It's gonna be okay, kid," he said. "Stop crying, huh?"

Johnny nodded and rubbed at his face with both hands.

Mac looked at him for a long moment; his face

seemed almost angry, but when he spoke, his voice was soft. "Tomorrow I'm going into Major Henderson's office and have you transferred to my unit," he said.

Johnny swallowed hard, trying to understand. "What?"

"I said, you're coming with me. You're not going back to your old unit."

"Thank you," Johnny whispered. "I . . . just, thank you."

They were quiet for awhile, then Mac stood. "I'm gonna go finish what I started in there," he said. "You zip your pants and get the hell out of here."

"Okay, Mac, whatever you say. I'll wait for you back at the hotel, huh?"

"Sure, fine."

Johnny sat on the floor and watched until Mac had disappeared inside. Then he stood, zipped his fly, and left. He went back to the hotel and waited for Mac to come home.

-FIVE-

For the first time in weeks it wasn't raining as Mac made his way through the knee-deep mud that covered the compound. It was too bad, he thought, that the breakfast waiting for him in the mess tent wasn't worth all the trouble it took to get there.

Crazy George was standing outside the tent.

"Morning, George," Mac said, stopping to scrape his boots on the large rock set by the door for that purpose.

George only scowled at him.

Mac shrugged and went inside. He paused long enough to roll his trouser legs down again, then went to pick up eggs, toast, and coffee, which he carried to a table. "Morning," he said, unloading the tray.

"Good morning," Johnny said cheerfully.

Mac, the lifelong loner, still couldn't quite get used to the idea that someone was actually glad to see him every morning, but for whatever reasons existed inside his poor befuddled head, John Griffith apparently was. He made an effort at returning Johnny's smile, then bent his head over the eggs. They were cold, of course.

"How was the game last night?"

33

Mac grimaced. "Don't ask." He looked up, chewing diligently. "I haven't held a decent hand since that night in Saigon. Maybe you should come kibbitz again."

"No." The finality of the word allowed for no discussion.

Mac shrugged. "I was only kidding." He didn't understand Johnny's firm refusal to come watch him play cards, but he accepted it as just one more quirk in a personality loaded with them. Maybe poker bored him.

"How much did you lose?"

"All of it." He didn't bother mentioning the several I.O.U.s.

"All?" Johnny shook his head, a bewildered expression on his face. "Maybe you shouldn't play so much."

Mac stopped with the tin mug of coffee halfway to his lips and stared at Johnny. "Get the fuck off my back," he said coldly. "You're not my wife or my mother, so lay off. Butt out of my life."

Johnny flinched back from the words as if they were physical blows. "I . . . I'm sorry. I didn't mean to make you mad. I'm sorry." He fumbled for his wallet. "I have fifty left. Take it for your stake tonight."

Mac stared at the bills, then shook his head. "Keep your goddamned money," he mumbled. "I don't want it."

"Please." Johnny's voice cracked, and for one terrible minute Mac thought the other man was going to cry. "Don't be mad at me. I shouldn't have said that. It's none of my business what you do with the money."

"Half of what I lost last night was yours," Mac

said bitterly. "I guess you're entitled to bellyache."

"No, no, I'm not. I don't care. The money doesn't matter. Please, Mac."

After another long moment, Mac's fingers closed around the bills. "Hey," he said, "I shouldn't have blown up like I did." When Johnny didn't look up, Mac reached across the table and lightly punched him on the shoulder. "Hey, Johnny-boy, you in there?" He hated it when Johnny wouldn't talk.

Johnny sighed finally and raised his eyes. "Are we okay again?"

"Sure." Mac tucked the money into his shirt pocket. "We're okay, Johnny, of course we are."

Griffith smiled.

Mac could feel a knot of tension forming in his neck. That seemed to happen a lot lately. "I gotta go," he said, gulping the last of the cold coffee. "Staff briefing in a couple of minutes."

"Okay," Johnny said. "Have a nice day."

Mac stopped in mid-stride and turned back to Johnny, a helpless smile playing around the corners of his mouth. Jesus. Griffith sometimes said the damnedest things; there was just no way to figure the guy out. "You have a nice day, too," Mac said after a moment. Johnny nodded and Mac walked out of the tent.

Crazy George was still standing there. "Hey, Lieutenant," he said softly.

Mac paused. "Yeah, George?"

George stepped closer and lowered his voice. "I know the secret," he said.

"What?" Mac looked into George's eyes and saw the madness there. Entranced by that, he didn't even see the knife until the blade was already

moving through the air. "Hey, don't—" he started
to say.

The knife sliced through his upper arm and
blood spurted out over them both. George lifted
his hand again, and Mac fell away, crashing
through the side of the tent. George kept coming,
yelling something about God and Lyndon John-
son. Mac tried to get away, but his legs were
tangled in the heavy, muddy canvas. "Oh, hell," he
said aloud, thinking that this was a fucking stupid
way to die. "Damn."

The air was suddenly filled with a noise that
sounded like it came from an animal in mortal
pain. Through the mud and confusion, Mac was
aware of a blur flying past him and colliding with
George. The two tangled figures sprawled in the
mud and standing puddles.

Mac struggled to sit up, watching Johnny and
George roll around, the knife blade flashing between them. A crowd had gathered by this time,
and a couple of the men made a half-hearted attempt to stop the battle, but most just stood there
watching. George's arm jerked and the knife
slashed across Johnny's cheek. Johnny swung a
hand wildly in response, sending the weapon skidding away. Mac finally got himself untangled from
the tent and sat up, trying to stop the flow of blood
from his arm. "Johnny!" he yelled.

Johnny, if he even heard him, ignored the shout.
He was on top of George now, clutching the larger
man by the hair. In the sudden silence of the
crowd, Mac could hear the terrible dull thuds of
George's head against the rock upon which he'd
cleaned his boots earlier. Again and again flesh and
bone crashed against the rock. Two men tried to

pull Johnny away, but he shrugged them off almost nonchalantly. It was hard to believe that there was so much strength in the slender body.

Mac half-ran, half-crawled across the distance between them and plowed into Johnny with the full force of his body, sending them both into a puddle. Somebody immediately dragged George away. Mac lay heavily on top of Johnny, who still writhed and jerked from the emotional frenzy of the fight. "Johnny, Johnny," he crooned, like a man trying to calm a distraught animal. "Take it easy, babe, take it easy."

Slowly Johnny relaxed and his breathing returned to normal. "Did he hurt you, Mac?" he asked in a hoarse voice.

"No, kid, I'm okay. Just cut my arm a little." Mac rolled off Johnny. A short distance away, a medic was bent over George. "Sit up," Mac ordered.

Johnny struggled up. Both his eyes were already starting to discolor and the cut on his cheek was bleeding. "You really okay, Mac?" he persisted.

"Yeah, yeah," he said, although his arm was throbbing like hell.

"He was trying to kill you."

"Well, I guess. George is crazy."

"Is he dead?"

"No, of course not," he said reassuringly, although he didn't know.

"I wish he was." Mac looked up in surprise. The expression that he could see in Johnny's eyes was scary, a little too much like the look he'd seen in George's eyes just before the attack. "He was going to kill you, Mac," Johnny said by way of apparent explanation. "He deserves to die."

Mac sat speechless for a moment, then jerked his head around. "We need a goddamned medic over here!" he yelled. "Can't you see we're bleeding to death?"

He felt dizzy suddenly and leaned against Johnny to keep from falling into the puddle again.

-SIX-

He walked across the compound to the supply tent, knowing that Johnny would be there taking inventory. That was all Johnny did, by Mac's order. It was a good job for him, because he could work alone, and by the time he finished counting all the bandages and cases of corned beef hash and the bullets, it was time to start over again. Everyone knew, of course, why Dumb Johnny had been assigned the task. Everyone except Johnny.

He was there, bent over the omnipresent clipboard. All that remained of the fight with George was the healing scar on his cheek. Mac leaned against a case of powdered eggs. "How's it going, kid?"

Johnny looked up, startled, until he saw who it was, then he smiled. "Okay. Except I think I need glasses. The numbers keep getting smaller."

Mac cleared his throat. "I got my orders."

"Your orders?"

"Shipping home. Next Wednesday."

Johnny lowered the clipboard. The scar suddenly stood out, vivid red against his pale skin. "Wednesday?"

"Yeah."

39

He shook his head, the eyes even more bewildered than before. "But, Mac, I—"

"Hey, you'll be okay, kid," Mac said quickly, trying to sound a hell of a lot more sure than he felt. "You've only got eight weeks left, right?"

"I won't make it."

The words should have sounded melodramatic, but they didn't. Instead there was the simple starkness of truth. Mac didn't say anything and after a moment, Johnny sighed and raised the clipboard. "Johnny, hey—"

"It doesn't matter," he said quietly. "Fifty-two, fifty-three—"

"What the hell is that supposed to mean, it doesn't matter?"

"Nothing. I'm glad you're getting out of this mess. Sixty-four, sixty-five—"

"Johnny . . ."

"I'm trying to count this stuff, Mac. It's my job. Seventy-three, seventy—"

Mac suddenly moved toward him, grabbed the clipboard, and threw it across the tent. "Forget the fucking inventory," he said. "Nobody cares if you stand in here counting things."

Johnny's hands dropped to his sides, and he stared at the floor.

"Johnny?"

The silence rang loudly in the tent.

"Johnny, say something to me."

But he didn't.

Mac clenched his fingers around the edge of a packing case. "Don't do this, Johnny. It's stupid."

Instead of answering, Johnny relaxed his legs and slid down the pile of boxes, huddling on the floor. Mac could feel a seething white anger well up inside him. "You stop it," he said raspingly. "Stop it now, or I'll . . . I'll. . . ." Words wouldn't come; he didn't even know what the hell he wanted to say. He crashed a fist against the top of the box. "Damn you. I don't care what happens. I don't care if you sit there until hell freezes over. You bastard. You crazy son of a bitch."

He turned around and walked out of the tent, not looking back.

Johnny didn't show up for supper. Mac sat alone, for the first time in months, but he didn't eat much. He pushed the food around on the plate for awhile, then left. Bumming a bottle of cheap wine from Wash, he crawled into his cot, resolving to drink until he passed out.

He almost made it.

But he couldn't stop thinking about Griffith sitting in the supply tent, huddled on the floor like a scared kid. The image finally propelled him off the cot. Gingerly walking what he hoped was a reasonably straight line, he made his way across the compound. Just to cover all his bases, he checked the mess tent and Johnny's quarters, but then he went back to the supply tent.

Johnny was still there, sitting on the floor, with his legs crossed Indian-style, and a .45 in his hand. Mac stumbled into the circle of pale yellow light. "What the hell are you doing?" he demanded, wishing that his tongue didn't feel quite so thick.

Johnny looked up at him. "I don't want to stay here by myself," he said quietly.

"Shit, man, everybody ain't leaving, just me. You'll still have lots of company."

Johnny's glance at him was filled with scorn.

"You know what I mean," he said. "I don't want to stay here by myself."

Mac nodded. "Okay. I know what you mean. But what the hell are you gonna do about it?"

"Go away, Mac."

He didn't go away; he sat down facing Johnny. "This is great, you know, really great."

"What?"

"We have a problem here, kid, and what happens? Do you give me a chance to handle it, to figure out what to do? No, sir, all you want to do is blow your fucking brains out. Assuming you have any brains in there, which I doubt very much. Some buddy you are. Christ."

Johnny stared at the gun for a moment, then lifted his gaze to Mac. "I'm sorry," he said. "I just thought—"

"*You* thought? When the hell did you start thinking?"

"I didn't know it mattered what I did."

"Well, it matters." Mac was quiet for a moment, trying to clear his fuzzy brain. "It matters, you stupid son of a bitch."

Carefully Johnny set the gun down onto the floor. "You said you didn't care."

"Oh, shut up. Nobody else around this place pays a goddamned bit of attention to anything I say; why the hell should you?"

They were quiet for a couple of minutes as Johnny chewed thoughtfully on a fingernail. "What are we gonna do?" he asked finally.

"I don't know yet."

"I could just go AWOL," Johnny suggested.

"Oh, sure, that's a terrific idea. Then they could stick you in Leavenworth or in front of a firing squad." Mac rubbed his temples. "Look, will you just let me handle it? Leave the thinking to me. I promise I'll get you out of here, okay?"

"Okay."

Mac sighed. "But right now I have to get some sleep." He pushed himself to his feet wearily and started out. "Good night," he mumbled.

"Sleep tight," Johnny returned cheerfully.

Mac didn't know whether to laugh or cry. He did neither, just shook his head and kept moving.

-SEVEN-

Mac was drunk. But it was his bon voyage party, so he figured he was entitled. They were drinking some punch Washington had created. It seemed to be nothing more than an uneasy mingling of all the booze in camp, with a can of fruit cocktail dumped in to give it an air of festivity.

Mac sat in one corner, trying to dig a green grape from the bottom of his glass. He looked up blearily as Wash dropped next to him. "Great party," he said.

Washington surveyed the roomful of drunk men glumly. "I guess."

Mac almost captured the grape, but at the last minute it slithered away. "Damn. Slippery little fucker."

"I got a question for you, Lieutenant-buddy."

Mac looked at him.

"What are you gonna do with the zombie when you get back?"

They both glanced across the tent to where Johnny sat alone, watching the proceedings with a faint smile. Mac shrugged. "I'm not gonna do anything. He wanted out and I got him out. That's all."

Washington wiped his sweating brow. "You

know the guy is a real screwball, don't you?"

"Ahh, he's okay. A little weird, but okay."

"Mac, John Griffith is sick." The black man's voice was flat.

Mac took a gulp of the punch, wishing they weren't having this conversation. "Hell, Wash, so is everybody else around here."

"Whenever you ain't around, he don't talk, man."

There was a by-now-familiar knot of tension in Mac's neck, and despite the punch he felt sober again. "He gets scared, is all."

"That's not all." A hand rested firmly on Mac's shoulder. "Take my advice and get him into a hospital."

"You mean turn him over to the shrinks?"

"He needs help."

"No," Mac said flatly. "I can't do that." He was quiet for a moment, letting the memories wash over him. "My old lady bought it in one of those places. I can't do that to Johnny."

"Fine," Washington replied. "What will you do? Dump him on the street in Frisco and walk away?"

Mac finally captured the elusive grape and pulled it out of the glass. He studied it, then threw it across the table, watching as it bounced and rolled to the ground. "Once we're out of here, he's on his own. He knows that."

Washington snorted. "Shit, he don't know what his own name is unless you tell him every so often."

The hammer was pounding in the back of Mac's skull. "He'll be okay."

"Yeah, sure, Mac. Zombies probably make out real good on their own."

Johnny had seen Mac staring at him. He grinned

and started to make his way through the crowd toward them. Washington got to his feet. "But I guess that's not your problem, is it? It will be though, unless you get out from under, and soon." He smiled, suddenly and without humor. "Or else adopt the bastard." He walked away.

Mac watched Johnny approach. Get out from under . . . out from under. Damn it, maybe Wash was right. If he didn't set this thing straight right now, he was liable to have Griffith around his neck for a long time. "We have to talk," he said abruptly when the blond reached him. "Let's go outside."

"Sure, Mac," Johnny agreed, as usual.

Mac led the way across the room and outside. They wandered across the compound aimlessly as he lit a cigarette. Back at the party somebody's eight-track was blasting Beatles music. "What are your plans, Johnny?"

"Plans?"

"What are you gonna do when we get back home?"

Johnny shook his head. "I don't know, Mac."

"Well, you better start to think about it."

The younger man looked genuinely bewildered. "I thought you were going to do all the thinking, Mac. That's what you said. Leave the thinking to me, you said."

Mac took a long drag on the cigarette. "I only meant while we were here, Johnny, not forever. When we get Stateside, you're on your own. You understand that, don't you?"

"Oh." The word was soft.

Mac kept his eyes on the ground. "I mean, we have to get on with our own lives, right? I have things to do, you know?" He wondered as he spoke just what the hell he had to do. He was finished in the army; his own promise not to re-up was part of the deal he'd struck for Johnny's early-out. This wasn't the time to think about that, though. "There must be people you want to see and stuff to do, right?"

"No."

"Well, you'll think of something." The words were sharp.

"Sure, Mac," Johnny whispered.

He tried to ignore the tightness in his gut. Shit, he was only getting out from under. It was the smart thing to do. He sure as hell didn't need to have John Paul Griffith hanging around his neck like some kind of goddamned millstone. He was going to have a hard enough time keeping himself afloat. Given a burden like that, they'd probably both go under. So it was best to dump him now, like Wash had said.

So what if the guy was glad to see him every morning?

Suddenly, irrationally, he knew, Mac was angry at Wash. Where the hell did that black bastard get off butting in to say that Johnny was crazy and that Mac would be better off without him? Sure, the kid had some problems, but who the hell didn't? Given a little time, they could work it out.

He glanced sidewise at Johnny walking next to him.

Wash was a good guy, and a good friend, but this time he was wrong. Griffith was okay. He liked the kid, damn it, and to hell with what anybody else thought. When the rest of the fucking world kept out of it, he and Johnny got along just fine. Where the hell was it written that Alexander McCarthy couldn't have a friend?

He stopped walking and turned to face Johnny.

"Hey."

Johnny raised his head, looking like a puppy dog that couldn't understand why its beloved master has suddenly kicked him. "What, Mac?"

"We could sort of stick together for awhile. Until we get our bearings. I have some connections in New York, so we might head east and see what happens. If you want." He was surprised to realize how much he wanted Johnny to say yes.

Johnny was staring at the ground again. "What do *you* want?" he asked very softly.

"I think it sounds okay."

"I think so, too. I don't get so scared when I'm with you." Johnny's face was suddenly anxious, as if he'd said too much. "Is that okay?"

Mac smiled. "Yeah, sure." He was quiet for a moment, then shrugged. "You want to know something, Johnny?"

"What?"

He dropped the cigarette and crushed it under his heel. "I don't get so scared when I'm with you, either." He heard his own words with bemusement, figuring he wasn't as sober as he'd thought, and hoping to hell he wasn't going to regret this in the morning.

Johnny laughed, as if he'd said something very funny. "You're never scared," he said complacently.

Mac opened his mouth to set the kid straight on that, but then he only shook his head helplessly. "Let's go back to the party," he said instead.

"Sure, Mac, whatever you say."

They turned and walked back across the compound.

-EIGHT-

It was a good night for Johnny. His Bowie knife style of throwing the darts was right on target time after time, and he won three straight games, raking in a total of thirty dollars. Prudently, he decided to go out a winner, despite the mild protests of his defeated opponents, who wanted a chance to get even. They didn't press him too hard, however, because they realized that there would be other nights.

Johnny was a familiar figure in the Pirate's Cove Bar, although nobody really knew any more about him than his name. He came in several nights a week with a grim-faced poker player. The card game took place in the back room, but Johnny never went in there. He stayed in the front, perfecting his dart throwing skills to a deadly degree of accuracy. Although he was always willing for a game if asked, the other players soon discovered that it wasn't easy to carry on a conversation with him. When a few words were pulled out of him, they were said in tones so soft as to be almost impossible to hear.

Mostly he just sat in the rear booth, drinking a beer or two—never more—and waiting until the poker player came out. Then the two of them would leave.

Johnny fingered the three tens as he sat drinking a beer. This was the most he'd ever won at darts and it gave him a good feeling. Maybe, he hoped, the money would make Mac feel better, too.

A frown creased Johnny's brow as he thought of his friend. Mac's luck hadn't been too good lately. The first few months in New York were okay, although Mac's "connections" never came through as he'd hoped they would. They both still had some army money left, though, and for a while the cards seemed to run his way more often than not. Life was turning out okay.

But then things started to go wrong and for the past three months it had all grown steadily worse. Johnny didn't mind getting along on a diet of cheap hamburgers, or moving from one grimy, depressing room to the next. None of that mattered much to him. But he did mind a whole lot seeing what it was doing to Mac.

He took a thoughtful sip of beer. At least the angry outbursts didn't scare him so much anymore. He'd learned finally that Mac's rages were not directed at him, but at the circumstances, and that though he might smash a glass or put his fist through the plasterboard wall of whatever cheap room they were in at any given moment, he would never turn the anger toward Johnny.

Johnny frowned again. It was true that Mac said things sometimes, things that hurt more than a blow might have. Especially when he threatened to just take off and leave all of his problems behind. They both knew that he meant Johnny himself was

the biggest problem. But Johnny also knew that
Mac didn't mean those things when he said them.
And he always apologized when the outburst was
over, not in words, maybe, but with a candy bar or
just by hanging around the room a little longer
than usual to keep Johnny company.

The door to the back room opened suddenly and
Mac came out. Johnny bit his lower lip, knowing
from the expression on the tall man's face that
tonight's luck hadn't been any better than all the
others lately. Mac stopped at the bar for a drink,
paying for it with a handful of change, then came
and slumped down across from Johnny.

Neither of them spoke for several minutes.

Johnny finally broke the silence. "Guess what?"
he said softly.

"What?"

"I won thirty dollars." He pushed the crumpled
bills across the table. "Here."

Mac looked at the money for a moment.
"Where'd you get this?" he asked, picking it up.

"Playing darts. I won three games. Thirty
dollars." Johnny smiled, feeling proud.

"Shit," Mac said. "I just dropped two hundred
dollars in there." It was the last of the money from
the pawn shop. The cassette player. Johnny's gold
watch. The cheap portable TV. Their possessions
endured a nomadic existence, bouncing back and
forth between them and the hock shop with regu-
larity. "I just lost everything we had, kid. What
good is thirty fucking dollars?" He threw the money back across the table at Johnny. The bills hit
him in the face and fell, landing in a puddle of
spilled beer. Mac downed the rest of his drink and
got to his feet. "You coming?" He stalked toward

the door, not waiting for an answer.

Johnny carefully picked up the bills and put them into his shirt pocket, before hurrying to catch up.

It was a fifteen minute walk to their fourth floor furnished room, a journey that passed in complete silence. Once inside, Mac took a lukewarm beer out of the haphazardly operative refrigerator, and sat down in front of the only window, apparently hoping for a breeze. He propped his feet on the sill and stared glumly out at the flashing neon sign across the street. ANCI G IRLS.

Johnny stripped to his shorts in an effort to feel cooler and stretched out on the couch which doubled as his bed. He could hear the faint sound of a TV next door and listened until he could iden-tify the show. MANNIX. He couldn't make out much of the action, but in a couple of minutes he'd heard enough to know that he'd already seen that episode. Taking off his glasses, he rubbed his eyes wearily.

Mac cleared his throat finally. "You must be getting pretty good at throwing those darts."

Johnny shrugged.

"Thirty dollars, huh?"

"Uh-huh. I probably could've won more, but I was afraid of losing the thirty, so I quit."

Mac sighed. "That's why you're always gonna be a loser, Johnny. You're too damned scared to take a chance. You have to live dangerously if you want to be a big winner."

"I guess you're right, Mac."

"Sure as hell am, kid." He was quiet for several moments. "Still, thirty dollars is pretty good."

"You think so?" Johnny got up from the couch,

picking up his shirt from the floor. He pulled the money out and handed it to Mac. "Here."

Mac held the beer-damp bills tentatively. "You don't have to give me this, you know."

Johnny was bewildered. "But you need a stake. I don't need it for anything."

"You could get the TV out of hock."

Johnny thought about that for a moment; he sure missed having the small set around for company. Then he shrugged. "Ahh, hell," he said. "Nothing on now but reruns anyway."

After a second, Mac grinned. "Yeah. Hey, you know what?"

Johnny was smiling now, too, feeling good again. "What?"

"This dough might just change my luck. And if it does, we could get a brand new set. A color one. Maybe before the new season starts. Wouldn't that be great?"

"Yeah, sure, Mac. I'd like a color set."

"Terrific. So we'll just let that crummy little black-and-white stay where it is, and I'll use this to get going again. I feel really lucky now, Johnny."

"Good." It was terrific when Mac was up like this. Johnny went to the refrigerator and took out a Coke. He'd join Mac at the window and they could talk.

But Mac had a familiar expression on his face, a sort of hungry look that Johnny knew well. "In fact, why wait until tomorrow, huh? If I'm feeling hot right now?" He shoved the money away and got to his feet. "You want to come back to the Cove with me?"

Johnny shook his head. "Think I'll just go to bed."

"Okay, kid." Mac drained the beer can on the

way to the door, then tossed it into the waste-
basket, where it landed with a thud. "See? That's a
sign that my luck is changing." He paused by the
door. "Hey, that's really great, you winning all this
money, Johnny. Really great. I'm gonna have to
watch you play sometime, okay?"

Johnny felt his face grow hot with pride over the
unexpected praise. "Sure, Mac," he said shyly.
"Anytime."

"Terrific." Mac was keyed up, ready to go.
"Good night," he said.

" 'Night, Mac."

The door closed. Alone, Johnny went to stand
by the window and looked down at the sidewalk.
He leaned against the wall, sipping soda, and listening to the end of MANNIX from the next
room, and watching until Mac disappeared around
the corner.

-NINE-

By the time fall arrived, they weren't going to the Pirate's Cove anymore. Mac explained it by saying that in his line of work "fluidity" was very important. A new game, new money, it was all crucial. Mac didn't bother to explain that his line of credit at the Cove had been cut off and that a couple of people were beginning to get uptight about late payments. He figured that Johnny wouldn't understand all that financial stuff anyway, so why bother him with it? All the kid really cared about was having his TV to watch and plenty of Coke to drink.

So they moved to Brooklyn, to a small room over a pizzeria, and Mac found new games. Each beginning brought the same hopes of a break in his streak of bad luck, and in fact, there were enough wins to keep his hopes alive, though never quite enough to get him out of the hole. Johnny surprised the very hell out of him by getting a job washing dishes for the old dago downstairs. Mac didn't like the idea very much, because Johnny was too smart to have to put up with a chickenshit job like that. But, of course, there wasn't any way the rest of the world could know how smart he was when he was also too damned scared to open his mouth. Down there, he didn't have to talk; all he had to do was wash the dishes and haul the garbage and keep the floor swept. He was invisible, as the people who do that kind of work always are, and he was content. Once a week he brought his pay envelope upstairs and gave it to Mac. The money, once they paid rent on the room, was hardly enough to keep Mac in cigarettes, but it was something, and it seemed very important to Johnny.

And at least he had a job. Mac tried. He worked for three days in a shoe store, but he figured a week of that and he'd be as spaced-out as Johnny, so he quit. For awhile after that he read the classifieds every morning over breakfast, solemnly discussing the offerings with Johnny, but they never found anything that seemed suited to his particular talents. So he played cards and Johnny washed dishes for the dago and they got by.

Chinese Eddie raked the chips across the table with both his tiny hands. "Sorry about this, Mac," he said cheerfully. "You been going through a cold streak lately, ain't you?"

Mac threw his cards down in disgust. "All my fucking life," he mumbled. "Well, that finishes me. Unless you'll take my marker?"

But Eddie shook his head woefully, causing his several chins to jiggle. "No can do, man. I'm already getting static from upstairs."

"I'm good for it."

The other players had suddenly become very interested in their drinks; he and Eddie might have been alone in the dimly lit room. Eddie was slowly shuffling a new deck. "Have you totaled your markers lately?" he asked casually.

"No, but—"

"They come to almost four thousand dollars, Mac, between here and the Cove. That's a lot of money."

The amount stunned Mac a little, and he reached for a cigarette, trying not to let his fingers tremble as he lit it. "Well, yeah, I know it sounds like a lot. Hell, it *is* a lot, but—"

Eddie carefully cut the deck, not even looking at him. "There are no 'buts', Mac. The boys would like you to arrange some settlement for this account."

The atmosphere in the room had turned vaguely ominous. Mac took a couple of quick drags on the cigarette, then smiled. "Sure, look, I know how it is. But, see, I've got a couple of very hot prospects that ought to start paying off real soon."

Eddie smiled, beaming as if his fondest dreams had been realized. "I'm very glad about that, Mac, because I like you." A faint, a very faint hint of worry crossed the vast expanse of his face. "I can only hope that these prospects start paying off within the next twenty-four hours."

Mac's mouth was dry, but there wasn't any whiskey left in his glass. "But that's not enough time. . . ." His voice dwindled off as he realized the futility of protest.

Eddie spread his fingers helplessly. "I don't make the rules, Mac."

"Sure, Eddie," he said bitterly. He jerked his coat on and left the room.

It was almost two A.M., time for Johnny to get off work, so instead of going up to the room, Mac pushed open the door of the pizzeria. The old dago

was sitting bent over the racing form and he barely
glanced up. "He's in the alley taking the garbage,"
he said, already studying the sheet again.

Mac nodded and walked past him to the rear of
the place. "Hi," he began, pushing the back door
open. He stopped. Johnny wasn't alone.

Two gorillas had him against the fence that lined
the alley. One of the apes had both hands on
Johnny's shoulders. The glow from the streetlamp
reflected off the lenses of Johnny's glasses, hiding
his eyes from view, but Mac knew what expression
he would have seen there. "What the hell is going
on here?" he asked quietly, recognizing both men
from the Cove game.

Frank, one of the tough guys, turned. "Why
nothing's going on, Mr. McCarthy," he said. "We
was only leaving a message with your friend here."
The massive fingers dug into Johnny's shoulders
and he winced visibly. The men were built like bull
elephants stuffed into polyester suits. Johnny was
six-one and Mac six-four, and while the other two
may not have been any taller, they were con-
siderably heavier. Not to mention the fact that beneath each shiny jacket could be seen the obvious
outline of a holster. The fingers squeezed again.
"You get that message straight, dummy?"

Johnny nodded jerkily.

"Good." The hands released him, and Johnny
slumped against the fence. Frank and his buddy Al
grinned at Mac and disappeared down the alley.

Mac moved, grabbing Johnny by one arm. "You
okay?"

"Yeah."

"You sure, kid?"

"Yeah, Mac, I'm okay."

He nodded, releasing his breath in a long sigh, then turned to look off into the darkness as they heard a car start up and drive away. "Bastards. They don't have any business coming around here bothering you."

Johnny took several deep breaths. "They said to tell you twenty-four hours. What's that mean?"

"Nothing." He realized that Johnny, in his shirt sleeves, was shivering as the sharp November wind hit him. "Get your coat and let's go home."

Some home, he thought bitterly as they climbed the stairs. A room about four feet square, stinking all the time of tomato sauce and olive oil. Johnny stood in front of the space heater and tried to get rid of the chills that still wracked his body. Or maybe it was fear. Mac poured two slugs of dago red and handed one to him. "Drink it," he ordered when Johnny made a face.

"Mac, what's happening?"

"Nothing."

"But those guys—"

"Shut up, Johnny," Mac said sharply. "Drink your wine and shut up about it."

Johnny shut up and drank the wine.

Mac sat down on his bed. "Ahh, Johnny," he said after a long time. "I've really screwed things up."

Johnny shook his head. "It wasn't your fault."

"Goddamnit, Johnny, listen to me for once, willya? I owe these people a lot of money. Four fucking thousand dollars." He stared at the empty glass in his hand, then suddenly threw it across the room. It shattered against the wall. The room was quiet for a moment. "Oh, Christ, Johnny, I'm scared. I'm really scared."

Johnny came over and sat beside him. He patted
Mac's arm. "It'll be okay."

"These people aren't playing games, you idiot.
They had guns."

Johnny's face was pale, but his voice was steady.
"You'll take care of it."

Mac sneered. "Oh, yeah, sure. I'll take care of it.
Superman lives, right? You gotta stop watching so
goddamned much TV; it's rotting away what few
brains you have left." He felt so tired. All he
wanted to do was get out of this lousy room, away
from the hassles, away from those damned blue
eyes that were always watching him. Trusting him.
God, he didn't want to be trusted anymore, not
anymore. The walls were closing in, suffocating
him. Almost desperately he reached for his jacket
and pulled it on again. "I gotta go out for awhile,"
he mumbled.

"But, Mac . . ."

"Don't worry." He opened the door, then
paused. "I'll be back, Johnny. I'll be back, but I
just have to get out for a while, okay?" He left before Johnny could speak again.

He walked for a long time, rode the subway for
awhile, and ended up in the New Amsterdam
Theater on Forty-second Street. His was the only
white face in the crowd. He made his way up the
aisle, which was sticky with spilled soda, cigarette
butts, and discarded hot dogs, and found a seat in
the last row of the balcony. Lighting a cigarette, he
propped both feet on the back of the seat in front
of him and stared at the screen.

He had no idea what movie was playing, but it
didn't matter. Half-asleep, he watched the flicker-

ing images on the screen until his eyes grew tired of staring at the garish pictures, then tipped his head back to gaze at the vast, vaulted ceiling overhead.

He dozed, waking once to find a hand on his thigh, edging upwards toward his crotch. Without opening his eyes, he spoke. "Get away from me, you mother-fucking fag bastard," he said very softly, "or I'll ram this chair up your ass."

The hand vanished. Mac scrunched further down in the seat and watched the movie.

-TEN-

Johnny sat in the room for a long time after Mac left. He was trying to think about what to do. Mac needed help and Johnny wanted desperately to help him. Finally, he got up and left the room.

He knew all about the faulty lock on the back door of the pizzeria. It took him only a couple of minutes to snap it free and push the door open. As he stepped inside, his father's voice rang clearly in his mind, sounding as if the old man were standing there next to him. "Thou shalt not steal," the harsh voice said.

Johnny brushed the words away impatiently. This wasn't stealing. The old man had money. Mac needed money. It was as simple as that, really. You didn't need a whole religion and lots of rules to know right from wrong, he decided. Things just were what they were, and the only thing to do was make the best of it.

Carefully he made his way through the kitchen, into the small cubicle that served as an office. A narrow sliver of light leaked in from outside. He started opening desk drawers at random, until he reached the bottom drawer, which was locked. He pulled out his pocket knife again and started to work. This one took a little longer than the lock on the door had, but finally it, too, snapped open. A small steel box sat there. Now he had to get that open. He knew that it would have been easier to just take the box along, but that wouldn't be fair. He didn't want all the dago's money, just four thousand dollars, the amount that Mac needed. So he began a studied attack on the padlock securing the box. His breathing was quick and raspy as he worked, but his fingers were steady.

Blinding white light suddenly exploded in the room. Johnny looked up, surprised, blinking against the sudden invasion of brightness. A massive black cop stood in the doorway, his gun leveled at Johnny. "Freeze."

Johnny froze. "Don't shoot," he whispered. "Please, don't shoot me."

"I'm not going to shoot, if you do what you're told. Just put the knife down on the desk and stand up slowly."

He dropped the penknife and stood.

Another cop slipped into the room, coming forward to frisk him quickly and efficiently. "What's your name?"

Johnny's head turned toward him. "Huh?"

"Your name, buddy, what is it?"

Johnny's hands were still in the air. "John Paul Griffith," he said hoarsely.

"Okay, Griffith, you're under arrest." The cop pulled a worn card out of his pocket and glanced at it. "You have the right to remain silent. If you give up that right, everything you say can and will be used against you in a court of law. You have the right—"

The voice faded away slowly until, although he

could still see the man's lips moving, Johnny
couldn't hear any of the words. He stared dumbly
at the moving lips as the terror filled him, con-
sumed him.

The black cop said something and then Johnny's
arms were jerked around behind his back and
cuffed there. Johnny wanted to tell them that he
hadn't been doing anything wrong, that he'd only
wanted to get the money for Mac. But the words
wouldn't come. The cops took him out through the
front, past the other tenants from upstairs, and
past Giancarlo, who pointed a finger, like a parent
scolding a small child. "Thief, thief," he said.

Johnny was pushed into the backseat of the radio car. He huddled against the door, staring at the
mesh screen that separated him from the cops in
front. A taste of hot bile rose in his throat, but he
swallowed the bitter fluid back down, afraid of
what might happen if he threw up all over the police car.

Mac is going to be so mad, he thought dimly. Oh
God, where *was* Mac? Even if he was going to be
mad and yell, Johnny wanted him there. "Mac?"
His lips formed the word, but no sound came out.
Mac, please, I need you.

They took him to the precinct house four blocks
away, turning him over to a heavyset man in a
rumpled brown suit. The man shoved a paper into
the typewriter. "Name?" he snapped around an un-
lit cigar.

Johnny's hands, freed from the cuffs, were
clasped together in his lap. Someone, he thought,
was talking to him, but the words were muffled and
he had to strain to understand them.

"What's your name, pal?"

A familiar face, the black cop who'd busted him, appeared briefly, a papercup of coffee in one hand. "He told us it was Griffith. John Paul. Then he just clammed up. Acts like he's stoned."

The detective typed the name. "Address?"

The room was filled with a strange empty darkness, but the void didn't scare him. It was safe where he was. He slid down in the seat, smiling a little.

"Hey, Griffith, where do you live?"

With Mac, he thought, but he didn't tell them that. He just kept smiling and waiting for Mac to show up and take care of this.

They gave up finally, and took him away for booking, prints, and pictures. When all that was done, Johnny was taken to a holding cell. He curled up on the cot there, watching and waiting.

-ELEVEN-

Driven almost equally by weariness and the need for company, Mac finally went home. It was almost noon by the time he got back to the empty room. He sat down on his bed, a little bewildered. The pizzeria didn't open until two, and Johnny rarely went anywhere else alone. Except to the movies. Then he remembered that there was a spaghetti western playing down the street. Johnny loved the noisy shoot 'em ups. Mac was a little disgruntled, wishing Johnny were there. They needed to talk.

The soft tapping at the door startled him.

He got up to answer it; the old woman from across the hall was there, looking even more fluttery than usual. Mac knew her only slightly. Johnny would sometimes help her carry groceries or something. "Yes?" he said, trying to sound polite.

"I thought you ought to know," she stage-whispered.

"Know what?"

"They took him away."

Mac's eyes felt gritty after his long night, and he shook his head a little, hoping to clear away the fog in his brain. "Excuse me, Mrs. Jakubjansky, but what are you talking about?"

She sighed, as if impatient with his stupidity. "The police took him away. In the handcuffs. They said he stole money from Mr. Giancarlo." She shook her head sorrowfully. "John is a good boy. I don't think he would take money."

Mac managed to thank the woman and get rid of her, although he felt like someone had just delivered a quick punch to his mid-section. When she was gone, he rested his forehead against the door and closed his eyes. Johnny? Busted? Hauled off in cuffs?

He felt sick, like he might throw up. Oh goddamn, he thought, the kid did it for me, because I need money. That idiot. That goddamned stupid fucking idiot.

Christ, he must be scared to death.

Mac left the room, clattering noisily down the stairs, and running all the way to the police station. By the time he reached the front desk, he was gasping hoarsely for air. The desk sergeant looked up without much interest. "Yeah?"

He stood still for a moment, trying to catch his breath. "Uh, Griffith," he finally managed to say. "You have John Griffith here?"

The sergeant started pawing through some papers. "Griffith?"

Another cop looked up from his magazine. "That's the flake up on three," he said helpfully.

"Oh, yeah, right. Go to the third floor and ask for Lieutenant Mazzeretti."

When he asked, Mac was directed to a small office at one end of the squadroom. Mazzeretti, a dark-skinned, slender man in a grey sharkskin suit, frowned at the rumpled, unshaven figure before him. "Alex McCarthy? What's your interest in Griffith? You're not a lawyer? Or a relative?"

Mac shook his head. "No, I'm just a friend. He doesn't have a family or anything. Can I see John?"

Mazzeretti was toying with a gold ballpoint pen. "He's in the holding cell around the corner, but I don't know about seeing him." He clicked the pen open, studied the point for a moment, then clicked it closed again. "I have a transfer order pending."

"Transfer to where?"

"Bellevue."

Mac kept his face poker blank, although an icy hand seemed to be squeezing at his gut. "No, don't do that." The cop seemed startled by his tone and Mac forced himself to speak more quietly. "I mean, he's okay. He doesn't need Bellevue. Just let me talk to him for a minute."

Mazzeretti frowned. "That's the problem, man. He won't talk. Hasn't said word one since they brought him in."

The icy hand gripped more tightly. "He'll talk to me," Mac mumbled, hoping to hell it was the truth.

After a moment, Mazzeretti shrugged and stood. "Come on."

They left the office and walked around to the holding cell. Johnny was curled on the cot, staring blankly at the activity swirling around him. Mac stopped, gripping the bars with both hands, wanting to rip them aside and get Johnny out of this cage. "Hey, John," he said quietly.

Mazzeretti was standing next to him. "See what I mean? Nothing."

"Can I go in?"

The dapper cop hesitated. "He might be dangerous."

Mac gave him a look. "Him?"

The lieutenant had the grace to look fleetingly sheepish, then he unlocked the door. He closed it behind Mac, but didn't secure the lock.

Mac crouched on the floor next to the cot. "Johnny?" he whispered. "Listen up, kid. It's me, Johnny."

Slowly the foggy eyes cleared; the lips lifted in a tentative smile.

Casting a triumphant look toward Mazzeretti, Mac spoke again, more softly so only Johnny could hear. "What the hell are you doing?" he asked fiercely. "You stupid dumb jackass."

The hesitant smile faded and Johnny squeezed back against the wall.

"See?" Mazzeretti said. "That's why the order for Bellevue. The guy obviously has problems."

Mac ignored him, reaching out to take one of Johnny's hands between both of his. "Johnny?" he said, softening his tone. "Please. Don't do this. They're gonna take you away and lock you up in a padded cell someplace. Is that what you want?" His hold tightened helplessly. "Please, kid, snap out of it."

The inert hand moved a little and the smile slowly returned. "Hi, Mac," Johnny said. "I was waiting for you. I knew you'd come."

"Well, of course I came," Mac said, relief making his voice hoarse. "So you just knock off this zombie stuff, willya?" He squeezed the hand once more, then released it.

Johnny bit his lower lip. "What are they gonna do to me?"

"Nothing, kid, I promise. Everything is going to be okay. You just cooperate with them and I'll take care of it."

Johnny's face was anxious, and his eyes stared into Mac's. "Are you mad at me? I'm really sorry, Mac. I didn't mean to get into trouble."

"Shh, it's okay, never mind that." He was quiet for a moment. "No, I'm not mad. I know why you did it. Shit, Johnny," he said, "nobody ever cared enough before to . . . well, never mind. But thanks." He got up from his position by the bed. "Can I talk to you?" he asked Mazzeretti.

The lieutenant nodded and Mac started out. Johnny's hand around his wrist stopped him. "Mac?"

"I gotta go now, kid. But I'll be back in a little while. You just take it easy, okay?"

Johnny nodded, letting his fingers slip slowly from their grip.

Mac followed Mazzeretti back to his office, where the lieutenant paused long enough to light a thin black cigar with a gold lighter that matched the pen. "Griffith is a head case," he said succinctly.

Mac drew a level breath. "The guy has some problems," he admitted. "He was in Nam."

Mazzeretti nodded. "Doesn't surprise me much."

"But he doesn't need to be locked up. The help he needs, he's already getting." Was it really a lie? Mac didn't think so. Johnny needed help, yeah, needed to be . . . taken care of. But not by a bunch of shrinks. He helped Johnny just by being his friend, and when everybody else left them alone, it was just fine.

"He's never been busted before." It wasn't a question; apparently they'd checked.

"No, John is a good kid."

Mazzeretti raised his brows. "Kid? How old is he anyway?"

Mac had to stop and think. "Twenty-nine," he said after a moment. The figure surprised him a little; somehow, he always thought of Johnny as being so much younger.

"Hardly a kid," Mazzeretti murmured almost to himself.

"He wouldn't hurt anybody, Lieutenant, really. What happened last night was a . . . a mistake. He honestly thought he was doing the right thing." Like a child, Mac thought. Yeah, he was only trying to help. To help me.

Mazzeretti watched the lengthening ash on the tip of his cigar. "Well, McCarthy, I sympathize, but as long as Mr. Giancarlo insists on pressing charges, there's absolutely nothing I can do."

Mac nodded. Maybe there was nothing the cop could do, but he had no intention of letting them haul Johnny off to some nuthouse. "Thank you," he said, getting to his feet. Perhaps Mazzeretti knew that he intended to go see Giancarlo, but neither man said anything about it as Mac left.

He skirted the area of the holding cell, not wanting Johnny to see him again right then. Outside, the day had turned grey and overcast, and the gloom fit his mood perfectly.

Was Johnny crazy?

Mac had wondered about that before, of course. Ever since their first meeting amid the horror of Tan Pret, the issue of Johnny's sanity had plagued Mac. He seemed to be the only one with any doubts on the matter. Everybody else was so damned sure that they knew better than he about Griffith.

Well, Johnny *was* different, that much was true enough. He had a lot of weird habits. Like clamming up whenever things got tough. That wasn't normal, for sure. And his hang-ups about sex. And his dependency on Mac. He was just like a kid sometimes, no matter how old he really was in years.

So? They were friends, and shouldn't friends depend on each other? Hell, he depended on Johnny, too.

Yeah, I do.

What would happen to Johnny if they sent him away? Mac remembered the hospital where his mother had died. He could still smell the gagging odor of disinfectant that mingled with rather than hid the other smells of the place. He could still hear the screams, the animal cries, the low anguished moans that echoed in the hallways. Most of all, though, he remembered the people themselves, like his mother, with their various madnesses written on their faces. Bony hands reached out toward him as he walked past, swaggering a little so the nun wouldn't know how scared he was. Even now the horror of it all filled him whenever he thought about it.

Johnny, quiet, sweet-natured, childlike Johnny, wouldn't last ten minutes in a place like that.

Another question came to Mac. What'll happen to *me* if they send him away? He stopped abruptly on the sidewalk. A fat man dressed in filthy work clothes bumped into him and snarled an obscenity, but Mac ignored him. He stared into the window of a dress shop, seeing only his face reflected among the swirl of colors there. His own eyes stared back at him as if they were seeing a stranger.

Does it make a fucking bit of difference to me if Johnny is as crazy as everybody else says he is?

The answer came back in almost the same moment.

No.

Giancarlo was behind the counter of the restaurant, scribbling figures into a worn black ledger, and he looked up sullenly as Mac entered. "You come to make trouble," he said, "I gonna call the cops again."

"No trouble," Mac replied quickly. "I just want to talk."

"About John?"

"About John, yes."

"I got nothing to say. He's a thief."

Mac hadn't seen old lady Jakubjansky come in just behind him, but she spoke up now. "Antonio, you old fool, John is a good boy."

"He was trying to rob from my store. A crook, that's what he is."

Mac leaned across the counter and Giancarlo scooted back a little. "I think we all know that John has problems," Mac said softly, feeling a twinge of disloyalty, but dismissing it impatiently.

Giancarlo tapped his forehead. "Yeah, I always know he is a little funny in the head, but I never think he also be a thief."

"He's not, not really."

"We caught him right here."

Mac picked up a paper napkin and twisted it in his fingers. "John was doing that for me. I told him

I needed money and he . . . he just didn't think. He was only trying to do what he thought was right."

"Why should he take my money? He belongs in jail."

Mac glanced around at Mrs. Jakubjansky and she seemed to see the despair he was feeling reflected in his face. She came closer to the counter. "Antonio, you always been a big talker about how wonderful is this country. Well, John was a soldier fighting for you. Is it his fault the war made him a little sick in the head? He's a good boy now, but if they put him in jail with all the killers and crooks, who knows what will happen to him? Mr. McCarthy takes good care of John, better than a jail."

Giancarlo seemed to waver just a little. "But he was stealing. . . ."

Mac crumpled the napkin and tossed it onto the counter. "Look, if you'll drop the charges, they'll let him go. We'll leave; I'll take him away right now, today, and we'll never bother you again. I swear to God, all we want to do is get away from here."

It took about ten more minutes for the two of them to convince Giancarlo, but he finally put up his hands and surrendered. As the disgruntled man went off to the precinct house, Mac ran upstairs to pack. He also shaved and changed, before piling their meager belongings just inside the door for easy pick-up. As he was finishing, old lady Jakubjansky appeared at the door again, a foil-wrapped package in one hand. "My sugar cookies," she said. "John likes them."

Mac took the package. "Thank you," he said awkwardly.

"He is like a little boy sometimes."

"Yeah."

Her face grew stern and she pointed a skinny finger at him. "He is your responsibility. Take better care for him."

Mac nodded and she left. He stared at the package of cookies for a moment, then set it on top of the luggage and left.

By the time he got to the station, Johnny was already out of the holding cell, sitting in the squad room, drinking a Coke and listening to Mazzeretti. Johnny didn't seem to be saying much, but he nodded occasionally in response to something the cop was saying. As Mac got closer, Johnny looked up and saw him coming across the room. His face broke into a broad grin. Mac grinned in response and walked a little faster. He felt good now, and ignored Mazzeretti's troubled dark gaze that rested on them as he and Johnny greeted each other. "How you doing, kid?" he asked, giving Johnny a light punch on the arm.

"I'm okay, Mac," he replied softly.

Mazzeretti stepped forward. "McCarthy, I want to talk to you."

"What about?" Mac asked, only wanting to take Johnny and go.

"In my office."

Mac glanced at Johnny, who was watching the conversation.

"John can wait here," Mazzeretti said.

Giving the suddenly frightened blue eyes a quick A-OK sign, Mac followed the detective. They sat facing one another across the desk. Mazzeretti lit another cigar, and Mac took out a cigarette.

"Tell me about John."

Mac shifted in the seat. "I thought you said he

could go, if the charges were dropped."

"He can go. As soon as we've talked."

"I don't know what you want me to say." Mac
took a deep drag on his cigarette.

"I want to know what his problems are."

"I already told you; he was in Nam."

"So were a lot of people."

The small office was quiet for several moments.
Mac finally sighed. "Some people can hack war,"
he said. "Some can't. Johnny didn't belong there."
He looked at the cop. "But that was all a long time
ago. Johnny's okay now."

"Except when he gets scared, like tonight,
right?"

"He's okay," Mac repeated stubbornly.

"You said he's getting help?"

"Sure," Mac lied.

"What's his doctor's name?"

He frowned, glancing out to the other room.
"He goes to the VA hospital," he improvised.
"Look, can we go now?"

After a moment, Mazzeretti nodded. "All
right," he said. "But I suggest you keep an eye on
him. Next time he might get into more serious
trouble."

Mac was already at the door. "Sure," he said
quickly. "I'll take care of him."

Johnny looked up from his intent contemplation
of the floor and smiled as Mac approached. "Can
we go now?" he asked softly.

"Sure, kid, come on." He took Johnny by one
arm and guided him through the squadroom, feeling Mazzeretti's eyes on them all the while.

-TWELVE-

Mac spent the next two days running all over the city, trying to parlay his pitifully small stake into four thousand dollars before the people he owed could catch up with him. He hustled like he never had before, chasing down guys he hadn't seen in months, scrounging every cent he could.

They had a new home, a cockroach-ridden room behind a second-hand furniture store, and Johnny stayed there. He was restless and a little bewildered, but as always, he obeyed Mac's orders unquestioningly. The last thing Mac needed was to have Johnny wandering the streets, easy prey for Frank and Al, the two gorillas.

At the end of forty-eight hours, he'd managed to turn his pittance into three-hundred and seventy-five dollars. A tidy sum, yeah, but still a helluva long way from what he needed. It was nearly ten P.M. when he finally gave up and started home. He was very tired, a little drunk, feeling the almost unbearable loneliness of the deserted side street. The chilling wind cut through the heavy denim jacket he wore as if it were made of paper. He walked a little faster, wanting to be home, not wanting to be alone anymore.

He was three blocks from the room when Frank and Al stepped out of an alley and stopped in front of him. Mac pulled his hands out of his pockets, tensing. "Hi," he said.

"Hi, there, Mr. McCarthy. We've been looking for you."

"I've been around."

"So we hear."

Mac ran the tip of his tongue across his lips. "You want something?"

"Yeah, sir, we want something. In fact, we want four thousand somethings. And we want them now."

"Oh, yeah." He reached toward his pocket. "I have three-hundred and seventy-five dollars," he said. "You take it. Well, look, on second thought, take only three, why don't you, and leave me the seventy-five for a stake, so I can—"

He never finished the sentence. A fist, augmented by brass knuckles and backed by Frank's well-over two-hundred pounds, crashed into his stomach. Grunting, Mac bent over. The same fist collided with his jaw, sending him reeling backwards. He collided with a brick wall.

"See," Al said kindly, "you don't owe three-hundred. You owe four thousand. And on top of that, see, you ran out so we had to chase you all over the city."

"I . . . wasn't trying . . . to run out," Mac gasped. "I was only . . . trying to raise the cash."

"Yes, well, that's fine and good. But you didn't get it, did you? So now we have to collect the interest." Al stepped aside.

Mac tried to avoid the next blow from Frank. He sidestepped, shoving both arms into Frank's mid-section. The fat man grunted a little. Before Mac could take advantage of that momentary victory, Al crashed what felt like the butt of a gun into the back of his head.

Colored lights exploded in his skull. Mac sprawled onto the gritty concrete, tasting the hot blood that gushed from his nose, feeling the surface of his palms scraped raw. He rolled onto his back, hoping to be able to kick upwards and make his escape.

Before he could move and put his plan, such as it was, into operation, a steel-tipped shoe was propelled into his side once, then again and again. The heel of another shoe was pressed slowly, deliberately, into his outstretched palm. All of this took place in an eerie silence, broken only by the sound of his own raspy breaths.

Absently Mac kept a tally of the bruising kicks to his body. He could feel the bile rising up, threatening to choke him, and he turned his head, letting the hot liquid roll out the side of his mouth. It made him mad to realize that he might die here, amid the over-turned garbage cans, finished off by a couple of shitheads like these two. It also made him sad, although he didn't know why. Life hadn't been such a barrel of laughs that he should mind very much checking out a little early.

The beating had stopped without Mac's really being aware of it, and someone was pawing through his pockets. The hard-earned money was removed. "We'll be around for the rest," a voice said. "Understand?" Another kick. "Understand?"

He managed to nod. They walked away, leaving him alone in the alley to die.

A long time passed, and he didn't move at all. It was kind of peaceful there, actually, just him and a couple of roving tomcats. Or maybe they were rats; he really couldn't see too well. The flow of blood from his nose had slowed to a trickle. He wondered how long it took to die.

"Oh, shit," he mumbled suddenly. "I forgot about him."

So much for a nice quiet death here in the alley. Johnny was waiting for him in that terrible little room above the furniture store, and if he didn't come back, that idiot would probably just sit there until he died of starvation or something.

Mac tried to roll over, and on his third attempt, he made it. The effort brought tears to his eyes, but he didn't take time to catch his breath before pushing himself to his knees. *"Ohjesus,"* he said. *"Ohchrist."* Putting his hands against the side of the building, he managed slowly and excruciatingly to push himself to a standing position. He leaned his face against the cold surface of the bricks. It felt so good that he just wanted to stand there forever, but after a while he knew that it was time to move on.

The first step nearly finished him. He shuffled about six inches and then stopped, doubled over in pain, throwing up again. "Help me," he whispered to the emptiness. "Help me, Johnny." Oh great, he thought, things were so bad that he needed help from the dumbass kid. His breath came in sharp, gravelly gasps that whistled every once in a while. With shaking fingers, he poked and probed until he came to the conclusion that no matter how much they hurt, all of his ribs were still somehow intact.

Finally, by sliding his feet along the pavement, he managed to move. He kept both arms wrapped

around his stomach, stopping every once in a while
to catch his breath. Think about something else, he
ordered himself. Shit, it was so damned cold.
Almost Christmas. Yeah, think about Christmas.

When he was ten, he spent the holiday with some
minister's family. What the hell was their name?
Loomis, that was it. The Loomises were Episco-
palians, but the nuns were so anxious to find
a home for the gangly, solitary boy that they decided to forget liturgical differences and let him go.
The minister was a nice man. Dumb, but nice. His
wife baked cookies all the time. While the minister
wrote his Christmas Eve sermon and the wife
turned out seemingly endless pans of cookies, Mac
spent time with their son. The boy was fifteen. Mac
hadn't thought about Brian Loomis in a long time.
The minister's son and the orphan boy hid in the
cellar, where they smoked illicit cigarettes and
looked at dirty pictures. Whenever Brian got a
hard-on, he would make Mac jerk him off. That
happened a couple times every day during his one-
week stay.

He wondered what had happened to Brian
Loomis.

Mac looked up and realized that he still had a
block to go. Think some more. Christmas. Last
year he and Johnny had humped down to the
Salvation Army for a free meal. His luck had been
on a bad streak then.

He tried to laugh, but it hurt too much.

Still, the meal hadn't been so bad. Turkey and
everything, and they even let Johnny have seconds
on the pumpkin pie. Afterward, he treated Johnny
to a double feature, both westerns. Johnny, shyness
making him even more tongue-tied than usual, pre-

sented him with a carton of cigarettes.

Hell, when he stopped to think about it, last Christmas had been pretty good. Better than most. Maybe even the best.

He reached the corner. Just a little further, he thought, and I'll be home. Then everything will be okay. That thought kept him moving, when all he really wanted to do was fall into the gutter and let blessed oblivion wash over him. But finally, finally, he dragged his weary body up the stairs and reached the door to their room. Without even enough strength left to knock, he lifted one hand and scratched feebly at the chipped painted surface. He waited a century or two, then scratched again.

"Who's there?" said a soft voice from within.

"John," he gasped out. "It's me, Johnny."

The door flew open. He got one look at Johnny's scared face before everything started to spin around, the blackness taking over at last, and he pitched forward into Johnny's arms.

His next awareness was of a dull, throbbing ache in his side, and then of a soft insistent whisper very close to his ear. "Mac? Hey, buddy? Please, Mac, don't die."

He couldn't even open his eyes yet. Instead, he lay very still and took a groggy inventory. The bloody clothes were gone, his body had been cleaned, and he was lying in bed, feeling warm and almost comfortable. It was nice and he was tempted to just drift away again.

But there was that whisper. "Mac, please, wake up."

Allowing himself to be dragged back from the

edge, he managed to move his hand a little, searching, until his fingers closed around Johnny's wrist. He squeezed lightly. "S'okay," he mumbled through swollen lips.

"Mac?"

Finally he opened his eyes. Johnny, pale and wearing a T-shirt that was caked with blood, sat on the edge of the bed. His eyes, wide blue pools behind the glasses, were panic-stricken. "Hey," Mac said, "s'okay, really."

"Should I get a doctor or something?"

"Uh-uh. Hurts like hell, but I don't think anything's broken."

Johnny released his breath in a long sigh.

"Thanks for patching me up."

"Yeah, sure." Johnny grinned. "Maybe I should've been a doctor, right?" The smile vanished as suddenly as it had appeared. He stood and walked a few steps away from the bed, not looking at Mac. "I was so damned scared," he said hoarsely. "I thought you were—" He broke off.

"I must've looked like death warmed over," Mac said, trying to speak lightly.

Johnny whirled around to face him. "I was so scared, Mac. I'm sorry to be so scared all the time. I don't like being a coward."

Mac tried to lift his head, but immediately gave it up as a bad idea. "That's a stupid thing to say. You're not a coward."

Johnny shivered a little. "Yeah, Mac, I am, and that's no good. I hate myself sometimes and you must hate me, too."

"Stop it," Mac said wearily. "Just knock off the crap, willya? I'm really not up to it right now. I don't hate you."

"I'm sorry."

"Yeah, kid, I know." Every inch of his body hurt. "Shit. We have any booze?"

Johnny got an almost empty bottle of whiskey from the cupboard and brought it to him. "Who did this to you?"

"Al and Frank, of course. That shouldn't surprise you."

"Because of the money?"

"Yeah, because of the money." In one long drink, Mac drained the bottle. "Took my fucking three-seventy-five, too."

Johnny kept wiping his hands on his blue jeans, as if he were still trying to get rid of the blood. "They almost killed you."

He handed the empty bottle back. "Yeah, well, that was an oversight I'm sure they'll correct the next time." He leaned back and closed his eyes as the alcohol began to work on his system. "Gotta sleep, babe," he mumbled. "Ev'rythin' be okay, ya'know."

"I know."

Johnny's voice sounded faint and far away as Mac finally let the warm darkness wash over him and sweep him away.

-THIRTEEN-

He watched Mac sleep for a long time.

When at last he was convinced that the reassuring up-and-down movements of the other man's chest would continue, Johnny stood, stretching his cramped muscles. The bloody T-shirt stuck to his body unpleasantly, and he grimaced a little, pulling the offending garment over his head and tossing it into the trash.

He washed away the last traces of Mac's blood and put on an old khaki shirt that was a little too large. After checking on Mac again, Johnny went to the battered dresser and quietly slid the top drawer open. Inside the drawer there was a jumble of Mac's things, all dumped there indiscriminately. It was the way they lived, from one cheap room to another, an existence that made objects more of an annoyance than anything else. A thing that had no value at the pawnshop meant nothing. The drawer held socks and underwear, mostly G.I. Discharge papers for both men. Lieutenant's bars. Old matchbooks. A couple back issues of *Playboy*. Johnny scooted all the junk aside, reaching beneath the clutter until his fingers closed around the grip of the Army issue .45. The one item of value that never went to the pawnshop.

Johnny pulled the gun out, frowning a little. The feel of the cold metal in his hand reminded him fleetingly of something, but the memory was lost in that void he had in his past. Fragments came back once in a while, mostly at night, causing him to wake up trembling and drenched in sweat. At times like that, he would wake Mac, and Mac would talk to him, quietly and calmly, not about the dreams or what caused them, but about other things. Like the trip to Hollywood they were going to take soon. Or he told stories about some of the funny things that had happened to him back at the orphanage. It didn't matter what he said anyway; it was just the sound of the deep voice that drove away the demons.

Johnny shook off the thoughts and went back to the chair, holding the gun easily in one hand. Just as he sat down, Mac stirred restlessly, mumbling something Johnny couldn't understand. He reached out with his free hand and pulled the blanket up, tucking it more tightly around the sleeping man. "S'okay," he soothed. "I'm not scared now."

He checked the gun, saw that there was a full clip inside, and tucked the weapon into his waistband. Like Steve McGarrett, he thought. Or Matt Dillon. Leaning forward a little, he spoke again, his fingers resting lightly on Mac's arm. "I'll be back as soon as I can, buddy," he said softly.

Shrugging into his dark blue ski jacket, he turned off the overhead light, leaving a small lamp on, and went out of the room. The air outside smelled of approaching snow. Johnny shoved both hands into his pockets, ducking his head against the bite of the wind as he walked quickly toward the subway.

There was only one other person waiting for the train, a middle-aged black woman carrying a brown paper shopping bag. They eyed one another with mutual suspicion, before Johnny smiled blankly and moved several yards away.

It was nearly five minutes before the train roared to a stop. The car was crowded with a noisy bunch of teenagers, all of whom seemed to be high. They pushed and shoved up and down the aisle, singing, laughing, exuding an excitement that hovered on the near edge of violence. Johnny huddled in a seat by the door, careful not to look at any of the kids, afraid, terrified that they would notice him and . . . and what? He didn't really know what they might do, but the fear was so strong that he could taste it, metallic and bitter in his mouth. Only the thought that Mac was counting on him kept Johnny from fleeing the train at the next stop.

The fifteen minutes it took to reach his stop seemed endless, but at last Johnny could scurry out of the car and up the steps, emerging onto a crowded sidewalk. Despite the late hour and the cold, there were still plenty of people out and about. Hustlers, night wanderers, funseekers, moving in and out of the bars, massage parlors, and bookstores that lined the street. Surrounded by a universe of threatening strangers, Johnny drew further into himself, edging cautiously through the crowd, one hand resting on the gun. The lump of steel dug into his belly, but rather than being an annoyance, the presence of the weapon, Mac's gun, was reassuring. Almost like having Mac himself there.

Johnny's feelings were as jumbled as had been the contents of the drawer earlier. Fear, certainly. But not of the moment, itself, or even of what he intended to do. Only fear, as always, of the people swirling around him, watching him. Two hookers, one female and one male, approached him in the space of half a block. He ignored their graphic invitations.

Even the fear, though, was over-shadowed by his sense of purpose. It was the first time that he could ever remember feeling really important. Except maybe for the time he made the speech at graduation. The whole auditorium listened to him that night. He could still remember the speech. "As we the class of 1960 embark upon the great adventure of life," he whispered into the knife-edged wind, "we are strengthened and emboldened by the lessons learned here. The road we are about to set foot upon will not be easy. The dangers are many, but we face them unafraid. No one knows what the future may hold, but I am confident. I look into the next decade with all its promises and all its problems, and I feel a great sense of exhilaration."

They all applauded and cheered when he finished. Of course, it was maybe a little bit because they felt sorry for him, his parents being just dead and all. But still it was a good speech.

So now here he was, finally *doing* something, finally taking action. This was almost like those holy missions his parents used to go on. They went to save souls from the Devil. Well, Al and Frank were like devils. They were evil and cruel, and it was his duty to save Mac's soul from them, to save Mac. The wages of sin is death, and they had sinned by the terrible thing they had done to Mac.

And they might do worse unless he stopped them. Their evil could not be allowed to triumph over Mac's goodness.

When he reached the Pirate's Cove, Johnny didn't go in. Instead, he ducked into the alley and walked to the rear of the building. Loud rock music from bars on either side of the Cove filled the air. He hunched down behind some empty packing crates and leaned against the side of the building to wait.

It was getting colder. He blew on his fingers every couple of minutes to warm them a little. Hope this doesn't take too long, he fretted. Mac shouldn't be by himself, in case he needs me.

And, the thought came, what will Mac say about this?

Johnny chewed on his chapped lower lip. I gotta do everything just right, or he'll get mad at me. I hate it worse than anything when Mac is mad at me.

He sighed and gripped the gun more tightly. Where the hell were Al and Frank? They always turned up sooner or later at the Cove; it was a part of their routine. Johnny's knowledge of what went on around him would have startled even Mac, who was fully aware that he wasn't nearly as spaced out as everybody else thought. But even Mac had no idea how completely Johnny assimilated his surroundings. The vague blue eyes missed nothing. No one knew Johnny; he knew everyone.

His legs were beginning to cramp. Without standing, he straightened first one and then the other, trying to ease the kinks.

It wasn't that he really hated Al and Frank. Hatred implied feeling and he felt nothing at all for

them. They existed only insofar as they posed a
threat to Mac. They wanted to kill him. The very
thought made Johnny shake deep inside, and he
pushed it away quickly.

After what seemed like a very long time, the
back door of the Cove creaked open. Johnny
tensed, then leaned forward a little, until he could
see two dark profiles standing just a few feet away.
They talked together in muffled tones as Al struggled to light a cigar in the wind.

Johnny rested his arm across the top of a crate,
sighting carefully as if he were throwing a dart at a
target, and squeezed the trigger of the .45. The first
bullet struck Frank in the back of the head and the
big man toppled over, already dead. Al lifted his
head in startled reaction. Johnny fired again, the
sound of the shot nearly swallowed up by the wind
and the music, and this bullet hit Al in the chest.
He fumbled inside of his coat desperately. Johnny
fired again, and this time the bullet smashed into
Al's forehead.

Johnny waited a moment, the gun still poised,
but neither of the men moved. He slipped out of his
hiding place and knelt next to Al, rummaging
through the dead man's pockets until he found a
fat money belt. Quickly he counted out exactly
$375, then shoved the rest back.

An instant later he stepped out of the alley,
mingling once again with the crowd on the sidewalk. Inside the jacket pocket, one hand still
clutched the gun.

Now that it was over, he felt numb. Two men
were dead and he was the one who'd killed them. It
wasn't the first time he'd killed, of course. But, no,
he wouldn't think about that, wouldn't try to focus

on the grey memory that haunted him. Mac said it didn't matter.

He stopped to buy an Orange Julius and carried it down to the subway to wait for the train that would take him home. That was all he wanted. To get home, back to the small room that meant safety, back to Mac.

-FOURTEEN-

He woke once and stirred restlessly, feeling strangely alone. But that was stupid, because he knew that Johnny was there, sound asleep probably, just across the small room. It was senseless to wake him. Mac wanted to turn his head for a quick look, just to be sure that everything was okay, but the effort involved in such a maneuver seemed beyond his meager resources at that moment. With the thought still half-formed, he fell asleep again.

The next time he woke, Johnny was there, sitting next to the bed. Mac grunted a greeting, trying to focus his fuzzy gaze. Johnny, he noted, idly, was fully dressed and holding the gun in his hand.

The gun?

Now Mac was wide awake. "Hey," he managed to say through a dry throat.

After a beat, Johnny glanced up. "Hi," he said dully.

"I could use . . . some water, babe."

Johnny nodded, but otherwise didn't move.

Mac was bewildered, as if the beating had scrambled his brains and maybe it had. "Johnny? What's wrong? What're you doing with the gun?"

Johnny looked at the gun in surprise, as if he'd forgotten that it was clenched in his fingers. "Don't be mad," he whispered. "Promise you won't get mad at me, Mac." Before Mac could respond, Johnny set the gun carefully on the floor and went over to the sink. He let the water run for a minute to get cold, then filled a glass, and brought it back to the bed. "Here."

Mac raised himself a little and sipped tentatively. Everything seemed to be working okay, and he relaxed slightly. "Why should I get mad?" he asked when his throat felt better. "Johnny, what's going on?"

Johnny sat on the edge of the bed. He ducked his head, staring at the blanket, fingering a small hole in the cheap material. "Please, Mac. Promise."

"I promise," Mac said after a moment, suddenly afraid without knowing why.

Johnny sighed, watching his fingers enlarge the tear in the blanket. "I killed them."

"What? Who?" Mac realized that the poor guy was having another nightmare about Tan Pret. There hadn't been so many lately, but they still upset the kid a lot. "Hey, we've talked about this before, right?"

"No. This is something else. I killed Al and Frank."

Mac heard the words and even understood them, but the meaning didn't register. "What?"

"I killed Al and Frank a little while ago. I shot them both."

"*Ohmygod*," Mac breathed, drawing back a little. "You did what?" He gripped Johnny's arm with a strength he didn't think his battered body still had. "Is this a dream, John? That's it, right? Some kind of a crazy dream?"

But Johnny shook his head. "No," he said, still whispering. "It's not a dream. It really happened."

"*What* happened?" Mac realized that his voice was cracking. He finished the water in a gulp and took a deep breath. "Tell me all about it, Johnny. From the beginning." Something in Johnny's face made him add, "I'm not mad, kid. I just want to know."

Johnny relaxed a little. "After you fell asleep, I took your gun and caught the subway over to the Cove, 'cause that's where they hang out. I waited in the alley for a long time. It was really cold, too," he added. "Finally they came out, Al and Frank. I shot Frank first, because he was closest. I shot him in the head. Then I shot Al, but the first bullet didn't kill him, so I had to do it again. They were both dead." He fumbled in his pocket. "I got your money back. Three hundred and seventy-five, right? He had a lot more, but I only took yours." When Mac didn't reach for the bills, Johnny dropped them onto the floor next to the gun. "Then I bought an Orange Julius and caught the subway home." He made the entire recitation flatly, without the slightest trace of emotion, sounding like a TV anchorman delivering the evening news on a dull day. Finished, he raised his eyes and met Mac's gaze. Now his voice was strained. "I had to do it, Mac. They hurt you and they were going to kill you next time; you said so."

Mac suddenly remembered the expression in Johnny's eyes the day he tried to grease Crazy George; that same look was there now. The water he'd just finished threatened to come right back up. "Oh, Johnny," he said helplessly. He shook his head. "Ohchrist, kid."

Johnny's brow wrinkled anxiously. "You're not mad, are you? Please, don't be. You promised."

Mac released his hold on Johnny's arm. "No," he said absently, his mind on other things. "I'm not mad."

Johnny smiled a little. "Okay, then, it's all right."

"All right?" Mac leaned back and closed his eyes, trying to think. There was no way that the weapon used could be traced to him. He'd won the gun in a poker game in Nam, won it from a guy who'd bought it on the black market in Da Nang. At least they were safe on that front. "Nobody saw what happened?" he asked, opening his eyes. "You're sure?"

"Nobody saw, Mac. It was dark. The music was so loud that they couldn't even hear the shots."

"Well, thank god for that, anyway. Maybe we can pull this off."

"You understand why I had to do it, don't you?"

Mac stared into the guileless blue eyes that begged for approval like a child would, or a pet dog seeking the loving attention of its master. "Yeah, Johnny," he said finally, "I know why you did it." That was a lie, of course, because he didn't understand, not really, not completely anyway. But the blue eyes needed reassurance and so he lied. "Don't think about it anymore right now, okay? It's over and done with, so now things will be better. Understand?"

"Sure, Mac, just as long as you're not mad at me." Johnny stood and began to undress.

Mac watched him absently, rubbing the bridge of his sore nose gently. Well, it wasn't as if those two bastards would ever be missed by anyone. And, hell, they really might have killed him. Probably would have, if he hadn't come up with the rest of the cash. He sighed.

Johnny, stripped to his shorts, stood in the center of the room, looking around helplessly, as if he couldn't remember what the hell he'd been doing. Then a frown crossed his face. "Mac?"

"Huh?" Mac replied vaguely, still finding it hard to believe that this bewildered man-child had just finished blowing away two of the toughest collectors in the city. "What, kid?"

"Could I . . . could I stay over here with you for a while? I don't want to be by myself."

Mac hesitated, then attempted a shrug. "Okay, come on." He scooted over to make room, grimacing a little as his body protested.

Johnny turned off the lamp and stretched out next to him, giving a long sigh. "Thank you."

"What for?"

"Everything. For not being mad, and for letting me stay here with you."

Mac wanted to smash somebody's head against the wall, but whether it should be his own or Johnny's, he didn't know. "Ah, shit, Johnny," he said finally. "Go to sleep."

"Okay. Things are gonna be better now, huh?"

Mac closed his eyes. "Yeah, kid, sure," he said. "Things are gonna pick up."

"Good."

"But for now go to sleep, willya?"

Johnny didn't answer, but in only a few minutes, his breathing had taken on the regular pattern of sleep. Mac finally turned his face to the wall and slept as well.

-FIFTEEN-

Despite the morning chill that touched the room, the two bodies lying together in the narrow bed created a damp heat of their own, and it was that warmth which woke Mac finally. He shifted uncomfortably, trying to ease out from under the weight of Johnny's arm across his chest. The pressure and the heat combined until he felt as if he would suffocate. He moved again and Johnny moaned a soft, wordless protest, but didn't awaken. Mac finally managed to plant both feet on the floor and get up from the bed.

The cold air hit like an electric shock against his hot, flushed skin, and he stood still for a moment, feeling strangely breathless. At last he began to move, albeit slowly. His body ached all over, and the brief glimpse he took in the mirror revealed a face that would take two weeks to heal. But despite all that, Al and Frank were—had been—pros, and they hadn't really intended to do him any serious damage last night. This first time was only meant to serve as a warning. Well, there wouldn't be a second time. He glanced at Johnny, still curled in the bed, sleeping as deeply as a child. It was still almost impossible to believe what he'd done.

Moving carefully, Mac got dressed. When he'd donned cords and a sweater, and finished a can of flat soda pop he found on the table, he went back to crouch by the bed. "John?" he whispered.

Two bleary eyes snapped open. "Huh?"

"I have to go someplace. You stay inside today, understand?"

Fear flickered through the sleepy blue gaze. "Where are you going?"

"Just out. I want to see if there's anything going down about what happened."

"About what I did, you mean?"

"Yeah." Mac picked up the money from the floor where Johnny had dropped it the night before. "You okay?"

"I guess so."

Mac patted his shoulder absently. "Sure you are. See you in a little while." Grabbing his coat, Mac left the room quickly. Outside, he paused, taking deep gulps of the icy air. He felt like a drowning man being given oxygen. The cold seemed to steady him a little, and he was able to walk almost briskly to the Coffee Cup Cafe three blocks away.

Taking a seat at the counter, he ordered coffee and a Danish, and reached for the communal copy of the morning paper. Of course, he realized that it was too soon for there to be anything on the shooting, but he read each headline anyway, just in case.

When that task was complete, he gestured for another cup of coffee and glanced down the length of the counter, spotting a familiar face. "Working so early in the morning, Shirl?" he asked lightly.

The scrawny blonde grinned. "Rent's due, Alex. A girl's gotta keep a roof over her head."

"Yeah, I guess." He watched Shirley sip Coke

through a straw. She was young, about Johnny's age, but she looked older. Not bad, though.

"You walk into a door or something?" she asked.

"Huh?"

"Your face. Looks like a meat grinder worked you over."

"Close." He grimaced. "You know how it is."

She nodded glumly. "Sure do. How's John?"

"Okay," he replied, feeling the familiar tightening of tension in his gut. "Why?"

She shrugged. "Just wondering. I like John. He's funny."

"Funny?"

"Uh-huh. He makes me laugh sometimes."

Mac didn't particularly like the idea of people laughing at the kid. He was weird, yeah, but he had feelings like everybody else.

Shirley must have seen the disapproval on his face, because she suddenly spit the piece of ice she'd been sucking on back into the glass. "Hey, I didn't mean anything bad, you know? I don't laugh at John because of . . . well, because of the way he's kinda slow and all. I just meant that he makes jokes sometimes."

"Yeah, sure," he said. "Johnny's a regular Bob Hope once he gets going." Shit, if the kid ever made a joke, it must have been an accident. He probably wondered why the hell everybody was laughing. "He's not really slow, you know," he said. "Johnny was the valedictorian of his high school class."

"Yeah? That's good, huh?"

"Means he was the smartest one there." Mac glumly crumpled the last of his Danish. It wasn't even noon yet, and the rest of the day stretched out endlessly in front of him. He could spend the time walking the streets trying to find out what anybody might know about the killings. Or he could go back to the room, that damned room that threatened sometimes to suffocate him, and try to carry on a conversation with Johnny. Right at the moment, though, he didn't feel up to that challenge.

"You feeling down, Alex?" she asked.

"Yeah, I guess so."

"Why?"

He sipped the cooling coffee and wondered what she would do if he actually told her all his problems. Fall asleep, probably. "Why not?" was all he said.

"I got a couple of joints, if you're interested."

"No. Thanks anyway." Not about to mess up my mind like that, he thought. Booze is one thing, but I don't need any of that other shit. Hell, one spaceman in the family was enough.

Maybe there was something else he could do to kill some time until the late editions hit the street. "Fifty bucks pay your rent?"

"And then some."

He shoved the empty cup away. "How about I pick up a bottle and we go to your place?"

She pushed blonde strands out of her eyes. "Sounds good. Beats the hell out of standing on a street corner in this weather." She grinned. "Besides, sometimes it's nice making it with a friend, you know?"

It was already dark when he finally left Shirley's place, still a little drunk, groggy with too much sleep and sex and alcohol. He walked home slowly, stopping at a candy store for a paper; as an after-thought to appease his guilt over having left Johnny sitting alone in the room for so long, he also bought a candy bar.

Johnny was slumped in the chair, half-asleep, a copy of *TV Guide* open in his lap. Crazy kid read the guide every week, even though they didn't have the set anymore. He woke with a start when the door opened, then smiled. "Hi."

"Hi, buddy." He tossed the candy into his lap. "I got that for you."

"Thanks."

Mac grunted and sat down on the bed, opening the newspaper. The story was on page three. "Two men found shot," he read aloud. "You want to hear this?"

"I don't care." Johnny was carefully unwrapping the chocolate.

" 'Police are investigating the shooting deaths of two men reputed to have ties to local gambling interests. The bodies of Francis Muldair and Albert Nueman were found behind the Pirate's Cove Bar in Manhattan. According to a police spokesman, there are no leads thus far in the double slaying. The two men reportedly worked for Daniel Tedesco, local gambling kingpin.' " He looked up. "That's all it says."

Johnny nodded. "They don't know I did it."

Mac threw the paper aside and began unlacing his shoes. "Everything go okay today?"

"Yes. I stayed here, just like you said to."

"Good boy." Mac grinned. "To tell the truth, babe, I'm a little drunk."

"I know."

"You can tell, huh? How?" Mac pulled off his sweater and pants.

"Because whenever you're drunk, you have this

stupid-looking smile on your face," Johnny said mildly.

"Thanks a lot." He flopped back onto his bed. "Tomorrow, Johnny, we really gotta talk."

"Sure, Mac, whenever you want."

He lay there for a long time in a sort of fuzzy glow, all the tension of the morning gone, watching Johnny finish the candy bar and then undress for the night. It was a pleasant moment, and he wished it could be like this all the time. Johnny pushed the chair and footstool together and spread out the blanket, as Mac still watched. " 'Night, Johnny," he mumbled as the light went out.

"Good night, Mac. Thanks for the candy."

He nodded, although Johnny couldn't see him in the dark, and fell asleep.

-SIXTEEN-

They didn't talk the next day after all. Somehow the right moment never seemed to arrive, and as several more days went by, they both seemed more than willing to simply forget what had happened. Although deep inside himself Mac knew that a day of reckoning would have to come sooner or later, he decided to just go with the flow as old Wash used to say. Go with the flow. Mac's luck was on an upswing suddenly and he was winning regularly, winning big. He got the TV out of hock and even blew a wad on a pair of genuine leather gloves for Johnny. The kid, meanwhile, was overdosing on soda and television.

All this good fortune lasted exactly one week. On Wednesday afternoon, they went to see the new western playing up the street. Afterward, they parted company amiably, Johnny going over to the Coffee Cup for a hamburger, and Mac eager to get an early start on the night's game.

He should've gone to eat instead.

His luck was suddenly as sour as it had been good, and in only a few hours, he was down seven hundred dollars. At that point, he quit. The cards were just running cold for him, and there wasn't much sense in blowing his last hundred and fifty bucks. Tomorrow night would be better.

He left the store front where the game was currently operating and started home, his mood gloomy. Why the hell couldn't they ever get far enough ahead to relax? One lousy week of feeling good, of spending money, of having some frigging fun, for chrissake, and now things had to turn rotten again. Shit. Just when he'd gotten John all keyed up about maybe taking a trip to California. Shit. Well, the trip would just have to wait. And Johnny wouldn't care, of course. He wouldn't even utter a word of complaint, but only smile that same idiotic smile and say, "That's okay, Mac."

Yeah, sure, that's okay, Mac.

Just once, he wished that Johnny would haul off and hit him. Then he could hit back, and everybody would be a whole lot happier. He kicked at an empty beer can and swore, but whether the anger was directed at John Griffith or himself wasn't really clear.

Lost in somewhat weary contemplation of his life, he wasn't aware that a car had pulled up behind him, or that two men had gotten out, until one of them touched his elbow. "McCarthy?" The tone was polite, but steely.

He spun around. "Huh?"

"Please get into the car."

He tried to pull away from the abruptly vise-like grip on his arm. "Why the hell should I?"

"Because I asked you to. Besides, you have an appointment and we wouldn't want you to be late."

"I don't understand," Mac said doubtfully.

"Please, Mr. McCarthy, into the car."

A gun barrel pressed lightly into his spine, and he decided not to argue anymore. Discretion and all that. He climbed into the back seat of the limo. One of the men joined him and the other got in front with the driver. The situation was absurd, of course. Like something out of one of those really bad gangster flicks Johnny loved so much. He opened his mouth to ask just where the hell they were going, but after a glance at the man sitting next to him, changed his mind and kept quiet. Go with the flow, Alex, go with the flow.

It was only a few minutes before they pulled into an alley behind a large warehouse and stopped. "Get out," the watchdog ordered. "Don't try anything funny, or I'll blow your guts all over the sidewalk."

"I wouldn't think of it," Mac replied sincerely. Christ, even the dialogue was right out of a B feature. He had a feeling, though, that the bullets in the gun weren't props.

The four of them entered the warehouse and walked across a vast empty area. Mac wondered if maybe they were taking him someplace secluded just for the purpose of killing him. That didn't seem unlikely, and he suppressed a sigh. Talk about your fucking losing streaks.

The office they went into was filled with oak and leather. Class stuff. Mac was pushed gently but firmly into a chair. He rested two sweaty palms on his knees and looked at the man sitting behind the desk.

He was stocky, grey-haired, and he cleared his throat elegantly. "My name is Daniel Tedesco," he said in a soft, musical voice.

Surprise, surprise. Mr. Big himself. Mac just nodded.

"We have a little business to discuss."

Mac tried for a grin. "Hey, yeah, the money. Well, look, I haven't forgotten that, ya'know."

Tedesco almost smiled. "I wasn't speaking of the money. We can deal with that matter later. At the moment, I have something else on my mind."

Mac slumped in the chair. "Yeah? What's that?"

"There is the question of my two employees. Or more correctly, my two late employees. The two men you killed."

Mac straightened quickly. "Me? I didn't—"

Tedesco held up a hand. "Denials are a waste of time. I am quite sure that you killed Al and Frank."

"But I—"

"Please," Tedesco said gently. "Either you killed my boys, or you know who did. If it wasn't you, then give me a name." He waited patiently.

Mac tried desperately to moisten his dry mouth. He lowered his eyes and stared at his fingers. Hell, he thought. Goddamnit to hell anyway. "Okay," he said after a few moments of rapidly considered and summarily rejected alternatives. "I did it." His voice was flat.

"Very good. Now we can begin to talk. Honesty is very important to me." Tedesco paused. One of the lackeys held out an intricately carved humidor, and with great deliberation, the old man made a selection. "You know," he said parenthetically as he prepared to light the cigar, "it wasn't very bright on your part to take only the three seventy-five. Since that was exactly the amount recorded in their book as having been collected from you earlier in the evening, it aided our investigation immensely."

"Yeah, I'm sure it did," Mac agreed bitterly. That dumb bastard Johnny. If there was a way to screw things up, you could always count on him to do it. I oughtta just turn the son of a bitch over to Tedesco and solve all my problems at one time. "So what now? You going to burn me, too?"

"Well, that's certainly an option," Tedesco said a little too quickly to suit Mac.

He wondered how they'd do it. A quick bullet to the head? Or maybe a trip over to the Hudson. Concrete and chains? Hell, I've been seeing too many of those damned movies with Johnny. And thinking of Johnny . . . well, that was a line of thought best left alone. There wasn't a damned thing he could do for the kid now, except keep his name out of it. John would cope. Somehow. He realized belatedly that Tedesco was talking to him. "Sorry, sir?"

"Please give me your complete attention. I dislike having to repeat myself."

"Yeah, okay."

"I find myself in the need of a new collector to replace the late and much-lamented Mr. Nueman. Would you be interested in the job?"

"Me?" Mac laughed sharply, until he realized that there was no hint of humor in Tedesco's flat, grey eyes. He leaned back in the chair. "You're serious, aren't you?"

"I'm always serious, Mr. McCarthy. Correct me if I'm wrong, but you're in a rather precarious position at the moment, are you not? Shall I enumerate? You owe this organization four thousand dollars. Plus interest. On top of that, you admit to killing two of my best boys." He paused and studied the glowing tip of the cigar. "Of course, perhaps you've already managed to devise some way to extricate yourself from these various complications?"

Mac shook his head. "No," he said softly.

"I thought not. So perhaps you should give my offer serious consideration."

"Just exactly what is your 'offer'?"

"You will handle my collections. A percentage of your cut will be applied toward liquidating your debt. In no time at all, you'll be free and clear once again."

"Uh-huh," Mac said noncommittally.

"Additionally, I am prepared to forgive and forget the matter of my boys being killed like they were. It would become a family matter and go no further."

Mac sighed, looking around the plush office. What chance did he and Johnny have against somebody like Tedesco? They were just a couple of losers in way over their frigging heads. If it was just him. . . . He sighed again, realizing that it wasn't just him and hadn't been for a long time, maybe even since that first day in Tan Pret. At that moment, more clearly than ever before, he was aware that it would never be just him again. Somehow, without really understanding why or how, he seemed to have made a commitment to John Griffith. There would always be someone else to consider. He rubbed his hands along the sides of the chair. Felt like real leather. "Can I have some time?"

"Of course. Take twenty-four hours."

He stood. "Thanks. How can I reach you?"

"Don't bother."

"Can I go now?" He wanted to be home very much.

"Certainly. Can my boys drop you someplace?"

He didn't want any of them near the place. "No. Thanks." He walked to the door, then paused. "This job. It's just making collections, right? Nothing else? No rough stuff like Al and Frank pulled on me?"

Tedesco spread his hands, looking for the moment like a genial uncle. "The job is yours. Handle it anyway you wish. Just bring me my money, and I'll be happy." He smiled. "We'll be in touch."

"Yeah," Mac muttered as he left the office. "I'm sure you will." As he walked across the empty warehouse again, the only sound was the eerie echo of his own footsteps. He resisted the urge to run.

After nearly a week of clouds, the next day brought a bright sun and clear sky. The weather, unfortunately, didn't do much to improve Mac's mood. He toyed unenthusiastically with his scrambled eggs, and watched Johnny across the table at the Coffee Cup. "Hey, I just got an idea," he said finally, dropping his fork.

Johnny was ladling strawberry jam onto toast, his face a study in the same intensity he devoted to every task, no matter how mundane. He finished the job and carefully replaced the spoon in the jelly dish before looking up. "What idea?"

"Why don't we take a ferry boat ride?"

"Today, you mean?"

"Sure. Now. Right after breakfast."

A smile crossed Johnny's face; he dearly loved the boat rides. Then he sobered and chewed the toast thoughtfully, before asking the primary question. "Can we afford it?"

The question irritated Mac. "Of course we can, damn it. Would I suggest it if we couldn't?"

Diplomatically, Johnny refrained from answering. "Okay," he said, smiling again. "That would be fun."

Mac felt dragged out, wondering if he'd gotten even twenty minutes' sleep the night before. He gulped coffee impatiently as Johnny took his own sweet time finishing breakfast. At first, he had considered accepting Tedesco's "offer" and simply not tell Johnny anything about it. But that could lead to all sorts of complications he wasn't really sure he was ready for.

And besides. Yeah, besides. It wouldn't be fair to Johnny to get him mixed up in something like this totally ignorant of what was going on. Even Johnny—spaced-out, screwed-up John—deserved the chance to make a decision like this for himself. Mac wondered if maybe he had a small streak of honor somewhere inside himself. He liked to think so.

On the other hand, there was one more thing, something Mac had admitted to himself only after hours of tossing and turning the night before. He was scared. Just plain scared. If he was going to do what Tedesco had said—and what real choice did he have?—he didn't want to be doing it alone. He wanted Johnny there, too. After all, he admitted in a burst of brutal honesty, Johnny wasn't the only one who needed somebody.

Last night it had all seemed fairly simple. But now, in the sharp glare of the winter morning, with Johnny watching him, it wasn't quite so simple. In fact, it was damned hard.

He didn't say much of anything else until they were actually on the return trip, heading from the Statue of Liberty back to the city. Johnny leaned over the railing, the sharp wind off the water making his face red and tousling his hair. Mac stood back a few feet, watching, both hands wrapped around a cup of hot chocolate from the snack bar. At last, he took a deep breath and walked over to stand beside Johnny. "Want some?" he asked, holding out the cup.

"Thanks." Johnny took a couple of sips, then handed it back. "What's wrong?" he asked suddenly.

Mac took a gulp of chocolate. "Wrong?" He stared back at the Statue of Liberty, before looking at Johnny.

Johnny smiled. This wasn't one of his usual bland grins, but a much rarer expression, one filled with a kind of wry self-awareness. It was an expression Mac had come to enjoy, hoping perhaps it signified that the kid was sort of snapping out of it a little. "Hey, Mac, I know you pretty good by this time."

Mac returned the smile. "Yeah, kid, I guess you do."

The moment passed, and the blue eyes clouded again. "Did I do something wrong, Mac? 'Cause if I did, I'm sorry."

Mac crumpled the empty cup and dropped it into the water. "No, you didn't do anything." He was quiet for a moment and Johnny waited patiently. "I won't bother to apologize to you for screwing things up again. I could spend a whole lot of time doing that."

Johnny's eyes flickered over Mac's face. "You don't have to."

"I know. I know, and that makes it worse, because I *don't* have to apologize. Makes it too easy for me to be a bastard."

Johnny shook his head. "You're not."

Mac shrugged. "Well, anyway. You ever hear of a guy called Daniel Tedesco?"

He thought for a moment. "Uh-huh. He's the guy who runs the gambling stuff. Like your card games."

"Right. He's also the guy Al and Frank worked for, remember?"

The color faded from Johnny's chilled face. "Yeah," he whispered.

Mac shoved both hands into the pockets of his cords. "A couple of his apes snatched me last night, and I had a personal meeting with Mr. Big himself."

Johnny's teeth were chattering, but whether it was from the cold or from fear, Mac couldn't tell. He lifted a hand, as if to touch Mac, then lowered it again. "Did they hurt you?"

Mac shook his head impatiently. "No, no, of course not. Tedesco just wanted to talk. About Al and Frank."

"*Ohmygod.*" Johnny clutched at the railing, his fear-blanked eyes staring at Mac. "Do they know what I did?"

"No." Mac grinned. "They think I did it. And I just let them go right on thinking that." He pulled his hands out and ducked his head to light a cigarette.

"But, Mac. . ." Now Johnny grabbed him by one arm. "You didn't kill them. I did and it isn't fair for you to take the blame."

"Shut up, willya, dummy?" Mac shook off Johnny's hand, aware of the other passengers standing nearby. "You did it because of me. That makes me responsible, too."

Johnny moved away from the railing and huddled against the wall. Mac swore to himself and tossed the cigarette away. People were beginning to look at Johnny, and Mac moved over very close to him. "Johnny, it's okay, kid, everything's gonna be okay."

Johnny just shook his head.

"Come over here," Mac muttered through clenched teeth, dragging him around the corner to where they could be alone, at least for the moment. He stared into Johnny's vacant face. "Man, don't fold up on me now. I need you."

A new, unfamiliar, look came into Johnny's eyes. "Yeah?"

"Yeah. Goddamned right."

The idea of being needed seemed to amuse Johnny fleetingly.

Mac shook him by the shoulder. "Are you listening to me?"

"I'm listening."

"Good. Now look, Tedesco isn't going to do anything to me at all. At least, not if I go along with what he wants."

"What's that?"

Mac shrugged. "He wants me to take over Al's job. To become his collector."

"Are you going to?"

"I don't know. That's why I'm talking to you about it. So we can decide together."

In a couple more minutes, the ferry docked. They disembarked, not talking much again until they were on the subway platform, waiting for a train to take them home. Johnny broke the silence finally. "What's going to happen, Mac, if you say yes?"

"Tedesco told me that I could just do the job anyway I want. Part of what I make goes to pay off the money I owe. I figure when that's taken care of, we could save most of the money, and then get out of this town. Go to L.A. and make a fresh start."

Johnny nodded thoughtfully. "And what happens if you say no?"

Mac gave a sharp laugh. "Then I think that my future will pretty much take care of itself." He bit his tongue, tasting blood. Shit. That was just the kind of thing he hadn't wanted to say. "Oh, hell, we could figure out something," he said quickly, but the look in Johnny's eyes told him that the damage was already done. He averted his gaze, studying the graffiti on the wall beyond. One extremely ambitious spray-canner had scrawled his message in large red letters that seemed to go on forever, like splashes of blood against the concrete. I'VE GIVEN UP SEARCHING FOR THE TRUTH, it read, AND NOW I'M LOOKING FOR A REALLY GOOD FANTASY. "I thought maybe we could handle the job together," he said at last.

"Yeah?" Johnny replied.

"Yeah. It might be a way out of this hole. But only if you want to, John. Otherwise, I'll just tell Tedesco no deal, and we'll think of something else." Sure we will, he thought hopelessly.

It was several minutes before Johnny spoke again, and by then they had boarded the express. "There is something else I could do," he said.

"What?"

His voice was very soft and Mac had to lean close to hear him. "I could go to the police and tell them what I did. Then nobody would bother you."

Mac could only look at him, stunned by the unexpected suggestion. "Don't you know what they'd do to you?"

"Put me in jail, like that other time."

Mac snorted. "Shit, man, they'd shove you into a padded cell so fast that your head would be spinning."

"But it would help you."

"Oh, yeah, sure, John, sure," Mac said in disgust. "How long have you had this Jesus Christ complex? Well, you might as well climb down off your fuckin' cross, 'cause I'm not gonna play that game. If we go down in flames, we go together. We're not heroes, either one of us."

Johnny relaxed. "Thanks," he said. "I didn't really want to do that."

"No kidding?"

Johnny's fingers twisted around the edge of the seat. "If we work for Tedesco, I wouldn't have to do anything by myself, would I?"

"No," Mac said firmly. "And neither would I."

He sighed. "Okay, Mac. If you think we should do it, that's okay with me. Whatever you say."

Mac couldn't look at Johnny. Instead, he watched the tunnel lights flash by. God, he thought, God, what am I doing? Whatever I say is okay? I don't know what to say, you poor dumb bastard, except that I'm scared. And that's the one thing I can't say, not to you, because I'm supposed to be strong enough for both of us. Christ, how did I ever get myself into such a fucked-up place? "Oh, hell, Johnny," he said suddenly, "sometimes I get so tired."

"I know," Johnny replied unexpectedly.

Mac rested his head against the window behind him and closed his eyes. Johnny began a soft, rhythmic patting of his shoulder, a childlike

gesture apparently intended to reassure or comfort
him. Mac appreciated the effort, although he
didn't say so.

-SEVENTEEN-

Her name was Toni and her picture had once been in *Playboy*. She told Mac all about it when they were finished and he was getting dressed. Her body, covered only by a thin sheet, stretched languidly. "Maybe you saw it?" she suggested hopefully.

He shook his head as he leaned over to tie his shoes. "No, I don't think so."

"Yeah, well, it was there. Page eighty-two." She tossed her head in a well-practiced gesture that sent amber curls tumbling over her shoulders. "You know, man, that was sort of a quickie. Sure you have to take off so soon?"

"Yeah. Well, I gotta go to work. See ya around."

"Sure," she replied, reaching one bare hand out to touch his arm, and then snuggling back under the sheet again.

Mac left the room and hurried down two flights of steps to the street, emerging into the soft darkness of the spring night. An almost warm breeze blew against him, lightly ruffling his hair. He glanced at his watch and grimaced. Damn. Nearly thirty minutes late.

Luckily, it was only three blocks to the restaurant. Arriving a little out of breath, he paused just inside the door to search the dimly lit room. The place really wasn't classy enough to justify the lack of lighting, but at least they were trying. After a moment, Mac grinned and moved to a corner table. "Hi," he said.

Johnny glanced up from his plate of spaghetti. "About time you showed up." The complaint was half-hearted at best, but he smiled anyway, as if to take any possible sting from his words.

"Yeah, sorry about that," Mac replied, dropping into a chair.

"Hungry?"

"Uh-uh. Maybe later." He picked up the salad fork and absently began wrapping strands of pasta around the tines. "You know, Johnny, we really have to do something tonight about this guy Karlin."

Johnny frowned. "Do we?"

"Yeah." Mac started on his second forkful of spaghetti. "Tedesco got on my ass about him this afternoon."

"Karlin told us last month—" Johnny began softly.

"Hell," Mac broke in, "he's been *telling* us everytime we see him, but he never *does* anything. Tedesco wants results."

"Or else?" Johnny asked, giving up finally and shoving the plate across the table toward Mac.

Mac gave him a sheepish grin and kept eating. "With Tedesco, kid, it's always 'or else.' You should know that by this time."

"I do know it."

Mac's lips tightened at the bitterness he could

hear in Johnny's usually mild voice. "It doesn't do any good to worry about it," he said. "We just have to do what we have to do."

"I know that, too, Mac."

"Good." He smiled again. "Look, babe, this shit isn't going to last forever. Pretty soon now we'll be living it up in Los Angeles."

"Uh-huh."

Mac shoved a piece of meatball around the plate and frowned. "If I hadn't dropped so much in that damned game last week, of course, we'd be in better shape."

Johnny looked at him sharply. "That was just bad luck, Mac. It wasn't your fault."

"Yeah, sure, kid, I know." He pushed the plate away. "We better go."

They left the restaurant, hailing a cab for the twenty-minute ride to Karlin's. The whole operation had become routine in the last six months, and they were very good at it. They knew it—or, at least, Mac did—and Tedesco also knew it, which was probably why he gave them a little more leeway than was usual before cracking down, as he had that afternoon about Karlin. Mac and Johnny showed a high rate of return and managed to do so with a minimum of fuss. Tedesco had no reason to regret the addition of John Griffith to his organization. In fact, it was quite likely that it was Griffith, more than McCarthy, who accounted for the success of the team. Mac talked a good tough line, and looked dangerous, but he had never yet laid a hand on anybody. It must have startled more than a few people when the tough guy smiled pleasantly, then stepped aside to watch as his blond and gentle-looking companion moved in to take over. Tedesco knew that he was onto a good thing here and he was pleased. Just so long as he didn't have to actually *see* Griffith. Something in the pale blue eyes caused a chill inside the old man, and so he met only with Mac.

Karlin lived in a small wooden frame house tucked between two factories. They left the cab waiting at the curb and walked around the house to the back porch. Karlin, a balding, paunchy man with a penchant for also-rans at the track, answered Mac's sharp knock and stepped outside, pulling the door closed carefully. "My wife," he explained. "She gets upset."

Mac leaned against the porch railing, lighting a cigarette and tucking the cheap lighter back into his pocket before speaking. "I think maybe she has good reason to get upset, sir," he said politely. "Our employer, he's a little upset, too."

"I know I've missed a couple of payments, but—"

"Four," Mac interrupted gently. "You've missed four payments." He took a long drag on the cigarette, and with off-hand deliberation, blew smoke into Karlin's face. "We want the money, you bastard," he said, his voice suddenly harsh. "Or else."

"But I don't have . . . give me more time . . . please."

"Everybody runs out of time, man, and you just did." He nodded toward Johnny. "You remember my associate?"

Karlin glanced toward the shadows. "Yeah, sure."

Johnny stepped into the circle of brightness cast by the porch light. Two blue chips of ice glittered in his pale face. He reached out and gave Karlin three quick open-handed slaps in succession. "You have to pay the money, sir," he said. Another slap, this one hard enough to knock Karlin backwards. "Please," Johnny added coldly. He took Karlin's face in one hand and pushed hard, crashing his head against the house. "Do you understand that this is your last chance?"

Karlin tried to nod. "Yeah, yeah."

Johnny nodded, satisfied, and released him, stepping back immediately into the shadows. Mac tossed the cigarette into the bushes. "Twenty-four hours, Karlin. Then it's out of our hands." He almost smiled. "And we're the nice guys. Good night."

He led the way back to the waiting cab. Johnny got in first, scooting over to the far door, and sat there, both hands folded neatly in his lap. Mac leaned toward him. "You okay?" he asked in a low voice.

Johnny only nodded.

"*Are* you?" Mac insisted.

"Yes."

It was only one word, muttered through clenched teeth, but it was enough for Mac. He relaxed. This was a helluva way to make a living, yeah, but they didn't have much of a choice right now. Someday, someday damn it, they'd get out from under. Out from under. The words had a familiar ring. Yeah, that's what Wash had told him a long time ago. He'd been talking about getting rid of Johnny, of course. But Mac had ignored that advice.

And look at me now, he thought glumly.

As if he were somehow aware of Mac's thought,

Johnny lifted his gaze and looked at him. "Hey, Mac," he said.

"Yeah, kiddo?"

"There's a new movie at the Variety. Will you come with me?"

Mac glanced at his watch. "I have a game," he began, but then he looked into Johnny's hopeful eyes, and shrugged. "What the hell; the game will be there later. Sure, let's go."

Johnny smiled.

-EIGHTEEN-

Mac was disgusted. The game hadn't gone very well, at least as far as he was concerned, and it didn't help his mood much to emerge onto the street close to midnight and find out that the temperature was still hovering somewhere around the ninety degree mark. By the time he'd walked half a block, he was already drenched in sweat. Summer in this city really sucked. Even Johnny seemed dragged out by the heat and humidity that blanketed New York day after day. He spent most of his time parked in front of the TV, swilling down gallons of soda.

When the car horn beeped lightly behind Mac, he closed his eyes in weariness for a moment, before turning to see, as he'd expected, Tedesco's limo sitting by the curb. It was something of a surprise, however, to see that the old man himself was in the back seat. He waved Mac over. At least it's cool in here, he thought as he climbed in and eyed Tedesco. "Yeah?"

Tedesco smiled, looking cool and unruffled in a white suit and Panama hat. "How is it going for you, Alexander?"

"Okay," he grunted. "But I'm sure you already

123

know how it's going for me. Right down to the last nickle. You probably already know how I came out of tonight's game."

It wasn't denied. "Every life has its little ups and downs, right?"

"Right."

"When you get as old as me, you'll know how to take these things in stride."

"Probably."

"And how is John?"

Mac knew that there would be no business discussed until all of these preliminaries were out of the way. "John is fine," he said, enjoying the feel of the sweat chilling on his body.

"Good, good, I like all my boys to be happy." Tedesco paused before continuing in a saddened tone. "We have a little problem, Alexander."

His mind moved quickly over the past couple of weeks to see if there were something he had done— or Johnny—to get them into trouble, but nothing came back to him. "What problem?"

"You are perhaps familiar with the name Mike Danata?"

He thought some more, then shook his head. "No. Should I be?"

"Probably not. He hasn't been in town very long. Out of Chicago, Mr. Danata is."

Mac just looked at him, wondering where the hell all this was leading. There had to be a point to it; the old man never talked just to make conversation.

Tedesco sighed. "Like so many young men, Danata is ambitious. That in itself is not bad, because without ambitious young men, where would this country be? Am I right?"

"Yes sir, you're right."

"Unfortunately, in Mr. Danata's case, his ambition has led him to make some foolish mistakes. Such as intruding into areas that are my concern. We have warned him about this, but he has chosen to ignore us." The musical voice turned hard. "I want Danata taken out. For good. And I want you to do it."

Mac straightened slowly in the seat. "Me?" he said hoarsely. "You must be kidding." The chill he felt now was not pleasant.

"I told you once before that I'm always quite serious about what I say."

"Then you must be smoking something funny in those damned Havanas of yours. Hey, man, I'm a collector. Period. Not some two-bit hitman."

"You're my employee, Alexander."

"That doesn't mean I'm a killer."

"Come now," Tedesco said, smiling. "It wouldn't be the first time you've killed."

"I never, except for the war, I never—" He broke off. Shit, he thought.

Tedesco's black eyes glittered in the dim light. "Well, we mustn't forget Al and Frank, right?"

"Yeah, right," Mac mumbled, slumping in the seat again. "Those two."

"Except for one minor point."

"Which is?"

Tedesco discovered a small spot of dirt on his right trouser leg. He frowned and brushed at it. "You didn't kill them, did you?"

"Sure. Of course I did."

"No," Tedesco said gently. "You just said that Alexander McCarthy is not a killer. I believe that."

Mac's face was stony. "Look, this whole conversation is a lot of shit. Cut it out, huh?"

"All right. To the point. John Griffith killed Al and Frank, didn't he?"

"No. It was me," Mac said.

"Your sense of loyalty is admirable, but totally unnecessary. At any rate, it's quite irrelevant. I want Danata eliminated. You will do it. Or John will do it for you. He does whatever you tell him, doesn't he? I don't care very much either way, just so long as the job gets done. Otherwise . . . well, we won't discuss the various unpleasant alternatives right now, will we?"

Mac realized suddenly that the car had stopped in front of their apartment building. "I don't want to talk about this," he said.

"Fine. It's late. Go upstairs. Sleep on it, as they say. Perhaps discuss it with John. If you can talk to him about such things," Tedesco added, tapping his forehead significantly.

Mac opened the car door. "John isn't crazy," he said, wondering why the hell it mattered now.

"Whatever. We'll be in touch."

Mac got out of the car and hurried into the building, not waiting to watch Tedesco leave.

His gut hurt.

This was the nicest place they'd ever lived in. It wasn't luxury, by a long shot, but at least the hallways didn't smell of piss, and the apartment itself had two beds and a small kitchen. Life had been sort of okay lately. Until now.

Johnny was sitting in the middle of his bed, watching TV, the small fan aimed right at his body, a can of Coke in one hand. He looked up and grinned when Mac came in. "Hi, buddy."

Mac tried to smile and went to get a beer. He

flopped down onto his bed. "Things okay with you, John?"

"Oh, sure, fine." Johnny reached over and turned the fan slightly, so part of the air flow hit Mac, too. "Things okay with you?"

Mac took a long drink of beer. "Yeah, babe, fine."

Johnny looked at him for a moment, then turned back to the TV. "This is a good movie. *Paleface*, with Bob Hope."

"Yeah? Well, you watch it, huh? I'm tired." Standing, he pulled off his clothes, gulped down the rest of the beer, and then stretched out on the bed again. Maybe they should just get out of town. Yeah, like that other guy. What was his name? Bright? Something like that. He'd crossed Tedesco. Mac didn't know any of the details, but he knew that Bright had left town, figuring that would solve his problems. All it did was to get him wasted in Cleveland, instead of New York. Big fucking deal.

Mac turned to face the wall and closed his eyes. Maybe Tedesco would just let it drop. The meeting tonight might have been just a feeler, and now that he knew exactly how Mac felt, the matter might be forgotten.

He stopped thinking about it and finally fell asleep, listening to Johnny's soft laughter as he watched the movie.

It seemed like only moments, but it must have been a couple of hours later when Mac was jerked abruptly back into wakefulness. The room was suddenly filled with light and noise. He rolled over and found himself staring into the twin barrels of a sawed-off shotgun. "Oh, shit," he said.

The man with the gun smiled humorlessly. "Sorry to wake you up."

Mac slowly turned his head. Two more men stood by Johnny's bed, one of them holding a .357 Magnum, the barrel of which was tangled in blond hair. Without his glasses, Johnny peered myopically around the room, his face bewildered.

"What the hell's going on here?" Mac asked.

"Nothing to get excited about, Mr. McCarthy," said the man without a gun. He was slowly pulling on a pair of black leather gloves.

"Mac?" Johnny's voice was a hoarse whisper.

"It's okay, kid," Mac said quietly, realizing suddenly just what was going down. "I think they're just here to deliver a message."

"You got it, man."

"Well, I'm the one the message is for, not him."

The man flexed his fingers inside the gloves. "Oh, the message is for you, all right." He looked at Johnny. "You right-handed or left-handed, dummy?"

Johnny only blinked, obviously incapable of answering.

"He's right-handed," Mac said wearily. "Why?"

"We don't want to put him out of commission."

Mac swallowed. "Don't hurt him. I'm the one who's supposed to get the message and, believe me, I got it."

"But we're supposed to impress upon you the importance of the message. Just so there's no mistake." The man lifted Johnny's left arm.

Mac licked his upper lip. "I'm as impressed as hell. Listen, you son of a bitch, he doesn't even know what's going on."

The man shrugged. "It's nothing personal. We're just following orders."

Mac tensed and leaned forward to push himself up from the bed. "Don't do it, sweetheart," his keeper murmured, pressing the shotgun against his chest. "Unless you want to have yourself spread all over the walls."

He relaxed again.

Johnny tried to pull away from the hands gripping him. "No," he whispered. "Don't hurt me, please." The fingers closed around his wrist. "Mac? Help me. . . ."

Mac closed his eyes.

He had to. There wasn't anything he could have done for Johnny, except witness his ordeal, and that he wouldn't do. In the quiet of the room, the sound of bone snapping echoed like a gunshot. A faint gasp of pain was Johnny's only reaction. Mac felt hot bile rising in his throat; he leaned sideways and threw up. "Nonono," he whispered to the floor, one long, almost soundless, word.

The gloved hands released Johnny, who slumped back against the wall. The three men walked to the door. "He'll be in touch," the spokesman said.

Mac nodded, wiping his mouth with the back of one hand. When the three men were gone, he sat very still, staring at the closed door.

"Mac, it hurts," Johnny said quietly.

"I'm sorry." He got up from the bed, carefully avoiding the pool of vomit on the floor, and went to sit next to Johnny. "God, kid, I'm sorry."

"You didn't do it."

At last, he forced himself to look into Johnny's eyes, seeing the unshed tears gathered there helplessly. "But it's my fault."

Johnny just shook his head. He drew a deep, shuddering breath. "Damn, Mac, it hurts."

Mac tried to look at the arm without moving it,

almost retching when he saw the swelling, discolored wrist. "Ohjesus, baby, this needs a doctor."

"Yeah."

Mac tried to remember his first aid training. Immobilize it, he thought, until we can get to the hospital. He stood, looking around the room for something to use as a splint.

"Mac, why'd they do this? We don't even know those guys."

He didn't answer immediately. He picked up a copy of *TV Guide*, and yanked a tie out of the closet, then sat down again. His hand moved restlessly across Johnny's shoulders, touching sweat-damp curls that clung to his neck. "Later, kid, I'll explain. Later, okay? Right now, we have to get you to the hospital," he whispered. What magic words he could say later that would make this all okay, he didn't know, but there was no time now to wonder. He tucked the magazine around the wrist and secured it with the tie. Johnny didn't make a sound during the procedure, although Mac knew it had to hurt like hell. "Think we can get some clothes on you?" He tried for a smile. "Don't want you running around in your skivvies."

"Yeah, I think so."

Mac pulled his own clothes on, then helped Johnny into blue jeans and sandals. He draped his windbreaker over Johnny's bare shoulders. By this time, Johnny was a sick white color. Sweat poured down his face as he watched everything Mac did with two glazed eyes. "It hurts," he kept saying. "It hurts, Mac."

"I know, I know," Mac muttered, urging him out the door and down to the sidewalk. He managed to get a cab almost immediately and eased

Johnny into the back seat carefully.

By the time they walked into the emergency room, Johnny was trembling continuously, his flesh felt cold and clammy, and his eyes seemed unable to focus. But he wasn't bleeding and his breathing, though shallow, showed no signs of stopping immediately. A skinny Spanish nurse waved them to the waiting room, which was already jammed. Mac managed to find some space on a plastic couch in one corner, and he lowered Johnny onto it, then sat next to him. He lit a cigarette and draped one arm lightly around Johnny's shoulders. "How you doing, kiddo?"

" 'Kay," Johnny said thickly. "Killed my dog."

"What?"

"He killed my dog."

Mac hunched closer to him. "I don't know what you're talking about, babe."

"Had a dog. Raffles. Nice dog. Mine. Dog loved me."

"Yeah, dogs'll do that," Mac agreed, massaging the back of Johnny's neck.

"I stole money from my mother's purse. Five dollars." He shivered. "Cold." It must have been eighty-five degrees in the room. Mac gently tugged the windbreaker more closely around Johnny. "Took the money, you know, so I could buy candy. Thought the kids would like me, but it didn't work. They took the candy and then they ran off. Then my father found out. He hit me. That was okay . . . deserved it." Johnny turned his head and looked blindly at Mac. "But he didn't have to kill my dog, did he?"

"No, man. He shouldn't have done that. It was mean."

"Yeah. He was mean."

Mac reached toward the ash tray and crushed out the cigarette. "But that was a long time ago, kid. Forget it, huh?"

"Yeah, forget it. You're my friend now, so everything is okay. You're a good friend, Mac."

"Oh, sure thing," he replied bitterly. "I'm a blue ribbon buddy, I am."

They didn't talk anymore. Finally a door opened and a tired-looking black nurse stuck her head out. "Mr. Griffith?" she called out.

Mac pulled Johnny to his feet and walked him over. The nurse nodded and took hold of Johnny's good arm. "Wait here, please," she said to Mac.

"But can't I just—"

"Please sir, we're busy, and it's very crowded back here. Just have a seat."

He wanted to protest further, but the nurse gave him no chance. She closed the door. He went back to the couch and lit another cigarette. Anger and pain and guilt were tearing up his insides, causing him to ache. He pressed a hand to his side. Goddamn, the world was a rotten place. People. Motherfucking people, anyway. Why the hell did they have to hurt somebody like Johnny? It wasn't fair. He stared across the aisle, watching distantly as an old black woman pressed a bloody towel to a young boy's shoulder.

"Sir?"

The voice sounded impatient, as if it had been speaking to him for some time. He turned. "Yeah?"

Another nurse. "We need some information for the records. Please come to the desk."

"You know how long it's gonna take back there?" he asked, as they both sat at the desk.

"No, sir. What is the patient's full name?"

"John Paul Griffith."

"Age?"

"Thirty."

"Address?"

The door to the treatment rooms opened and Mac answered absently, his eyes on the people coming out, but Johnny wasn't among them.

"Is the patient covered by Blue Cross?"

Mac managed not to laugh. "No. He doesn't have any insurance."

She frowned. "How will the bill be taken care of?"

Send it to Tedesco, he wanted to say. Better yet, I'll take it personally and shove it up his ass. "I'll pay it," was what he said aloud.

"Your name?"

"Alex McCarthy. Same address. Look, could you maybe just check and make sure he's okay? He gets kind of upset sometimes and—"

"How did the injury occur?"

Mac slid down in the chair. Bitch. Cold-hearted cunt. Thought nurses were supposed to be nice, to care about people. All she cares about are the frigging forms. "He fell on the steps."

"Name of his next of kin?"

"He doesn't have any family." Just one fucked-up friend. Poor John Paul Griffith. No family. No Blue Cross. Just me.

"Will you make a preliminary payment now?"

"How much?"

"Fifty dollars."

He sighed, but handed her the money. After a couple more questions that seemed to have very little to do with a broken wrist, she sent him back to the couch to wait some more.

He had time to smoke three more cigarettes, read three very old issues of *Time*, and count the other people waiting several times before Johnny appeared in the doorway, a short cast gleaming on his forearm. He stood still, his eyes darting wildly around the room, until he spotted Mac and hurried toward him.

Mac stood, carefully gripping Johnny by both shoulders. "You okay?" he asked softly.

Johnny nodded.

They stood in the awkward half-embrace a moment longer, then Mac led Johnny out of the place. "They gave me a shot, Mac, so it doesn't hurt so much," he said, keeping a tight grip on Mac's arm, just as he used to do when they were walking through the jungles of Nam.

"I'm glad, kid." They walked for a couple more minutes, then Mac spotted an all-night coffeeshop. "You want to get something?" he asked.

"Yeah, I guess."

Once they were sitting in a booth and Johnny had ordered a Coke and a jelly doughnut, and Mac coffee, they sat in silence for a long time. Mac still found it hard to meet Johnny's eyes. He stared, instead, at the cast. "It seems like I just keep getting us in deeper and deeper," he said finally.

Johnny was examining the doughnut. "I don't understand."

"What happened tonight—Tedesco did it."

"I sort of figured that," Johnny said thoughtfully. "But why? Did I do something wrong, Mac?"

"No, of course not." Mac took a quick gulp of coffee. "It's me. He wants me to do something and I told him no. This is his way of getting me to change my mind." He set the cup down with a crash. "That bastard. That goddamned mother-fucking bastard. He could have come after me."

"Hey, Mac, it's okay. Don't get mad, please."

Mac didn't say anything.

Johnny licked sugar from his fingers. "What's he want you to do?"

"Kill a man," Mac said flatly.

"Oh." Johnny's face didn't change. He shook his head. "I wish that we had never got mixed up with Tedesco."

"Yeah, well, you can thank me for that piece of luck, too, can't you?" Mac said. He pushed himself out of the booth suddenly. "Man, I've been screwing things up for a long time. You'd have been better off never meeting me. You think I'm a friend? Well, the joke's on you, dummy. I'm just a fucked-up loser, so why don't I do us both a favor and get lost for good?" He turned and walked out, his back stiff.

Mac walked around the block slowly, smoking a cigarette. He passed a dancehall and paused awhile to watch the crowd milling restlessly on the sidewalk. Couples shared cigarettes and necked in the shadows. Everybody seemed to be having a good time. Nobody else was alone.

He didn't like being alone. Finally he sighed and walked back to the coffeeshop. He sat down in the booth, once again avoiding Johnny's eyes.

"Don't do that," Johnny said very quietly. "Don't you ever run out on me like that."

Mac reached for the Coke and took a swallow. "You knew damned well I'd be back," he muttered.

"Yeah?" Johnny thought about that for a moment. "Well, maybe I did, but that doesn't matter. It isn't fair for you to do that to me."

"All right, all right, I'm sorry." He was. "I won't do it again."

"Promise?"

The blue eyes gleamed. Shit, what a preacher the kid woulda made if he'd followed in the footsteps of his folks. "I promise."

Johnny nodded then, forgiving with the ease of a child.

"Come on," Mac said, leaving a quarter tip, "let's go home."

They left the coffeeshop and started walking slowly, half-heartedly looking for a taxi, but really content just to walk. "Who are we supposed to kill?" Johnny asked after a couple of minutes.

"Some guy named Danata. He's trying to muscle in on Tedesco's territory." Mac kicked at an empty beer can. "But let's not fool ourselves. This would only be the beginning."

"Tedesco still has an 'or else,' right?"

"Oh, yeah. Breaking a bone or two is just for openers."

Johnny stopped walking and fumbled in his pocket, pulling out a white envelope. He put two tiny yellow pills on his tongue. "It's starting to hurt again," he explained as they walked some more. "We have to do it, don't we?"

Mac took a deep breath. "Unless we want to risk Tedesco's 'or else.' And I don't know if we're ready for that." He reached out and touched the cast with a fleeting fingertip. "I'm not ready, at least. I don't have that much strength."

Johnny was frowning. "He might hurt you."

"I guess."

Johnny shrugged. "Then we don't have any choice, do we?"

"I guess not." They were quiet for awhile. Mac finally cleared his throat. "It's a helluva thing for a fifteen-year Army man to admit, but I'm not much of a shot." Self-hatred filled him, waves of it washing over him. At that moment, he hated himself more than he had ever hated anyone in his life, even Tedesco. Instead of looking at Johnny, Mac stared at the empty beer cans, cigarette butts, fast food wrappers, and other less identifiable pieces of litter that filled the sidewalk. People were such slobs.

"That's all right," Johnny said wearily. "I'll do it."

They looked at one another. "Thank you," Mac said softly.

Johnny shrugged. "You'll come with me, won't you?" he asked suddenly.

"Sure."

"That'll be okay, then. There's a cab. I'm tired."

Mac nodded and raised his arm to summon the taxi.

-NINETEEN-

The messenger, a skinny kid in an ill-fitting suit, handed a box to Mac and then was gone again immediately. Mac brought the package in and set it on the table. Involuntarily, he wiped both hands on the front of his dark green T-shirt.

Johnny was awkwardly trying to manipulate a shirt on over his cast. He looked up curiously. "What's that?"

"Tedesco sent it over," Mac replied shortly. "Must be the gun."

"We have a gun already."

"No good. He wants us to use this one. It's new. Clean. No way to trace it to anyone."

"Oh." Johnny finally got the shirt on and began to button it with one hand. "Open it," he ordered suddenly. "I want to see the gun."

"Why?"

"It's mine, isn't it?"

Mac looked at him, a little bewildered by the edge in his voice. "Yeah, it's yours," he muttered. With a quick jerk, he snapped the string and then ripped away the brown paper. He took off the lid and pulled aside the cotton wadding. A shiver ran the length of his spine as he stared at the blue-steel monster, with its eight-inch barrel. He shoved the box across the table toward Johnny. "There. Your toy."

Apparently oblivious to the sarcasm in the words, Johnny lifted the gun out with his right hand, hefting its weight thoughtfully. Some emotion Mac couldn't quite read flickered through the blue eyes. "Mac?" he said faintly.

"What?"

"I killed a lot of people in the war, didn't I?"

Mac began crumpling the brown paper. "What difference does it make now? That was a long time ago."

"I was just wondering. I did, didn't I?"

"You did the same as everybody else." Mac wondered, not for the first time, just what had happened at Tan Pret. What had turned John Griffith, high school valedictorian, into the shattered child he'd met? The child he was apparently stuck with for good. Well, he'd probably never know. Not that it mattered much now.

Johnny was squinting down the barrel of the gun.

"Be careful, willya? That fucker might be loaded."

"I know. When you're in a war, it's okay to kill, I guess."

Mac was clearing away the breakfast dishes. "I guess it is."

Johnny put the gun down and tried to scratch inside the cast. His face was thoughtful. A danger sign. When Johnny starting thinking, things usually started to get weird. "That's because you have to get them before they get you," he announced seriously.

"Yeah," Mac said heavily. "That's right, but why talk about it now?"

Johnny picked up the gun again. "Because that's what we're doing here, too, isn't it?"

Mac nodded.

Johnny thought for another moment. "I understand now."

He ran hot water into the sink. "You understand what, kid?"

"That you don't have to be brave to be a good soldier. You just have to be scared enough." He sighed and bent his attention to the gun once again.

Mac crashed the silverware into the sink.

Mac was enjoying the feel of the car beneath his hands as he guided the rented Camero over the Jersey roads. "We oughta get us a car," he said enthusiastically. "I had an old Dodge once that was great."

"Yeah," Johnny agreed. "This is fun." He had the radio blaring and the window rolled down so that the sun-drenched wind blew across his face. "When I was a kid, we never had a car."

"Well, we're gonna get one," Mac decided.

"Could you teach me how to drive?"

"Don't you know? Shit, I didn't think there was anyone who couldn't drive."

"I'm sorry," Johnny said.

"What for? If you don't know, you don't know. I'll teach you. Then we won't be so tied to the frigging city."

Johnny grinned. "Could we get a blue car?"

"Sure, whatever kind you want."

He finally found what he was looking for, a wooded area isolated from the main road. He parked the car behind some trees, and they got out, Johnny carrying the gun box with his good arm. They walked until the trees thinned out a little. Mac used a thumbtack to attach the centerfold from an old *Playboy* to a tree, then paced off about fifty feet. "Come here," he ordered.

Johnny walked over, eyeing the picture curiously. "You want me to hit that?"

"Yeah, boy, that's the general idea. Hit it."

He took the gun out of the box. "Who is she?"

"What the hell difference does that make? Miss April or something."

Johnny smiled faintly as he took position. "It's almost like throwing darts, huh?"

Mac nodded. "Something like that, yeah."

He lined up the shot, squinting a little, hesitated for a moment, then squeezed the trigger. The powerful gun exploded, startling him with its force, knocking him off balance. He straightened and watched eagerly as Mac walked back to the tree. "How'd I do?"

"You did good," Mac said after a moment. "Right through the middle. Damn good, kid."

Johnny beamed with pleasure at the praise. "It was easy, Mac."

Mac ripped that page down and put up another target, this one a magazine cover displaying the face of Richard Nixon. "Come closer this time," he ordered. "Pretend like you just knocked on the door, and this guy opened it. Be fast, because he probably has a gun, too. Understand?"

"Uh-huh." Johnny's face was a study in concentration as he acted out the scene as Mac had directed. He walked closer to the tree, raised his hand as if to knock, waited a moment, then lifted the gun and, without seeming to aim at all, fired again. The top of Nixon's head vanished. Johnny looked around, his face anxious. "Was it okay, Mac?"

Mac looked away for a moment, trying to swallow the bitter bile that threatened to gag him, then he managed to smile at Johnny. "That's good, kiddo. You're a damned good shot."

Johnny's grin threatened to split his face in two. "Want me to do it again?"

"No, that's enough." He pulled the page down and crumpled it savagely.

They were both reluctant to have the day end, so on the way back to the city they stopped for dinner. The place Johnny picked was an old country inn, all stone and wood, with an enormous fireplace that burned cheerfully at the same time the air conditioner worked overtime to keep the room bearable in the summer heat. Mac, feeling out of place in his T-shirt and blue jeans, wasn't even very hungry. Still, it was so nice being away from the city, just the two of them having a good time, that he managed to eat a little, as Johnny devoured prime rib. They shared a carafe of house wine and talked about everything except guns or Daniel Tedesco.

Mac pushed apple pie around on the plate for awhile and finally gave up. "Hey, Johnny," he said.

Johnny looked up, a slight flush from the unaccustomed wine touching his face. "Huh?"

"Did you ever get another dog after your old man killed Raffles?"

He looked puzzled for a moment, then nodded. "Yeah. My folks gave me another one. But it wasn't the same. I just kept him because I had to.

I mean, he needed to be taken care of. And I guess having him around was better than being all by myself. I never cared about him like I did about Raffles, though. Raffles really *belonged* to me, you know?" He licked ice cream from the spoon thoughtfully. "He finally ran away one day, but I didn't care very much."

He shrugged and bent to finish the pie a la mode.

At home later, Mac cleaned and reloaded the gun, while Johnny watched *Ironside* on TV. Mac picked up his beer and took a gulp, frowning at the snowy picture on the set. "You want a color TV for your birthday, kid?"

"Yeah, that'd be nice," Johnny said, not looking away from the screen.

"Well, Tedesco should pay us plenty for this job, so I'll get you one."

"Thanks."

Mac finished with the gun and replaced it in the box. He tipped his chair back on two legs, whistling softly to himself, wondering if he should go over to the game. Supposed to be some big uptown money in there tonight. Of course, after renting the car and paying for dinner, he was a little low on cash, but he had enough to buy his way in.

A commercial came on. "You know something," Johnny said as he went for a Coke.

"What?"

"I saw Chief Ironside on a talk show the other day, and he wasn't in a wheel chair at all."

"Of course not, dummy. That's just part of the story."

Johnny sat down again. "Yeah, well, I guess I knew that, but still, it was sort of strange to see him walking around like everybody else."

Mac's mind wandered a little as he stared at Johnny, once again engrossed in the story. Hey, guy, he wanted to ask, what do you really think about this whole fucking mess? Do you think about it at all? Don't you *care*? Why don't you hate me? Or maybe you do. What the hell makes you tick, John Paul?

The same old questions and never any answers.

Johnny must have become aware of the scrutiny, because he turned around suddenly, the familiar smile on his lips. The flickering lights and shadows from the television were reflected in his glasses.

Mac crashed his chair to the floor. "Going out," he said abruptly. "Probably be late." He was gone before Johnny could respond.

-TWENTY-

"Will you for chrissake quit playing with that goddamned thing?" Mac spoke more harshly than he had intended, tension and a hangover making him short-tempered.

Johnny looked up in surprise, then he carefully put the gun back into the box. "I'm sorry," he said.

"Yeah, I know." Mac swallowed some more aspirin and gulped cold coffee. "I have a headache." The remark served as an apology.

Without replying, Johnny walked over and stood by the window, watching the traffic on the street below. Finally, hearing mumbling, he turned back into the room. Mac was thumbing through an old address book, the pages long loosened.

"What did you say, Mac?"

"I was just saying that I can't remember exactly where the bastard lived. Probably moved halfway across the country by this time anyway."

Johnny sat down, watching him curiously. "You gonna call somebody, Mac?"

"I'm going to try." Mac was flipping through pages quickly, an idea that had been forming in his brain all day finally taking shape. "If we can just get out of the country for a while, babe, we might

145

be able to dodge Tedesco."

Johnny frowned. "I don't understand. I thought we were going to do what Tedesco wants."

"I can't." Mac looked up. "You don't know how sick it made me to see you shooting that gun yesterday."

"Didn't I do it right? You said I was a good shot." Johnny leaned forward and spoke earnestly. "I could practice, Mac."

Mac tried to swallow down his sense of despair and speak quietly. "You did fine, Johnny. Really. I just don't want . . . goddamnit, kid, you have to know what a terrible thing this is, don't you? I don't want us to turn into a couple of killers."

"But Tedesco will hurt you." Johnny walked back over and sat on the arm of Mac's chair. He reached out to touch Mac's hand lightly, stroking absently.

Mac had long since learned to accept the touching that Johnny seemed to need so much. When the kid got scared or upset or just seemed to be feeling lonely, he turned to Mac, seeming to crave the physical contact of a strong hand or maybe a hug. When Mac bothered to think about this at all, he decided that it all had something to do with Johnny's childhood. Probably nobody ever hugged him much. Mac returned the stroking for a moment, until he felt Johnny relax a little. "He can't hurt me if we're not here," he said, returning his attention to the phone book.

"Where will we go?"

"I don't know," Mac mumbled, running his finger down the page. "Mexico, maybe. Whaddaya think?"

"I guess. Whatever you say."

"I don't think even Tedesco can get us in Mexico. Yeah, here it is," he said, looking up. "Robert L. Washington."

Johnny was rubbing the cast on his wrist nervously. "Who, Mac?"

"Wash. You remember Sergeant Washington from Nam, don't you?"

After a moment, Johnny nodded. "Yeah. He didn't like me."

"He lives way the hell out on the Island, if he's still around, anyway," he said. "That's stupid. Why do you say he didn't like you?"

"He just didn't. Why are you going to call him?"

Mac stood, searching in his pockets for a dime. "To see if he can let me have some money. It's gonna cost a bundle to get us to Mexico." He went out to the hall phone and pulled some change out of his jeans. It took only a few moments before he had Washington on the line. "How the hell are you, Wash?" he said cheerfully.

"Fine, fine. Didn't know you were in the city."

"Yeah, sure. Look, man, I'd like to see you. Got sort of a problem and I need a friendly ear."

Washington seemed a little hesitant, but they finally set up a meeting for later that day, at the bowling alley in his neighborhood. He gave Mac directions on train and bus connections and they hung up.

Johnny was standing in the doorway, watching. "Can I go, too?" he asked.

"If you want to."

Johnny wanted to, so a short time later they caught a bus over to Penn Station and picked up the train out to Long Island. Mac read a *Times* that someone had left on the seat and listened to Johnny hum tunelessly.

"He said I was crazy," Johnny said suddenly.

"What?"

"Washington. He told me I was crazy and should be in a hospital."

Mac folded the paper carefully. "Yeah? Well, everybody's entitled to their opinion, I guess."

Johnny was quiet for several minutes. "Mac?"

"Huh?" He didn't look up from the sports page.

"Am I?"

"Are you what, kid?"

"Crazy."

He patted Johnny's knee. "No, of course not. You act a little weird sometimes, but that's okay."

Johnny gave a sigh and looked out the window again.

They found seats in the snack bar of the bowling alley and waited. Johnny finished off a Coke and an order of french fries doused in catsup, then he looked up. "They have some pinball machines back there, Mac," he said.

Mac pulled some change from his pocket. "Okay, go ahead."

Johnny smiled and took off in the direction of the noisy games.

Mac ordered another cup of coffee and settled back. In another moment, he saw a vaguely familiar figure enter and look around. "Wash," he said, half-standing.

The black man saw him and came over. "Mac, you son of a bitch, how're you doing?"

They shook hands and Wash sat down, ordering some coffee. Mac glanced toward the pinball machines, but Johnny seemed totally absorbed in his game. "So what're you up to these days, Wash?" he asked.

"Working in the Post Office, man. We just had another kid. That makes three."

Mac expressed the proper enthusiasm, and the talk shifted to Nam briefly, and the various fates of people they had known. Wash slowly stirred his coffee. "What ever happened to the zombie?" he asked suddenly. "Griffith?"

Mac hunched over the table a little. "Nothing," he said.

"He's probably living very happily in a padded cell someplace. You take my advice and dump him when the two of you got Stateside?"

Mac shook his head. He didn't realize that Johnny had approached the table, until he spoke. "I used up all that money, Mac," he said softly. "Can I have some more?"

Not looking at Washington, Mac hauled out some more change and handed it over. "But that's all," he mumbled, "so don't come back looking for more."

"Okay, Mac." Johnny hurried away.

Washington released his breath in a long sigh. "No, I guess you didn't take my advice."

"I couldn't. He needed somebody to take care of him."

"Yeah, right. But why you?"

Mac didn't answer right away, as they both watched Johnny. "Maybe I just needed somebody, too, Wash," he said finally, quietly. "Maybe I was just tired of being by myself. Johnny likes me. I like him. We get along okay when the rest of the frigging world leaves us alone." He took a gulp of coffee. "I tried, Wash. I tried to dump him, a couple of times."

He looked across the room to where Johnny was

bent over some damned game, his whole body tense with concentration. "He just couldn't make it on his own."

"So you adopted him." Washington took a roll of mints out of his pocket. "Trying to quit smoking," he explained with a grimace. He popped candy into his mouth. "Why couldn't you let the Army handle it, Mac?"

"Hell. I know what they would've done to him." He smiled a little. "Henderson thought we were queer for each other." He shot Washington a look. "We're not."

"I didn't ask."

"Yeah, well."

"So what's the problem you mentioned on the phone?" Washington asked abruptly.

"I owe some guys money, Wash. They're starting to get nasty about it."

Washington didn't look surprised. "You never got smart enough to give up poker either, huh?"

"No. And things were going okay for a while. But then I had a run of bad luck and got in over my head."

The black man sighed. "Hell, man, you were always over your head."

Mac tapped the tabletop. "I know, but that's all over now. What I want, see, is for the kid and me to get out of town and make a new start someplace else." He wanted it so much that it hurt, deep inside his chest.

"Sure. Find a new game, you mean, right?"

"No, Wash, really."

They were quiet for a moment. "You ever think that maybe if you stopped treating him like a kid, he might grow up?" Washington asked mildly.

"Johnny's okay. I take care of him, you know?"

"What's with the cast on his wrist? He talk back to you or something?"

"What the hell is that supposed to mean?"

Washington ate another mint. "Buddy, I've seen you smash your fist through a door because you couldn't draw a good hand. I wouldn't want you mad at me."

"You think I . . .?" Mac glanced toward the games. Johnny had apparently spent all the money, because he was walking back toward them. "Jesus, Wash, what kind of a creep do you think I am? I wouldn't do anything like that to him." Then he lowered his gaze. "I told you these guys I owe the money to are starting to get nasty."

Washington's glance was filled with scorn. "Oh, yeah, you take good care of him."

Johnny slid into the booth next to Mac. "I scored 70,000 points."

"Good, Johnny."

"How're you, Griffith?" Washington asked.

"Fine." Johnny kept his eyes down.

"Wash, we need some money," Mac said urgently. "Johnny and I have to get to Mexico for a while."

"Mexico?" Washington gave a soft laugh. "Man, you don't want much, do you? I deliver the *mail*, buddy; it's nice, steady work, but it don't pay much. Especially when you've got a wife and three kids and a mortgage. You know how much all that costs?"

Mac shook his head wearily. "No, I don't know anything about that stuff."

"Right." Washington searched his pockets. "Damn," he muttered. "I forgot. If I eat another one of those damned mints, I'll throw up." He looked at Mac. "Why don't you stop being such a goddamned asshole and try earning a real living for a change? Lay off the cards, man. If you've gone and appointed yourself babysitter, then you damned well ought to do a better job of it. Shape up, Mac, and quit expecting other people to bail you out all the time."

Johnny leaned forward suddenly. "Stop it," he said in a shakey voice. "Mac does the best he can. It's not his fault if the luck just ran bad."

The three men were silent for a long moment. Mac spoke finally, his voice low. "Please, buddy. I'm begging you. We need the money and there's no one else I can ask. Please."

Washington sighed. "I just don't have it, Mac. I'm sorry."

Mac nodded, his fragile hope turning to ashes. He spread his hands helplessly. "Okay," he said flatly. "I understand. Thanks anyway."

"You want some advice?"

"What?"

"Turn Griffith over to the V.A. and hop the first train out of town." He tossed a dollar bill down onto the table and was gone.

They sat there a few minutes, not talking. Mac rubbed the back of his neck. "Let's go home, babe," he said finally.

"Okay. I guess we're not going to Mexico, huh?"

"No, I guess not. I'm sorry, Johnny."

"That's all right. I don't mind so much."

Mac pushed himself to his feet. "You don't mind much of anything, do you?"

"I guess not. Except this cast," Johnny said with a slight smile. "I'm kinda tired of it."

Mac dug into his pocket and came up with a quarter. "Here," he said, "get a candy bar to eat on the train."

Johnny took the money with another smile and disappeared in the direction of the counter. Mac started toward the door. He wasn't even scared anymore; like Johnny, he was just tired. So damned tired.

-TWENTY-ONE-

Mike Danata looked more like a TV star than a two-bit hood angling for bigger things. Or maybe he only looked like TV's notion of a hood. One of those actors who seemed to work steadily, always playing the bad guy, so that whenever he came onto the screen, you immediately knew that before the hour was up, the hero would have exposed the guy as the villain. Anyway, what Danata looked like or what he aspired to didn't matter much at this point.

Mac slid the eight by ten color glossy back into the manila envelope. "So that's him," he said. "According to what Tedesco said, he'll be alone after midnight."

Johnny was slouched opposite him in the booth, a sullen expression on his face as he ate a cheeseburger. "Yeah, yeah, I know, you told me all that before."

Mac leaned across the table and spoke in an icy voice. "John, this isn't a game. It all has to be planned; the odds have to be figured perfectly. I don't especially want to be cleaning your insides up from all over Danata's hallway."

Johnny ate a catsup-drenched french fry, pouting. "Okay, okay. You don't have to get so mad."

"I'm not mad, goddamnit, it's just—" Mac broke off and took a deep breath. Christ. They were both on edge, in danger of becoming a couple of basket cases. "I'm sorry, Johnny."

"Me, too." Johnny took a long slurping drink of his chocolate shake and frowned. "Listen, won't this guy get suspicious if somebody comes knocking on his door so late?"

"No, because he'll be expecting his broad. She's a dancer at some strip joint downtown, and she comes over every night after the show. But tonight a couple of Tedesco's creeps are making sure she's late." Mac finished his coffee and crumpled the styrofoam cup. "You done?"

"Uh-huh."

They left the fast food joint and walked three blocks to the outdoor lot where Mac had parked the rented car. There didn't seem to be anything else to say and so it was a quiet drive over to Danata's apartment building. When they got there, it was exactly twelve-fifteen. "Right on time," Mac said, pulling into the alley and shutting off the engine. He turned in the seat. "You okay?" he asked quietly.

"Yeah." Johnny picked up the gun from the seat between them and shoved it into his jacket pocket, keeping one hand on the grip. "Need a holster for the damned thing," he muttered. "How can I carry a gun without a holster?"

"You remember the apartment number?"

Johnny, his face patient, looked at Mac. "I remember everything you told me," he said softly. "I'm not stupid, buddy."

"I know that, Johnny, it's just—" Mac stared

out into the dark alley, gripping the steering wheel so tightly that his knuckles turned white. "Be careful, huh?"

"I will. Promise." Johnny opened the car door. "It's like a movie," he said, whether to himself or Mac wasn't quite clear. "It's just a movie, that's all." He got out and walked without hesitation into the apartment building.

Mac started the car again. He lit a cigarette and began to watch the clock. This was crazy. Really crazy. Johnny and him carrying on like a couple of creeps from a late movie. Did they really expect to get away with this? Johnny would probably get blown away, was probably getting his guts splattered all over the hallway as he sat here, blowing smoke rings and watching the lighted clock face.

And if that happened, what should his own next move be? Well, he might make a run for it.

Run where?

Home and hide under the bed, I guess.

Except that home wouldn't be there anymore, not really. It would be just an empty room. It had been too damned long since he'd lived in an empty room, and he wasn't sure he could hack it again. You got used to having somebody around. Maybe Johnny wasn't the greatest company in the world, but then again maybe he was. They got along just fine.

Mac touched the .45 tucked into his belt. So he better stay here and shoot it out. Shoot the bad guys and shoot the good guys; shoot any damned bastard that got in his way.

Oh, yeah, tough guy. You're so frigging tough, so goddamned hot to start blowing the bums away, how come he's in there and you're out here?

It seemed like hours, but was really only four

minutes ticking away on the clock before the door to the apartment building opened, and Johnny appeared. One hand was shoved into his pocket and the dirty cast caught the dim moonlight. He kept his head bent as he walked swiftly to the car and slid inside.

Mac pulled out of the alley immediately. "You all right?"

There was no answer from Johnny. He bent forward, resting against the dashboard, his face hidden, his breath sounding harsh and raspy.

"Johnny? Did you do it? You okay?" When there was still no answer, Mac pulled the car off the street, into another dark alley, turning off the engine. He switched on the interior light and stared at Johnny in the pale white glow. "Hey, man?" He reached over, putting a hesitant hand on Johnny's shoulder and pulling the unresisting form up. "Babe? Hey, say something, please."

Johnny took a deep breath and then bit his lip. "I did it," he said finally. "I knocked and he opened the door and I shot him in the face." He gagged a little, then recovered. "I closed the door. Nobody saw me." His eyes behind the glasses were bright as he looked beseechingly at Mac. "Was it right, Mac? Did I do what you wanted?"

"Oh, shit, Johnny," Mac said, pulling the other man closer. For a long time, he just held on, feeling Johnny's heart race. "Yeah," he whispered at last, the word muffled in blond hair. "You did fine, kid, real good."

It was Johnny who pulled away finally, straightening in the seat. His face looked confused and a little flushed. "Next time it'll be easier," he said; his voice sounded husky.

"Don't worry about that right now. Let's just take

this one step at a time." He started the car and they rode silently back to the parking lot, leaving the car there to be picked up by one of Tedesco's lackeys.

One of the Tedesco's *other* lackeys, Mac thought as they walked home.

When they reached the apartment, Johnny put the gun away in the bottom of a drawer, covering it carefully with an old sweatshirt. They stood awkwardly in the middle of the room, not looking at one another. "You mind if I go out?" Mac said at last.

Johnny shook his head. "Can I have some money?" he asked. "Maybe I'll go to a movie or something."

"Good idea," Mac said, handing him a couple of bills. "Be careful. Don't get mugged or anything."

"I won't."

Mac patted his shoulder. "See you later."

"Yeah." Johnny smiled a little. "Have fun."

Mac hesitated another second, feeling as if he should say something more, but not knowing what. "You have fun, too," he finally mumbled, then left.

He picked her up in a bar called Eddie's. The place was filled with people trying to make connections quickly, because the night was disappearing much too soon. Her name was Sherry. Or Carrie. Something like that. The music was very loud, and he wasn't really listening anyway.

They had a couple of drinks and then went to her place, which was located, conveniently, just around the corner from the bar. Once there, she disappeared into the bathroom. Mac took off his clothes and stretched out on the bed, lighting a cigarette. He stared at the cracks in the ceiling, trying to find some recognizable object in the criss-crossed lines.

He knew that the hit had come down too late to make the morning papers, but the later editions should have something. Tedesco had said that as soon as he knew for sure that Danata was dead, they'd be paid.

Shit, Johnny had been pretty cool about the whole thing. Blowing off a guy's head, after all, was a damned hard thing to do. But the kid did it. Of course, it wasn't the first time for him. He'd killed Al and Frank. And the people in Tan Pret. Almost iced Crazy George that time, too.

Always because of me.

That was an uncomfortable thought and one he wished he could deny. But it was true. Except for Tan Pret, which didn't really count, because it was war and all, every time Johnny killed or came close to killing, it was for him. Weird. Really weird.

Mac frowned at the cracks on the ceiling, deciding that they looked like the state of Oklahoma. Of course, Johnny was a little shook afterward, but who the hell wouldn't be? Hell, he thought, I was shook, too, and I didn't even do anything.

Could that be used in court? I didn't do anything, your honor. Except plan it all and drive him over and tell him the apartment number. Little things like that.

Mac ran through the whole evening again, replaying it like a movie in his mind. Pulling into the alley behind Danata's place. Watching Johnny go in. The waiting, watching the seconds tick away so damned slowly. Johnny coming back at last, all pale and spaced-out. The moments later in the car and the terrible crashing of Johnny's heart against his own.

The girl, whatever her name was, slipped into

bed next to him and put a hand between his legs.
She giggled. "All ready for me, huh? You don't
leave a girl much to do except lay back and enjoy
it, do you?"

Slowly, he crushed out the cigarette and then
rolled over on top of her. Ignoring the preliminaries, he pushed himself into her, moving
back and forth silently, still thinking about the kill.
Remembering it all in excruciating detail. He
clutched at the pillow beneath her head, closed his
eyes, and remembered.

He opened the door and I shot him in the face.

Mac pictured the eight by ten glossy looking like
the magazine cover of Nixon's face after Johnny
shot it.

Was it right, Mac? Did I do what you wanted?

The eyes, pleading, needing.

Oh, shit, Johnny.

Johnny's heart beating so fast, too fast.

Mac came much too quickly. He rolled off her
body and stared at the ceiling again. "Shit," he said
aloud.

She said something he didn't hear. A moment
later, she began to kiss his neck and chest, working
her hips against his. He sighed, then tangled his
fingers in her tawny hair, pushing her head down
between his legs.

A part of his mind was very aware of her presence, of her mouth on him, sucking, nibbling, urging, and the heat began to rise in his groin again.
Another piece of his consciousness, though, was
apart from what was happening, hovering somewhere up above it all, lingering up there by the
absurdist rendering of Oklahoma, watching with
weary bemusement.

They were murderers, he and Johnny, and that

truth bound them together in a reality that was much more interesting than the fact that a girl whose name he didn't even know was sucking him off in a cheap room around the corner from a bar called Eddie's.

He could hear the television as he walked up the stairs and unlocked the door. Johnny was sitting on his bed. "Hi, Johnny," Mac mumbled wearily.

"Hi."

"What's on?" Mac asked, getting a beer from the refrigerator and starting to undress.

"Bogart. The one about the truck drivers."

"Oh, yeah, you like that one." He turned out all the lights but one, then sat on the edge of Johnny's bed. "Did you go out?"

"Uh-huh. I saw a movie. A western."

"Terrific."

"And I had a giant Chunky and some popcorn and a lemonade."

"Quite an evening."

They watched the movie until the next commercial. "You okay?" Mac asked, staring at the ad for toothpaste.

Johnny nodded.

"You were great tonight."

"Thanks." He shrugged. "It wasn't so hard, I guess."

"Sooner or later, kid, we're going to figure a way out of this. Sooner or later, life is gonna turn around for us."

"Life is okay." Johnny shifted the weight of the cast with a weary sigh.

"Bet you're sick of that damned thing."

"Yeah."

"Three more weeks, the doctor said."

"I know." Johnny stood, pulling off his jeans. "Mac?"

"Yeah?"

"Stay here with me awhile, would you, please?"

Mac nodded. He reached over to switch off the lamp and turned the volume all the way down on the TV, leaving the image of Bogart flickering on in silence. He stretched out next to Johnny on the bed.

"Danata knew," Johnny said softly. "He saw the gun, and for just a second, he knew what was going to happen."

"Yeah?"

"His eyes got all sort of scared. He didn't want to die."

"Nobody does, kid."

Johnny sighed, his breath warm and damp against Mac's skin. "I wanted to explain it to him, you know? Tell him *why* it had to be this way."

"He knew why. Because he crossed Tedesco."

Johnny shook his head and blond strands brushed against Mac's chest. "No, not that. I wanted to tell him that he had to die so that Tedesco would leave us alone. Because if I didn't kill him, you might get hurt."

Mac stroked Johnny's hair gently. "Don't think about it anymore. Just forget it. Go to sleep, boy."

After a few more minutes, Johnny relaxed against him and his breathing softened into the steady pattern of sleep.

Mac was alone then in the dark, except for the tiny figures on the silenced TV screen. He sighed deeply. The tears were unexpected, but he didn't try to hold them back. He made no sound that might disturb Johnny, but let the tears roll down his cheeks unheeded, dampening the pillow and the blond strands that touched his face.

The movie ended, but Mac was still awake, still stroking Johnny's hair with a kind of quiet desperation, waiting hopelessly for the morning.

-TWENTY-TWO-

Mac kept running. The knife of pain stabbed against his left side every time his shoes hit the pavement, and he was starting to get dizzy, but he kept running. Finally, just before he collapsed completely, he reached his goal.

Johnny looked up, grinning. " 'Bout time you got here."

Mac gave him a dirty look and dropped onto the bench next to him. "Don't . . . forget," he panted, "you've got . . . some years on . . . me, you bastard."

"Hah," Johnny sneered. "Eight years. Big deal."

Mac managed to catch his breath and smiled, shakily. "Well, from where you're sitting, eight years may not seem like much, but it's a helluva lot from where I'm sitting."

"Not easy being over forty, is it?" Johnny asked, even at thirty-three managing to look about twelve.

"Remind me to ask you that in a few years." Mac became aware that the grey November wind was getting colder. He blew on his fingers. "I need some coffee."

Johnny jumped to his feet, jogging in place. "Let's go then, old man." He smiled again and

164

took off across the park. "See you at the drug-store!" he called back over one shoulder.

"Son of a bitch," Mac mumbled. He pushed himself up and started after Johnny, trying to remember whose bright idea it had been that they should start jogging. Probably his own. It sounded like the kind of suggestion he might make, especially if he was drunk at the time. And, of course, that idiot Johnny would agree. Hell, Johnny would agree to walking across a bed of hot coals in his bare feet if Mac suggested it.

Mac shrugged. After six years, he was used to Johnny.

"Mr. McCarthy?"

The quiet voice came from behind him. He tensed, as always half-expecting to feel a bullet crash into his body. When none did, he turned slowly. "Yeah?"

A husky man nearly his own height stood there. He obviously wasn't a jogger, because he wore a long leather coat and carried a briefcase. Automatically, Mac surveyed the immediate area. He wasn't surprised to see two gorillas hovering nearby. "Yeah?" he said again.

"Could we talk, please?"

Mac glanced around, but Johnny had already vanished. "What about? I'm supposed to—"

"Mr. Griffith will wait, I'm sure."

Mac gave the man a sharp look. A lot of people knew his name; not many knew Johnny's, and it didn't especially make him feel good that this guy did. He tucked both hands under the jogging jacket. Out of the corner of his eye, he could see the two apes straighten. "I'm cold," he said loudly enough for them to hear. They relaxed again.

"Who are you anyway?"

"My name is Hagen."

The name sounded vaguely familiar, and Mac thought for a moment. "From Philly, aren't you?"

Now it was Hagen's turn to be surprised. "Yes, as a matter of fact, I am."

"So? What do you want with me?"

"I have a business proposition to offer."

"We don't deal that way," Mac said shortly. "You're in the company; you must know how it works. All our deals come down through—a higher authority." He turned to walk away.

"I'm offering you a chance to get out from under Daniel Tedesco's thumb." Hagen spoke softly, but his words reached Mac clearly.

He stopped. "What?"

"Can we talk?"

Mac looked around the park again, wondering what the hell was going on. This wasn't part of the routine. Shit, he thought. "It's too cold here. Come on."

They walked out of the park and across the street to the drugstore. The two apes trailed behind, taking up position just inside the door. Johnny was already in a booth, two cups of coffee in front of him. He was spooning sugar liberally into one cup. "At last. Thought you were crawling on your—" He saw Hagen and broke off, looking at Mac, puzzled.

Mac slid into the booth next to him. "Mr. Hagen here wants to talk some business," he explained, wrapping his chilled fingers around the coffee mug.

"Oh." Johnny took a gulp of his over-sweetened coffee and added one more load of sugar to the cup. "Maybe I'll go look at the magazines," he mumbled.

"Okay." Mac moved to let him out, then waved Hagen into the booth.

Hagen sat down across from him, his eyes on Johnny, who was already engrossed in the magazine display. "He doesn't seem very interested in what I have to say."

"He's not."

"It concerns his future, too."

Mac lifted the coffee mug. "I'll take care of his future. You said you wanted to talk. I'm waiting to listen."

"You two make a good team."

"Uh-huh. I already know that, Hagen."

"Over the past couple of years you've handled some very tough jobs for Tedesco."

The coffee was as bad as usual, worse than the stuff Johnny made, and that was the pits, but at least it was hot. "Have we?" he asked after taking several sips.

Hagen smiled. "Thirteen, to be precise. Beginning with Mike Danata and then, last week, Karl Schmidt."

Mac shrugged. "I heard he was shot."

"Right. You two never miss. A lot of people are very impressed."

Mac smiled blandly. "I'm not sure I understand what you're talking about. And even if I did, like I said before, we don't take on outside jobs."

Hagen was searching his pockets. "This isn't really that kind of thing. It's very much within the company."

"Yeah? Then how come Tedesco isn't telling me about it himself?"

Hagen didn't answer.

Mac drank coffee and watched Johnny snicker over something he was reading. Suddenly, he looked at Hagen, realization dawning. "Hey, you mean. . . *him?*"

Hagen took time to light a cigarette. "Want one?" he asked, holding out a gold case.

Mac shook his head. "Trying to quit."

"Smart man. These things will probably get all of us sooner or later." He tucked the case away. "Tedesco owns you, McCarthy. He owns both you and your programmed killing machine over there."

They both glanced toward Johnny, who was oblivious. "You seem to know a lot about it," Mac said.

"I know everything about it."

Mac sighed. "I still don't know exactly what it is you're saying here, man."

"It's very simple, and very much a matter of company politics, which I'm sure don't interest you at all."

"You got that right. You guys can screw each other around all you want, as long as you leave us alone to do our job."

"Fair enough." Hagen folded his neatly manicured hands on top of the formica table. "Let me just say this much. Tedesco has fallen out of favor in recent months, and it's been decided by the board of directors that his territory should be redistributed."

"And Tedesco himself?"

Hagen sighed and looked unhappy. "Well, the old man was offered a very generous retirement plan. Which he, unfortunately, has chosen to reject."

"Uh-huh."

"So we have naturally decided that a more permanent solution is called for."

"Naturally." Mac waved the waitress over and waited while she poured him another cup of coffee. When she was gone, he leaned across the table. "What's in this for us? *If* we decide to go along?"

"Twenty-five thousand dollars."

The figure stunned Mac a little. He sat back. Shit. With that much cash, he could pay off every fucking I.O.U. he had, and still have plenty left. Enough for a car. A color TV. Maybe even enough to get out of this city. Go to L.A. Or Vegas. He glanced toward the magazine rack again. Johnny would love to get out of New York. "And then what happens?" he asked Hagen almost absently, still lost in thought over what they could do with that much money.

"You and Griffith could do whatever you like."

He smiled bitterly. "Within reason, you mean?"

Hagen shrugged. "Well, of course, we would still have, let's say, an option on your services. But at least Tedesco wouldn't be giving all the orders." The man smiled. "You could freelance. Does that sound good?"

"We'll think it over."

"Fair enough." Hagen stood. "But don't take too long, McCarthy. The bandwagon is rolling, and you're either on or off. I'll be in touch." He turned and walked out, both apes at his heels.

Johnny came back and slid into the booth next to Mac. "Everything okay?"

"Huh? Oh, yeah, fine, kiddo," he said absently.

"Who was that guy?"

"Hagen." He looked at Johnny. "He wants us to do a job." He smiled humorlessly. "He wants us to ice Tedesco."

Johnny's eyes gleamed for just a moment behind the glasses, then he lowered his gaze. "Good," was all he said.

"I don't know what it might mean in the long run. But at least we'll get our hands on some cash. A lot of cash."

"Enough for a car?"

"Sure. Yeah, we'll get a car this time. I promise."

"Okay." Johnny was quiet for a moment, then he looked up and smiled. "Think you can make it home, old man?"

Mac shoved him out of the booth. "Fuck off, punk," he said cheerfully. Zipping the jogging jacket again, he followed Johnny out of the drugstore.

-TWENTY-THREE-

Johnny woke abruptly, sitting straight up in the seat. He usually woke that way, as if something had startled him. He groped for his glasses. "Where are we?" he mumbled, his voice still thick with sleep.

"Just coming into Frisco," Mac replied, rubbing his eyes with the heel of one hand. He was tired after the trip from Vegas. Not for the first time, he wished that Johnny had been able to get a license so that he could share the driving. But although he'd passed the written tests with perfect scores in New York, Chicago, Vegas, and Los Angeles, he just couldn't hack the behind-the-wheel part of the test. Not that he couldn't drive—he could, as well as anybody. It was just that the pressure of having to perform with a complete stranger sitting next to him, watching and evaluating his every move, wiped him out whenever he tried. The first couple of times it happened, the kid nearly cried. Finally, he just gave up, and never mentioned driving again.

Several times over the last couple of years, Mac had been sorely tempted to just sell the car. The cash would have come in very handy on more than

171

one occasion. But Johnny was so crazy about it.
Spent hours polishing it whenever he could. He really loved the blue BMW, so Mac was stuck with it.
He sighed. "Hey, guy, what was the name of the
motel we stayed at the last time we were here?"

Johnny frowned thoughtfully. "Something
stupid . . . Welcome Inn, that's it."

"Yeah, right. Was it cheap?"

Two blue eyes peered at him. "Of course it was
cheap," Johnny said drily. "Didn't I just say we
stayed there?"

Mac shot him a glance. "Don't try to be funny
so fucking early, willya?"

Johnny snickered. "Sorry."

They found the Welcome Inn and got a room.
Johnny, as usual, was hungry and wanted breakfast, but Mac just wanted to sleep. He peeled off
his clothes and crawled into one of the beds, barely
aware of Johnny's departure.

It was early afternoon before Mac woke, feeling
groggy and joint-stiff from being in the car so long.
He staggered into the bathroom and got under a
hot shower. When he'd finished that, and shaved
and dressed, he felt halfway human again. Shoving
his wallet into the back pocket of his jeans, he
stepped out onto the motel balcony.

Johnny was in the parking lot below, his shirt
off, carefully buffing the car. He wasn't alone,
however. A young man in tight swimming trunks
had evidently wandered over from the pool, and
they were talking as Johnny worked. Mac stood
watching for a moment. It was obvious to him that
the conversation—probably about the car—was of
less interest to the young man than was Johnny

himself. He could scarcely take his eyes off Johnny's bare torso and sunlit golden hair. The kid was oblivious to the attention as he enthusiastically pointed out the advantages of his car.

Mac frowned and leaned over the balcony rail. "Hi," he said.

Johnny looked up, shading his eyes against the sun. "Hi, yourself," he replied, grinning.

The young man looked up as well, and it was his turn to frown when he saw Mac staring at him. "Friend of yours?" he asked Johnny.

"Yeah," Johnny said cheerfully.

Mac just kept his icy gaze on the intruder, until he shrugged. "I gotta get my laps done," he muttered.

"Fucking faggot," Mac mumbled, watching him go.

"What'd you say?" Johnny asked.

He looked down at him and grinned. "I said you're gonna rub the frigging paint off that damned thing one of these days."

"You think so?" Johnny gave one more swipe at the hood. "Okay, I'm done anyway."

"Look, I have to meet a guy in Golden Gate Park later. Want to get something to eat and then go on over? We could throw the frisbee around for a while."

Johnny reacted with his usual enthusiasm, grabbing his shirt and pulling it on hurriedly. "That sounds great."

Mac walked down the steps. "Who was that guy, anyway?"

Johnny paused by the car door, looking toward the pool vaguely. "Oh, I don't know. Rick or Rich. Something like that. He was asking me questions about the car. Said he thought it was very nice."

"I'm sure," Mac muttered, getting behind the wheel.

"Huh?"

Mac glanced at him. "Be careful who you talk to, willya?"

"I am." Johnny looked dismayed. "I wouldn't ever say anything about. . . anything I shouldn't, Mac."

Mac patted his knee. "I know that, kiddo. It's just . . . well, never mind. What do we want for lunch?"

"Pizza?" Johnny suggested.

Mac groaned. "Only you could be three blocks from Fisherman's Wharf and want pizza. You're hopeless."

He started looking for a pizza place.

The park was crowded, but they managed to find a patch of unoccupied grass, and tossed the bright orange frisbee back and forth for nearly an hour. Finally, begrudgingly, Mac glanced at his watch. "I gotta meet that guy, babe. See you at the car in a little while, okay?"

Johnny jumped into the air to carch Mac's final toss of the frisbee. "Yeah, sure."

Mac waved a half-hearted farewell and started across the park.

The man in the brown suit was waiting when Mac arrived. He eyed Mac's T-shirt and blue jeans with some surprise. "You McCarthy?"

Mac lit a cigarette, coughed, then nodded. "Yep."

The man handed him a large envelope. "A picture and all the particulars are inside." He studied

Mac again and frowned. "I hope you know what you're doing. Papagallos is no fool."

"Neither are we," Mac said coldly. He hefted the envelope. "The money is in here, too, right?"

"Yeah. Just like you said."

"Fine. That's it, then." He turned to walk away.

"Hey!"

"What?"

"Aren't you going to tell me about how you're planning to do this? I just gave you a lot of money. I know you come highly recommended, but—"

Mac stared at the man. "What we do, and how we do it, is our business." He nodded sharply and walked across the grass, back to where the car was parked.

Johnny was sitting on the front bumper, idly spinning the frisbee between his hands as he watched a softball game. He turned and smiled as Mac sat down next to him. "All done?"

"Yeah." Mac lit a cigarette and they settled back to watch the rest of the game.

They went down to Fisherman's Wharf for dinner, and then back to the Welcome Inn. Mac spread the material on Papagallos out onto the bed and began to figure the angles of the job. "I have a headache," Johnny complained.

Mac reached for the aspirin bottle and tossed it to him without looking up. Johnny dropped four of the pills into a can of Coke and stretched out to watch *Beau Geste* on television.

"I'm gonna need two days, I think," Mac said. "The hit comes down on Sunday."

"Okay," Johnny replied, his eyes glued to the screen.

Mac folded all the papers again, and shoved them back into the envelope. He stretched out, propping his head against the wall, and watched the movie.

Mac woke up first on Sunday morning. He showered and shaved and dressed quietly, making a cup of instant coffee out of tap water. He sipped the disgusting brew as he moved around the room in the early morning half-light. When he'd tucked his shirt in and zipped his jeans, and pulled on his cowboy boots, he walked over and jerked the blanket off Johnny's bed. "Wake up," he said.

Johnny sat up quickly. "Huh?"

"Time to go to work."

"Oh." Johnny swung his legs over the side of the bed and rubbed his eyes. "I forgot." He stretched. "What's the guy's name?"

"Papagallos."

"Oh, yeah." He got up and walked into the bathroom, emerging fifteen minutes later, toweling his hair dry.

Mac shoved a can of Coke into his hand. "You awake?"

Johnny took a long gulp of the soda, then nodded. "Yeah." He dressed quickly.

"You want breakfast?"

"Huh-uh." He pulled the holster on, settling its familiar weight against his body. "I saw a good movie last night."

"Yeah?" Mac shoved the omnipresent .45 into his belt.

"Yeah. It was all about this cowboy that was maybe a ghost and maybe not. He came riding into this town and he painted it all red and got revenge on the people who killed him, sort of."

"Sounds good." Mac was used to Johnny's rather unique synopses of the movies he saw. He tried to remember what he'd done the night before. He could recall the card game. Then drinking at some dive. A broad. It all added up to nothing. So what else was new? "Let's go," he said shortly.

They never talked much on the way to a job. Johnny propped his knees against the dashboard and whistled softly to himself. Mac pulled into the alley behind the apartment building. "Be careful," he said ritualistically.

Johnny nodded and got out of the car. Mac watched him go, watched as he worked on the door; then, as the slender figure slipped inside, Mac lit a cigarette and bent over the steering wheel to wait.

BOOK

II

-ONE-

His Christian wife refused to get up early on Sunday mornings in order to make his breakfast. Since it was the one concession to her faith that she held onto with any degree of seriousness, Simon Hirsch did not argue the matter. As the son of a rabbi, he felt obligated to indulge such religious fervor.

He stopped at the Dunkin' Donut shop on his way over to the stakeout and bought three glazed and a cup of coffee, black. The girl behind the counter was painfully ugly, with a voice like sandpaper and a grating, loud personality. She had only one saving grace, that being the fact that she dearly loved cops, so he flirted with her as she got his order together. He even let his denim jacket flop open, so she could see his holster. Why not. It was Sunday; give the broad a thrill. Cops, after all, had to take their friends where they could find them.

It was nearly twenty after eight by the time he reached the stakeout. He parked just behind the innocuous brown sedan and got out, bringing the doughnut bag. Delaney, red-eyed and bewhiskered, greeted him with a yawn. "You're late."

Simon leaned against the car. "Yeah? Anything happen?"

"Sure," Delaney said, taking the doughnut Simon offered. "Papagallos peed. Took a shower. Gargled." The last word was muffled around a bite of pastry.

"Gee, I'm sorry I missed all that. How's Mike sound?"

Delaney snorted. "How does Mike always sound before his morning coffee?"

"Mean?"

"You got it."

Simon grinned. "Poor Papagallos. The man may be a no-good rotten bastard, but what's he ever done to deserve Mike first thing in the morning?"

Delaney wiped crumbs from his face and started the car. "It's all yours, Hirsch."

Simon stepped back. "Thanks for nothing," he muttered. He walked back to his own car and got behind the wheel again, switching on his receiver with one hand as he snapped the plastic lid off the coffee cup with the other. Every noise made in the apartment nearly three blocks away came to him clearly.

The first voice he heard was not that of Papagallos, but of his own partner, one Wild Mike Conroy. "Coffee's ready, Mr. Papagallos. You want some?"

"No, but help yourself," came the reply from the gravel-voiced racketeer. "Me, I'm gonna wait until my guest arrives, and we'll have breakfast together."

There was silence then, except for the sound of someone turning the pages of a newspaper, and the soft clink of a spoon against a cup. Simon smiled a little, imagining the almost orgasmic expression that would cross Mike's face as he finally got his first gulp of coffee. The hyper redhead was worthless until that morning fix.

"When she gets here," Papagallos said, "you make yourself scarce."

"Yes, sir."

The servile tone of Conroy's voice was so totally out of character that it brought a soft chuckle from Simon. The guy shoulda been a goddamned actor, he thought admiringly. Over the past month the wily undercover cop had insinuated himself so well into the Papagallos organization that odds were being given around the squad room of just how long it would be before the aging gangster gifted Michael Francis Conroy with control of his empire.

Simon wasn't betting, holding out, insisting that the old fart would probably adopt Conroy inside of another month. Wild Mike thought that sounded pretty damned good. He'd always wanted to be an heir, and the only thing his own father had left him were ten younger siblings to support and a sizable bar tab.

Simon finished the coffee and crumpled the cup. He really hated this part of the job. The waiting. The subtle feeling of helplessness. It was much better when the situation was reversed. He liked being on the inside. Working undercover, the edge of excitement kept him on his toes every minute. It was partly fear, of course, never knowing exactly what was going down from one minute to the next. The fear, however, was balanced by the security of knowing that Mike was someplace close, waiting to back him up.

Mike, he knew, was feeling the same way now. It was amazing and a little scary the way they balanced one another so perfectly. The odd couple, as they were called around the squad room. The tough Irish street kid and the Jew from Boston.

Simon rolled down the car window, letting the fresh air from last night's rain blow gently against his face. Papagallos must be expecting his newest broad. Idly, he thumbed through the pages of his notebook. Karen Hope, that was her name. A looker, too, from what Mike had said. Well, that figured. Lookers always went for guys with money.

Of course, Kimberly was a looker. Blonde. Regal. The original ice princess. But that wasn't a very good example, because when they'd gotten married, she'd figured that she was hooking up with the future partner in some big deal Boston law firm. It had never occurred to her that she would end up married to a cop and living in a tract house in San Francisco. Hell, she could have married a WASP, if that was the kind of life she'd wanted.

Simon frowned a little, scratching at an earlobe. The fight last night still rankled. It was so absurd. He didn't even give a damn about the anniversary party, but suddenly the celebration of their fifteen years of wedded bliss seemed to have assumed painful importance to Kimberly. He'd given her carte blanche to do whatever the hell she wanted. Except for one thing.

Kimberly was flatly refusing to invite Mike and his wife.

"I will not have that drunken Irishman ruin another party," she said, sounding regal. "Remember New Year's Eve?"

He remembered. The memory brought a faint

smile to his lips. Wild Mike had been in top form that night. It wasn't even as if the vase he broke was an antique or anything. It was just a vase. And Mike had paid for it, a fact that didn't seem to mollify Kimberly at all.

When the fight ended, long after midnight, the issue wasn't really resolved. She just kept insisting that Mike wasn't going to be invited, and he simply said that, in that case, she shouldn't expect him to show up either. Hell.

Simon stopped thinking about it, focusing his full attention on what was happening in the apartment. It was a little after nine when he heard the knock at the door. "Aha," Papagallos said, sounding pleased. "She's a little early. Couldn't wait, I guess."

"I guess," Mike agreed.

Simon could hear the sound of footsteps crossing the tiled foyer and of the door opening. The muffled crack of the silenced gunshot seemed to roar through the car, startling Simon so that his head jerked around. A muscle pulled in his neck. "What the shit," he mumbled. A second shot followed almost immediately. Before its echo died completely, he had the car started. He turned the volume on the receiver all the way up. The door to the apartment closed softly, but he heard it. "Mike?" he said aloud.

Almost as if in response, a faint moan came over the radio.

Simon grabbed for the microphone and with a mouth that was suddenly dry, requested back-up and an ambulance. He careened around the corner, pounding the accelerator to the floor, just missing a fire hydrant and two pedestrians.

He was out of the car before it came to a complete stop, running across the lawn, and into the building as if demons from hell were on his heels. He pulled out his gun as he moved, clutching it in his left hand and pushing the door open with his right shoulder.

His running footsteps echoed hollowly in the corridor. The door to Papagallos' apartment was closed. Not wanting to touch the knob, Simon raised one foot and kicked until the wood cracked and the door flew open. He fell through the entrance, almost tripping over Papagallos' body sprawled there in a bloody pool. "Mike?" he gasped out frantically.

His partner was huddled in a chair. There was blood everywhere. Simon crossed the room in three leaps, bending over the chair, wrapping both arms around Conroy. "Oh, shit," he sighed. "Mikey?"

Conroy's eyes fluttered open. He wanted to smile. "Hey, partner." A trail of blood ran out the corner of his mouth and down his chin.

Simon tried to wipe the blood away with the sleeve of his jacket. "There's help coming, babe, so you just hang tough. Hang tough, okay?"

Conroy coughed. "Hell." His fingers scrabbled weakly for a hold on Simon. "Knew you'd get here, buddy." His soft brown eyes squinted as he tried to think. "Saw the guy."

"Was it somebody we know?"

"Uh-uh. Hurts, Simon. Simon?"

"It's okay, Mike," he said. "I'm here."

"Blond guy," Mike mumbled. "Tall."

"Yeah, okay, I'll get him. Don't worry, buddy, I'll get the son of a bitch who did this." Mike began to shake violently. Simon bent over him, pressing his face to Conroy's. "Mike? Oh, god, Mike, I'm sorry. I'm so fuckin' sorry."

His partner stilled, tried to smile again, and died.

Simon listened desperately for a heartbeat, then shook the body a little. "Mike? Oh, damnit, man, why'd you have to go and die?" His voice was angry. "Why'd you do this to me?" Bloody, trembling fingers pushed a limp auburn curl off Mike's forehead. "Why?"

Simon heard the other cops come in, but he didn't say anything to them. He just slumped next to the bloody chair, holding onto Wild Mike Conroy's body and crying.

The wheels of officialdom began to move quickly, in their roughshod, uncaring way. The room was soon filled with blue uniforms, with snapping cameras, with men in grey suits, all talking in low, urgent voices. Simon ignored them, not caring either. He only spoke once, to tell them that he was going in the ambulance with Conroy's body. A white-clad intern started to object, but Simon pushed by him, climbing in next to the stretcher. Michael Francis Conroy wouldn't take this ride alone.

Simon held his partner's hand, until the nurses at the hospital gently, but firmly, pried him loose. Lieutenant Troy was there, dressed in golfing clothes, his lined face grim. "What the hell happened, Simon?" he snapped at once.

Simon shrugged. "I don't know."

"You don't know? What the hell does that mean? You were supposed to be covering him."

Simon raised his head slowly and stared at Troy, his dark blue eyes cold. "I was covering him," he said very softly. "Goddamnit, I *was*. It was you who put the fucking stakeout three blocks away."

"That was necessary; we couldn't afford to tip Papagallos off." Troy wasn't looking at Simon.

"Yeah. Right." Simon returned his gaze to the swinging doors through which they'd taken the bodies. "It just happened so fast. Someone knocked at the door, Papagallos went to answer it, and then I heard the shots. By the time I could get there, nothing."

"Did he say anything before he . . . before?"

Simon nodded. "Yeah. Said the guy was tall. And blond."

"That's it?" Troy sounded disappointed.

"The man had a bullet in his chest. He was hurting." Simon stretched out his arms, bracing himself against the wall.

"Go home, Simon," Troy said quietly.

He shook his head. "No, can't. Too much to do."

"You can't do anything like that."

Simon lowered his arms and looked at his hands. They trembled. "I'll be okay."

"You're covered in blood," Troy said flatly.

He noticed the blood for the first time and his stomach lurched. "Christ," he said. "He was bleeding so much." His voice cracked a little. "All right. I'll see you back at headquarters."

Troy nodded.

Simon hitched a ride back to the apartment building with a patrol car. The sidewalk was still jammed with sightseers and the press. A couple of reporters spotted him as he crossed the street toward his car. "Hey, Hirsch," one called.

"Yeah?"

"What happened here?"

Someone shoved a tape recorder in front of his face; he stared at it dumbly. "What?"

"Can you give us the details of today's double murder?"

He shook his head. "No. I don't have anything to say." Quickly he got into the car and started the engine, barely giving the press time to scatter before he squealed away from the curb.

Details. They wanted details.

He shook his head again, trying to clear away the fog. The only detail he could remember was the sight of Conroy's face as he died. He had a horrible feeling that he'd never be able to forget that.

Without being aware of the journey at all, he soon turned onto his block. The neighborhood was Sunday afternoon quiet. The only noise came from some kids playing ball in the middle of the street. They interrupted the game briefly to let him go by. He parked in the driveway and hurried to the house, hoping no one would see his bloody clothes. The door was locked. He fumbled for the key, found it finally, and shoved the door open, stumbling across the threshold.

Kimberly was stretched out on the chaise, reading. She looked up in surprise that turned to shock as he burst into the living room. Her face paled. "My god, Simon! What happened? Are you hurt?"

He stared at her.

The book she'd been reading slipped from her fingers as she got to her feet. "Simon?"

He walked past her, across the room to the mantel. Stupid, fucking mantel, he thought distantly. Why have a mantel when there wasn't any fireplace? A large cut-glass vase sat on one end of the useless appendage.

"Say something," Kimberly pleaded.

Without even looking at her, he picked up the vase and deliberately smashed it against the wall. The glass shattered and a hairline crack appeared in the plaster.

"Simon!"

Their daughter appeared in the doorway, her just-painted, blood-red nails fluttering. "What's going on? Daddy?"

Kimberly waved her out, then walked over to Simon. "Have you gone crazy?"

He stared at the shattered vase, then leaned wearily against the wall. "Mike is dead," he said in a muffled voice. "Somebody killed Mike."

Kimberly took a step backwards. Death, he knew, didn't belong in her world, at least not this way. Dying should be quiet and filled with dignity; it should be neat. There shouldn't be a madman covered with blood running into her all-white living room, smashing things and talking about death. "Oh, no," she said at last.

Simon gave a rattling laugh, still not looking at his wife. "You don't have to worry about him ruining your goddamned party now," he said.

Her porcelain skin flushed. "That isn't fair, Simon. I never wanted anything like this to happen."

He sighed. "Yeah, I know. I'm sorry I said that. It's just . . . damn it, Kim, I heard the shots. I heard it all happen, but by the time I got there, he was dying. There wasn't anything I could do."

"It must have been terrible."

"Yeah." Simon ran a hand down the front of his blood-encrusted T-shirt, denim jacket, jeans. "He just . . . died."

Kimberly was recovering. He admired that quality in her. Probably it came from her Methodist past. Solid American stock, people who never let any adversity keep them down long. "I always told you something like this could happen. Thank goodness it wasn't you."

"Yeah," Simon said. "Thank God for that, huh? My partner is dead, but, boy, I'm just fine and dandy. I was backing him up. Great job I did." He crashed a fist against the wall. "Goddamn motherfucking bastards."

"Shh, Tammy will hear you."

He only looked at her, his wife, and the neat white living room. Sometimes, he got the feeling that he didn't belong here at all. It was as if he lived two lives. One was out on the street with Mike, where they saw the blood and pain and shit that went down with monotonous sameness year after year; and his other life was here, surrounded by nice clean things, with a woman who didn't like some words because they scared her. Because they reminded her that beyond the wall-to-wall carpeting and the patch of green lawn that surrounded this mortgaged haven, there was a universe that was dangerous and dirty.

Simon wondered which life was his real one. Or maybe his real life hadn't started yet. If there was such a thing as real life.

He shrugged. "I gotta clean up and get downtown."

"Maybe you shouldn't go. You look terrible. They can't expect you to work after what you just went through."

"I don't know what 'they' expect, Kim. I know what I have to do. Somebody killed my partner, and I'm going to find the son of a bitch."

She shivered. "It scares me to hear you talk like that," she whispered.

He grimaced and started out.

Kimberly knelt on the carpet and began carefully to pick up the pieces of jagged-edged glass.

Simon stopped. "Don't do that," he said sharply.

"What?"

"Leave it there."

She picked up another piece of glass. "Don't be silly, honey. I can't leave this—"

He took a step toward her. "Leave the fucking thing there!" he shouted.

Her hand dropped the shards. They stared at one another for a long moment, then Simon spun around and went into the bedroom.

Just about an hour later, he walked into the squad room. Although he had showered in the hottest water his body could stand, scrubbing until his skin was raw, and dressed in clean clothes, he still felt as if he were covered in blood. The too-starched white shirt and neat sport coat seemed to chafe his flesh.

He sat down, propping both feet on his desk. A couple of other homicide dicks were in the room, and they looked at him without saying anything. There wasn't anything to say. He lit a cigarette and tried to ignore the desk opposite his, with its familiar clutter.

Troy, clad now in a suit, came in. "You okay?"

Simon nodded shortly. "Anything turn up?"

"No. We're still waiting to get the bullets. None of the neighbors saw or heard anything."

"Yeah, that figures."

"Probably they really didn't. This was a smooth job, Hirsch, pro all the way."

"Except for one little thing," Simon replied,

flicking ashes toward the already over-flowing ashtray, and missing.

"What?"

"I think Mike being there was a surprise. There was just the slightest hesitation between the two shots, as if whoever was pulling the trigger had to . . . readjust his plan. Mike's death was an after-thought." Simon smiled bitterly. "Hell. An after-thought."

"You may be right." Troy gestured impatiently. "Which gets us absolutely nowhere."

"This is my case, of course," Simon said.

"Is that a good idea, Hirsch? You might be too close to things."

"I promised Conroy. It's my case."

Troy looked at him for a moment before answering. "All right. As long as I think you can handle it. When I decide you can't, that's it."

Simon shrugged. "I'll have the bastard before then."

Troy moved closer. "I know how you must be feeling right now, Simon."

"Yeah?"

"I lost a partner once."

Simon crushed out the cigarette. Yeah, he wanted to say, but you didn't lose Mike Conroy. Instead, he crashed his feet to the floor. "I gotta clean out his desk."

"Somebody else can do that, man."

He shook his head. "My job."

"At least wait awhile."

Simon sighed. "I have to sit here and work. I can't be looking at that mess."

Troy nodded and left the room.

Simon moved around and sat in Conroy's chair.

He pulled open a drawer and made a face. "God, that guy was a slob," he said hoarsely.

The other men in the room took pity on him and turned away.

Simon started piling old magazines, wrinkled report forms, and discarded candy wrappers on top of the desk. "A goddamned slob," he said, this time to himself.

-TWO-

Simon stood hunched over the snack bar, chewing on the rubbery hot dog and waiting. Sometimes it seemed like they spent half their lives just waiting. Just over sixty hours had passed since the shooting, and he'd spent a lot of that time in a sort of limbo. He hadn't been home since that trip on Sunday to get rid of the bloody clothes. Hadn't changed since then, or shaved, or slept. He took a gulp of too-sweet Coke. Thank God for caffeine.

Where the hell was Danny anyway? That was the trouble with a junkie snitch; they were too damned unreliable. Danny, of course, might not show at all, since the creep really wasn't his snitch at all, but Mike's.

At the thought of his partner, Simon glanced at his watch and frowned. It was getting late. Now there wouldn't be time for him to go home and change before stopping at the funeral parlor. Hell, if Danny didn't get here soon, he'd miss the visitation entirely. Not that he was looking forward to it, but it had to be done. Some things just had to be gotten through and then, hopefully, gotten over. Like the report that he still had to write on the shooting. And like the funeral tomorrow.

He looked up again impatiently and saw the gimpy little junkie crossing the street toward him. The two of them made a nice pair at the end of the counter as Danny arrived and sidled up next to him. "About time you got here," Simon complained.

"Couldn't help it." Danny sniffled. "Very busy."

Simon nodded glumly.

Danny shuffled his feet. "Damned shame about Mike. Damned shame. I was real sorry to hear it."

"Yeah, I'll bet."

"I mean, he was a good guy, y'know? Ain't that always the way? The good ones always get it."

"Yeah, Danny, that's the way it is. The good guys get it, and the garbage like you keeps right on walking around."

Danny could no longer afford the luxury of being insulted by anything Simon said to him. "Mike, he understood how it is, y'know? Always had a few bucks to slip a guy," the junkie reminisced.

Simon pushed a folded bill down the counter toward him, but kept a finger on it. "Mike was always a sucker for a sob story," he said coldly. "But not me. I'm different. When I pay, I want something in return."

"I always try and give good value," Danny said.

Simon released the bill. "So I'm waiting."

Danny pocketed the money quickly and wiped his nose on his sleeve. "Ahh, well, that's the thing about this case. The streets is real dead, Inspector."

"Yeah, well, Mike Conroy is real dead, too, you prick."

"Damned shame."

"You said that already. Come on, Danny, you must have heard something. Christ, man, you spend all your time in the gutter."

Danny picked up the remains of Simon's hot dog and shoved it into his mouth. He mumbled something, spraying drops of saliva and crumbs over the counter.

"Swallow first, asshole."

He swallowed. "Well, word has it that the job was done by imported talent."

"Imported from where?"

"Don't know." He belched. "Back east somewheres, I guess."

"I need a name, Danny."

Danny washed the rest of the hot dog down with the last gulp of Simon's Coke. "No names, man. There ain't no name. It was big time stuff, though. Big time." He began to edge away. "Sorry about Mike," he mumbled. "Damned shame. He was a good guy." Danny slipped out the door, melting quickly into the crowd on the sidewalk.

Simon slumped against the counter, burying his face in his hands. Nearly four hours it took just to track Danny down and set up this meet. And all for what? A big fat zilch.

"You okay, Inspector?" asked a quiet voice at his elbow.

He raised his head and saw the young patrolman. Aginisto, he recalled after a moment. The cop had a worried expression on his boyish face. Boyish? I'm only thirty-five, Simon thought bitterly. I'm not old. "Huh?" he said.

"I just wondered if you were okay," Aginisto said hesitantly.

Simon nodded. "Yeah," he said wearily. "I'm

fine. Thanks for asking."

Aginisto studied the wall. "Sorry about Inspector Conroy."

"Right." Simon gave him a smile and started toward the door.

He stopped abruptly, staring across the room. A tall, slender man with shaggy blond hair stood at the far end of the counter, concentrating intently on a slice of pizza. After a few moments, he apparently became aware of the scrutiny. He turned curiously, peering around until his gaze rested on Simon.

Simon broke the uneasy eye contact first and walked out the door, mentally kicking himself. Hell, he couldn't start suspecting every tall blond man he saw. A guy could get real paranoid that way.

The parking lot of the O'Boyle Funeral Home was crowded, and he had to drive around twice before finding a spot to pull his car into. He locked the battered VW and went up the steps leading into the imposing brick building.

His first stop was the men's room. He splashed cold water on his face, then straightened to look into the mirror. Rather hopelessly, he tried to pull his comb through his tangled mop of dark curls. He gave that up quickly and simply tried to smooth the mess a little. His clothes were fairly hopeless, as well, but he stuffed the shirttail in where it belonged, and gave a quick polish to each shoe on the legs of his trousers.

Well, he thought, that was as good as it was going to get, and to hell with it anyway.

A discreet sign directed him to the right room. He pushed open a heavy oak door and slipped in.

The young man standing just inside looked so much like Mike had when they were first teamed eight years ago, that it sent a stab of pain through him. The kid turned and looked questioningly at Simon. "Uh . . . I'm Hirsch," he mumbled, trying to smooth his hair again.

A familiar smile flickered across the young man's face. "You're Mike's partner."

"Yeah, I am. Was." Simon looked around the crowded room. "I just wanted to come by and . . . just to come by. I hope it's okay?"

"Sure. You belong here. I feel like I know you already, Mike talked about you so much. I'm his brother, Kevin."

"Yes."

"Siobahn's been expecting you."

Simon could see Mike's wife—widow—sitting in the front row. She looked pale, but composed. Turning, she saw him and smiled a little. He nodded.

Kevin leaned closer. "You can go up front if you like."

He didn't want to. He'd already seen Conroy dead once and that seemed like quite enough, but apparently it was expected, so he walked down the aisle toward the casket. A man and a young girl stood there. They each made the sign of the cross, then the girl leaned over and brushed her lips against Mike's cheek. Then she turned and followed the man up the aisle past Simon.

Walking more slowly, Simon approached the coffin. It was strange to see Mike in his dress blues, instead of jeans and a T-shirt. His face was waxen. He didn't look asleep, like people sometimes said about corpses. He just looked dead.

Simon dropped to his knees, touching the side of

the polished wood box. Ahh, Mikey, he thought wearily, was it worth it? Was any of it worth this? A guy like you, your life should've come to something more than just an afterthought of some bastard with a gun.

His thoughts drifted fuzzily.

He realized suddenly that he was about to fall asleep right there against the casket, and he got to his feet quickly, hoping no one had noticed. For one more minute he stood there, staring down at what was left of Wild Mike Conroy, then he bent and kissed his partner's forehead. "Thanks, buddy," he whispered.

Siobahn was waiting for him in the hallway. "Thank you for coming, Simon," she said. "Have you met Mike's brother, Kevin?"

"Yes." Simon was staring at a large crucifix over the door. "Siobahn, I don't know what to say. If I could've got there sooner—"

She put a finger to his lips. "Hush. Don't say that."

"Well, I'm just so damned sorry."

"I know that. We're all sorry, everyone who loved him."

"Yeah," Simon said.

"I have a favor to ask of you."

He brought his gaze back to her face. "Sure, anything."

"Will you speak at the funeral?"

"Me?" he said, surprised. "But I'm not family or . . . I'm not even Catholic."

She smiled. "Mike thought of you as family. In some ways, you were closer to him than anybody else, including me. He loved you, and I think it would please him." Her eyes darkened. "If you would like to."

Simon nodded slowly. "All right. I . . . I hope I can say the right things."

She kissed his cheek. "You will." She gave him a gentle push toward the door. "Go home and get some sleep. You look terrible."

He shook hands again with Mike's brother, whose name he couldn't remember, and left the two of them standing in the hall.

By the time he got home, all the lights were off. He let himself in quietly and switched on a small lamp in the living room. The pieces of broken glass were still there on the rug. Simon knelt and began to pick them up. A shadow fell across the room. "Simon?"

He didn't look up. "Sorry I woke you."

"That's okay. Don't cut yourself."

"I won't."

"Are you all right?"

He picked up the last piece of glass and got to his feet. "Uh-huh. The funeral is at two tomorrow."

"I know. I'll be ready."

"Thank you. Go back to bed, Kim."

"Aren't you coming?"

"Yeah, sure. Soon as I dump this into the trash."

She stood there a moment longer, then vanished. Simon walked through the house to the back door. The plastic trash can sat beside the porch. He lifted the lid and dropped all the pieces of glass but one in. He held that single jagged sliver thoughtfully. After a moment, he took it between the fingers of his left hand, and carefully ran the sharp edge across his right palm. A thin trail of blood appeared in the wake of the moving glass. It hurt. He stared at the cut for a moment, then dropped the glass in with the rest, and went back into the house.

-THREE-

Joey Belmondo was a punk.

It wasn't the first time Belmondo had faced Simon across the table in the interrogation room. If anything, they knew one another too well. That had the advantage, at least, of cutting down on the preliminaries. Simon, dressed in his best (only) black suit, a new white shirt, and a black tie, came into the room and sat down. He lit a cigarette. "I don't have a whole lot of time, Joey," he said flatly. "So let's just skip the foreplay and get right down to business."

Joey stared at him, grinning. "You look like a fucking preacher or something."

"Maybe I finally got religion."

That seemed to strike Joey's funny bone and he laughed. "Hey," he said, "I got it—they must be planting your late deceased partner today."

Simon took a long drag on the cigarette. "As a matter of fact, they are." He flicked ashes onto the floor, keeping his gaze on Joey. "So maybe you'll understand that I'm not in the best of moods this morning."

Joey shrugged. "Nobody ever did accuse you of being Mr. Nice Guy, far as I know."

"You got it. I've always been irritable. Now I'm mean." It had been at their first interrogation together that the roles were set. He was the bad cop and Mike was the good, buddy-buddy cop. Now he couldn't remember if the choice had been an accident, maybe decided by flipping a coin, or whether it had actually been an astute case of type-casting. Anyway, by this time, it came easier being hostile than being nice. Especially today. "Talk to me, Joey. Who wanted Papagallos dead?"

"Gee, I don't know," Joey said, scratching his head in mock thoughtfulness. "Who wanted your partner dead?" He brightened. "You know, that's an idea. Did'ja stop to think that maybe somebody was really after Conroy and got Papa by mistake?"

Simon just looked at him.

Joey shifted in the chair a little. "I got a question."

"Yeah?"

"I'd like to know how Conroy got so close to Papa. Hell, I worked for that bastard three years, and I only saw him once. Never talked to him at all. How'd he do it?"

Simon slowly crushed out the cigarette. "Conroy was smart," he said.

"Yeah?" Joey laughed again. "So how come he's dead, and I'm still here?"

There was a long silence in the room. Simon put two fingers inside his collar and tugged at the tie that was strangling him. "Joey," he said finally, gently, "I got a ten-year-old boy waiting in the wings. A kid named Teddy Newhouse. You remember Teddy?"

Some of the bravado seemed to drain from Belmondo. "Never heard of him," he mumbled.

"Gee, that's funny, Joey, because he remembers you real good. He especially remembers the night you took him behind the garage to play games."

Joey sank further into the chair, his face pushed into a fatuous pout. "Ah, shit," he said sullenly.

"I've been keeping Teddy on ice, because he's just a kid and I sort of hated to make him get on the stand and go over the whole thing again." He paused, checking his watch. "But, see, that won't wash anymore. Ask me why, Joey."

"Why?"

"Because I want to find out who killed Conroy. No, wait a minute, scratch that. I *will* find out who did it." He stood, carefully shaking down the crease in his trousers. "And I'll tell you something else, Joey. I don't much care who gets run over in the process." He smiled pleasantly. "I gotta go now, but we'll talk again. Count on that."

He walked out and found Troy, wearing his dress uniform for the funeral, standing in the hall. The lieutenant had been listening to the interrogation on the intercom. He turned and looked at Simon. "Did you mean that?"

Simon didn't glance up as he busied himself brushing some ashes from the sleeve of his jacket. "What?"

"About not caring who gets run over."

Now Simon looked at him. "I meant it."

Troy's face was suddenly older. "You're a cop, Hirsch, not a vigilante."

"I know that."

The other man nodded grimly. "Make sure you don't forget it."

Simon pulled at his shirt cuffs. The vivid gash across his palm made his hand feel stiff and awkward. "I won't."

"What happened to your hand?"

He shrugged. "Cut it, I guess. Hey, I gotta go. Kim's waiting. See you later."

The building was beginning to look strangely empty as all but the most essential office personnel left to attend the funeral. Simon hurried through the quiet hallways to the parking garage.

The traffic jam began four blocks from St. David's. Their car inched forward slowly, as Simon hunched over the wheel, his face closed and expressionless. Kimberly sat next to him, tugging at the hem of her black dress nervously.

"She should've come," he muttered finally.

"Why? It would only upset her."

"Maybe it's time she got a little upset over something. I don't think it shows much respect for her not to be here."

Kimberly sighed. "Honey, we've been all through this. Tammy didn't want to come, and I don't think it would have been a very good idea to force her." She glanced at him. "Besides, she has cheerleading tryouts today."

"Oh, yeah, sure." He shut up about it, but the fact that his own daughter wasn't there left a bad taste in his mouth.

He managed to get the car to within a block of the church. At that point, he waved to a traffic cop he knew slightly. "Hey, Jeff, I gotta get in there. Take care of this thing for me, willya?"

The cop nodded. "Sure thing, Inspector."

They got out of the car and Kimberly held his arm as they walked to the church and up the wide steps. Just before going in, Simon paused. He pulled a black yarmulke from his pocket and settled it on his head.

The large church was already packed. They stood for a moment, looking around for a place to sit, before Mike's brother came up the aisle toward them. "Hi, Inspector," he said softly.

Simon nodded, still not remembering the kid's name.

"Your places are down front." He led them to the second row, just behind Siobahn and the two kids, boys, aged five and seven. Siobahn turned her head and smiled. Simon sat straight-backed, both hands resting on his knees.

"So many people," Kimberly whispered.

"Mike had a lot of friends."

"I even saw a TV camera outside."

Simon's fingers moved a little against the material of the black suit. "He was a hero," he said softly. "The media loves a hero."

"Will they put you on the news, do you think?"

"Me? Why the hell should they? I'm just the guy who got there too late." He couldn't take his eyes off the coffin, draped in the flag, that sat in front of the altar. Outside, an airplane roared over, drowning out the soft hum of conversation, and the noise of people settling in.

It was nearly twenty minutes before the service began. The priest, a tall, gaunt man with steel-grey hair led the proceedings. Simon scarcely listened. He followed the lead of those around him in when to stand and sit. He couldn't kneel, though.

When the priest nodded at him, he took a deep breath and walked to the front, pausing only a split second as he passed the coffin. Standing behind the pulpit, he stared out over the sea of faces. He cleared his throat, wishing that he'd thought to write down what he wanted to say. Except that he didn't know. His first words were in Aramaic, then he translated. "Magnified and sanctified is the name of the Lord." He tried to focus on the faces below. "Those are the opening words of the Kaddish, the Jewish prayer for the dead. My father is a rabbi, and I know all the right things to say when someone dies."

His glance went to the coffin.

He sighed. "Yeah, I know the words, all right, but I don't think I can say them. Not for Mike. Because once the words are said, it all becomes very real." His voice was growing stronger. "Mike was a cop, and I guess every officer on the force knows that someday this could happen to him. We all think about it." He shook his head, smiling faintly. "Yeah, I figured it might happen to me. But I never once thought about it happening to Mike. That's kinda funny, isn't it? Guess I was tempting the fates."

He bit his lip, deciding that was probably the wrong thing to say in church.

"Being a cop is not a very nice job sometimes, but having Mike for a partner made it easier. Made it bearable. A lot of times when I wanted to cry over some of the shit we have to deal with, he would make me laugh instead." As he spoke, Simon absently rubbed one finger over the cut on his palm. "I guess I'll probably still laugh. I mean, life goes on, right? Yeah, right. It's gonna be a whole lot harder now, though." He was quiet for a moment, staring out over the crowd. "I said before that my father is a rabbi. There have been a lot of rabbis in my family. There had never been a cop before. Doctors, lawyers, yeah. But no cops. Until me." The cut began to bleed. "My father thinks I have chosen a degrading way of life. A dirty job. He's right. But it's also an important job. I guess."

He could see Kimberly watching him, and Siobahn, and Mike's brother, and other men from the department. And a lot of strangers—people, he realized suddenly, that had been a part of Mike's other life, the part that he didn't know.

Abruptly, he felt very tired. "But there is something I want to say. If being a cop brought me nothing but pain, if my father never speaks to me again, if the rest of my life goes to hell because of the job, if it all adds up to nothing more than a bullet for me, too . . . if all this is true, it still will have been worth it, because once I had a partner and a friend like Mike Conroy."

He looked down and saw the blood on his hand. He closed the fingers into a fist. "None of this is probably what I should have said up here. I don't know. Probably I should have talked about God, or faith, or how Mike is in heaven now. But I'm not a very religious person. If there is a heaven, I know Mike is there, but, see, that doesn't make me feel any better. I don't want him in heaven. I want him here." He stopped to take a breath. "Or maybe I should have talked about some of the things Mike and I did together. But those memories belong to me. I'm just not very good at talking in public. I only know about doing my job."

He leaned forward a little. "The Bible says 'an eye for an eye.' That's my job. Exacting justice." He raised both hands, palms upwards, in a gesture of total hopelessness. "But what kind of justice can there be for Mike?" He looked around and stared at the priest, almost expecting—hoping—that there would be an answer. But the man was silent, so

Simon turned back to the front. "Michael Francis Conroy was a good cop. A good man. And the best damned partner in the world. I'm sorry he's dead." He took two steps backwards and ducked his head a little. "I guess that's all I have to say," he mumbled.

He left the altar, this time stopping to rest his hand on top of the coffin briefly. A little of his blood stained the fabric of the flag.

The rest of the service was a blur for Simon, and without really knowing how, he found himself standing on the front steps of the church again. Siobahn was there, too, and she embraced him. "Thank you, Simon."

He shoved both hands into his pockets. "I didn't know what to say."

"You said what was in your heart. It was fine."

He tried to smile, then followed Kimberly to where the car was parked. They fell into place behind the winding motorcade making its slow way to the cemetery. Kimberly twisted •her handkerchief. "I hate funerals," she said.

"Yeah, they're not much fun," he agreed.

She looked at him. "That was kind of a funny eulogy you gave."

"Was it?" He had no idea what he'd said. "I'm sorry."

"Well," she said, obviously trying to put the best light on it, "they probably just assmed it's because you're Jewish."

"Probably."

The graveside ceremony was mercifully brief, almost military. Simon spent most of the time watching the birds overhead. When the rifle salute shattered the stillness, he flinched visibly, hearing all too clearly the echo of the shots that had come over his radio on Sunday. The flag was folded and presented to Siobahn. Simon joined the line of people walking slowly by the grave. He bent and picked up a handful of dirt, held it tightly for a moment, then sprinkled the soil on top of the coffin.

Back in the car, finally, Kimberly relaxed with a long sigh. "Oh, God, I'll be glad to get home."

"We have to go by Mike's . . . Siobahn's first," he said shortly, pulling the car out of the cemetery drive sharply.

"Why?"

"It's expected."

She didn't argue.

There was a table of food set up in the dining room, and a lot of people stood around eating and drinking and talking, mostly about Mike. Siobahn sat in a rocking chair in the living room, accepting the condolences with a kind of weary grace. Simon poured himself a shot of whiskey from the bar on the sideboard, and walked around the room, sipping the drink slowly. He stopped finally in front of a large framed photo of Mike and himself, taken some four years earlier, after an intra-departmental softball game. They were both sweaty and filthy, grinning like idiots.

He stood there for a long time, letting the crowd flow around him unnoticed. When he turned away finally, it was with the feeling that those moments, not the funeral, had been his own farewell to Mike.

They left soon.

When they got home, he pulled up in front of the house, but didn't turn the car's engine off. He jerked the tie from around his neck. "Take this inside for me," he said, handing it to Kimberly.

"Aren't you coming?"

He shook his head. "Gotta get downtown."

"You're going back to work?"

"Yeah. Don't know when I'll get home."

She looked at him in silence, then shrugged and got out of the car. Simon drove away immediately, his mind already centered on the case.

-FOUR-

Some cops are plodders. They accomplish their jobs not with muscle or with quixotic undercover escapades, but instead through the patient gathering of facts, the tedious linking up of disparate bits of information, the slow and careful drawing of a conclusion from the collage thus assembled.

Douglas Campbell was that kind of cop. The stocky, beginning-to-bald inspector spent a lot of time poring over written reports, comparing statements, checking and rechecking old crime records. He usually ate lunch at his desk, chewing thoughtfully on a tuna fish sandwich packed by his wife, his eyes sharp behind the old-fashioned bifocals.

Campbell was Simon's new partner.

When Troy first broke the news, two days after the funeral, Simon just stared at him, his caffeine and tobacco-numbed brain unable to fully assimilate the crisply worded order. "A new partner?" he mumbled thickly, wishing that his mouth didn't taste like last week's coffee. "What the hell are you talking about?"

Troy was in the middle of lighting a cigar; he paused and looked up. "What the devil do you

212

mean, what am I talking about? Nobody in this squad is the Lone Ranger. Everybody has a partner. Campbell is yours. As of today."

Simon felt a lurching in his stomach; he pressed a hand to his gut to help ease the pain. "God, you could at least wait until the body gets cold," he said.

Troy squinted. "That's uncalled for, Hirsch. And unfair. I'm not asking you to fall in love with Campbell, just to work with him. He's a good cop."

"This is *my* case."

"This is everybody's case, Inspector." Troy finally got the cigar lit. "You do want to break this thing, don't you?"

Of course he did. So he didn't argue anymore; he just sighed and got up to leave Troy's office.

"And, Hirsch—"

"Yeah?"

"Would you for chrissake go home and change out of that damned mourning suit? You're beginning to smell like an old tennis shoe."

Since then, every couple of days, Troy or someone would remind him to go home and change. Sometimes he even slept a little, before showering, shaving, eating a meal served by a silent Kimberly, and coming back. In between those trips home, he grabbed catnaps on a cot at headquarters, and lived on coffee and candy bars.

It was almost time for another pit stop.

He sat at his desk, feet propped up, glumly watching Campbell. "We should be out on the street," he said for the hundredth or so time in the last two weeks.

Campbell didn't even bother to look up. "We

already talked to everybody, Hirsch," he said patiently. "There isn't any sense in going over the same territory again and again."

"It beats the hell out of sitting around here like some kind of fucking file clerk, reading old reports. We never once made a big bust sitting on our asses."

Campbell closed the file he was working on and sighed. "Simon, can I say something to you?"

Simon shrugged.

"I know you were partnered with Conroy a long time—"

"Eight years."

"Fine. Eight years. And I know that you were a terrific team. Highest arrest and conviction record in the city. The dynamic duo. That was great." He toyed with the folder. "But I'm not Mike Conroy. I don't operate the way he did."

"I noticed," Simon muttered.

"Probably we won't ever be friends, but I think we *can* work together. If we both try. Why not ease up a little? Compromise isn't a dirty word."

Simon was quiet for a time, rubbing his stubbled chin. "Doug," he said finally, "let me try to explain something to you. I'm not really interested in how you operate versus how Wild Mike used to do the job. I'm not at all interested in cementing our relationship, or in pulling together to win this one for the Gipper. I don't give a frigging damn about compromising. I only care about one thing. I only want to find out who killed my partner."

"Your former partner," Campbell said mildly. "I'm your partner now."

Simon sat very still. Then, slowly, he lowered his feet to the floor and stood. "I'm checking out for a

while," he said quietly. "Going home to change
and get a meal. Later, I'm going out on the street.
See what I can pick up from some snitches. Rattle
a few garbage cans. Break this case." He walked to
the door. "What are you going to do?"

Campbell looked at him, studied him, and finally seemed to come to a decision. "I'll be here," he
said wearily. "Still waiting on that follow-up
ballistics check from Washington. They're so
damned slow."

Simon met the other man's eyes. Deciding that
they now understood one another, he allowed himself a small smile. "Okay, Doug. I'll be in touch."

Campbell nodded, reaching for his tuna fish
sandwich with one hand and another file with the
other.

Kimberly fixed him bacon and eggs, then sat at
the table with him as he ate. They didn't talk much.
Simon kept his eyes on his plate, concentrating on
the meal. Kimberly clasped her hands on top of the
table and stared at the wall. "You look like a zombie," she said finally.

"I'm okay," he said around a mouthful of food.

"You're never home. Tammy and I almost
forget what you look like."

"I'm busy. As soon as this case is over. . . ."

"This case." She sighed, toying absently with an
errant blonde strand. "Tammy won the election."

He looked blank. "Election?"

"For the cheerleading squad."

"Oh, yeah." He poured more milk into his glass
and gulped it. "That was why she wouldn't go to
the funeral."

"She thought you'd be proud."

"I am. If that's what she wants."

"She's thirteen years old, Simon; of course it's what she wants. Why shouldn't it be?"

He ran a piece of toast around the plate, wiping up egg and bacon grease, then swallowed it with the last gulp of milk. "I don't know. No reason, I guess."

She leaned forward suddenly. "When are you going to stop this?"

Simon shoved the plate away and lit a cigarette. "Stop what?"

"Working all the time. Not sleeping. Eating once every two days. Ignoring your family." She flattened her hands against the table.

He relaxed in the chair, closing his eyes. "I'm just doing what I have to do."

"That sounds like a line out of some old movie. You're not some kind of superhero."

"I know that. I'm just a dumb Jew cop, trying to do my job."

"Are you? I don't think you care about the job so much. I think this is some kind of private war you're waging."

He shut out the sound of her voice. Instead of listening, he ran through the killing in his mind again, watching it happen as if the whole thing were a technicolor movie. He could see it all— Papagallos going to answer the door, Mike sitting in the chair drinking coffee, the killer appearing in the doorway. And that was where his dream image always stopped, at the faceless man with the gun. Over the past two weeks, he'd replayed the scene countless times. At first, all he saw was Mike—the bullet smashing into him, the blood, the expression on his face as he died. But the vision expanded until now he felt as if he'd actually been there for the whole thing. He could even see the killer approach the door, see the tall, blond, faceless man pull the gun.

"Simon!"

The voice cut through his groggy thoughts. He jerked awake, straightening with a grunt. "What?"

"Why don't you go to bed?"

He rubbed a hand over his just-shaved skin. "Can't."

Kimberly stood and began to clear the dishes. "I think you should see a doctor. Or maybe talk to Manny."

He pushed himself to his feet, searching in his pockets for the car keys. "I'm not sick, just a little tired. And why the hell should I talk to my brother?"

She was rinsing the plates. "I just think it might help. You seem so . . . sad all the time." She glanced toward him, then away. "I called him last night."

Simon stared at her. "What the hell gives you two the right to talk about me behind my back."

"It wasn't like that. I was just worried about you. Manny said it was the right thing for me to do."

"Yeah? My fucking bigshot psychiatrist brother. Who the hell cares?"

Her hands sloshed through soapy water. "He said you're probably suffering from unresolved guilt feelings, because Mike is dead and you're still alive." She was obviously quoting a long-distance diagnosis.

He took his windbreaker from the back of the chair and pulled it on. "Manny is an ass. If you make any more calls to Boston to talk about my private life, I'll pull the fucking phone out of the wall." He walked to the door, opened it, then stopped. "I know this isn't easy, honey. But it's so important. I'm going to see this thing through. I have to find that man. He killed someone. He killed Mike. It's my duty to find him. You can understand that, can't you?"

She shook her head, banging dishes in the sink. "No, not really. I mean, I know you feel bad about Mike. I know he was your friend. But there are other people working on it, too. I don't know why you have to do it all."

Simon opened his mouth to answer her, then realized that he didn't know what to say. He simply shrugged and left the house, shutting the door carefully.

-FIVE-

The wind blowing through Golden Gate Park was unseasonably chilly, and the clouds skittering overhead looked ominous. Simon huddled on a bench, hands shoved into his jacket pockets, watching as a couple of hardy joggers chased one another in a seemingly endless circle.

At last, he saw Doug Campbell approaching. The stolid figure, clad in a black raincoat, sat down next to him. They were quiet for a moment. "Lieutenant Troy would like to see you," Campbell said finally.

Simon gave a hoarse chuckle. "Yeah, I bet he would."

Campbell reached into the pocket of his raincoat and pulled out a bag of unshelled peanuts. He began to crack and eat them. "It finally dawned on him that I've been at my desk almost every day for the past two weeks, and he hasn't seen you at all. He asked some rather pointed questions about our working relationship."

"And what did you tell him?"

"That things were going along fine."

"Good."

They were quiet again, watching as a well-developed redhead jogged and bounced by. Campbell sighed and cracked another peanut between his teeth. "Simon, he just dumped two new cases on us."

Simon straightened. "How the hell can he do that? We've got to keep right on top of this thing with Mike. Let him give this other stuff to somebody else."

Campbell spread his fingers helplessly. "Life goes on, man. The squad is only so big. Murders keep happening. It's been over a month now, and we haven't been able to give him one solid lead. He said we've just been spinning our wheels, and it's time to put Papagallos on the back burner."

"I don't give a fucking damn about Papagallos, but it's not fair for him to pull us off Mike."

"What can I tell you? Besides, he's not pulling us off; he's just spreading us out a little. And he has a point, Simon. You know that it's almost impossible to crack one of these inside pro jobs. How often can we do it? Face it, man, we haven't come up with shit." He offered the bag of peanuts to Simon. "So now we've got the hooker strangling and the stabbing on the cable car."

Simon took a nut, but instead of eating it, began tossing it back and forth in his hands. "I don't believe this, Doug. A cop got killed. One of our own buys it, and everybody is in such a goddamned hurry to forget it."

"Nobody wants to forget it, Simon. It's just that there are other things that matter, too."

"Not to me."

"Well, they better start mattering." Campbell shoved the bag back into his pocket. "Come on, Hirsch. Maybe it's time you stop feeling so sorry for yourself, and remember that you're supposed to be a cop. All these other dead people deserve some attention, too. Even the hooker. I located her pimp. Let's go ask the gentleman a few questions."

Simon got to his feet, swearing softly and savagely. He threw the peanut out over the grass as he followed Campbell to the car.

It wasn't until they were riding along Geary Street en route to the pimp's apartment that Campbell spoke again. "Oh, by the way, I found something that might relate to Conroy's case."

Simon blew out the match in his fingers and looked at Campbell through a curtain of smoke. "What?"

"Three days ago, there was a hit in Denver. Somebody eliminated a smalltime hood named Willy Simpson."

"Yeah? So?"

"It was the same M.O. He opened the front door early one morning and took a slug through the head. I haven't been able to get a ballistics report yet, but it might be worth checking on." Campbell negotiated a turn carefully. "And about eighteen months ago, there was a killing right here. Remember Lefty Bergen?"

"Yeah. Numbers, right?"

"Right. Well, he was the same thing. The bullet there was too damned messed up for a firm check, though. Same caliber."

Simon sat back, nodding. "You might have something, Doug. That case in Denver—you have any more on it?"

"No, but I figured you might want to talk to them."

"I sure as hell do. Now."

"After we see the man," Campbell said firmly.

"Shit." Simon glanced at him. "Thanks, Doug."

"Just part of the job. I don't have any intention of giving up on this either, Simon."

They finished the ride in silence.

The forty minutes they spent talking to the sullen black man were forty minutes wasted. He told them nothing, and there wasn't anything they could pull him in on. So they warned him not to leave town—as if he would, with a stable of six women still working the streets for him—and went over to headquarters.

Troy passed them in the hallway and stopped, looking surprised. "Well, Inspector Hirsch. Nice of you to drop in on us."

"Yeah, sure, Lieutenant," Simon replied hurriedly. "I gotta make a phone call." But as he began to dial, Simon suddenly changed his mind and replaced the receiver. "Doug?"

Campbell didn't glance up from the report he was typing on their talk with the pimp. "Huh?"

"I'm going to Denver."

Now the other man swiveled his chair around to look at him. "What?"

"I think I should go to Denver myself and see just what the story is. I have a feeling that this is my boy."

"You have a feeling, huh? Troy will love that."

Simon stood. "Well, whether he does or not, I'm going." He turned toward Troy's office, giving Campbell a quick thumbs-up gesture. Campbell shook his head and bent over the typewriter again.

Campbell was right. Troy loved it. He slammed a desk drawer shut with a bang. "Oh, I love this, Hirsch. We have corpses popping up all over the frigging town and now you want to fly off to Denver to check out some two-bit stiff there. Because it might—*might*—have something to do with a case here. A case, by the way, that's supposed to be in pending. You have a *feeling*?"

Simon nodded. "This is my boy."

"This is your boy. Great. Do you really expect me to authorize travel vouchers because you're getting psychic vibes halfway across the goddamned country?"

"This is him, Troy, the same guy who wasted Mike."

"You think. You 'feel.' " Troy shook his head. "Sorry, Simon, but I can't sanction an official trip with no more than that to go on."

Simon took a deep breath. "I'm going anyway. Sir. I have some sick days coming. I'll use that time and pay for the trip myself."

Troy looked at him curiously. "You're kidding. Aren't you?"

"Are you refusing to grant me the days?" Simon asked flatly.

After a moment, Troy shook his head. "No, I'm not refusing. Take the days."

"Thank you." Simon got to his feet.

"Hirsch."

"Yes?"

"I can understand what you're doing." He seemed to read skepticism in Simon's face. "Damn it, man, no one ever gave you a monopoly on caring."

"I know that."

"Good. But you can't let this thing screw up your perspective. Make this trip to Denver, and I hope to hell something turns up for you. But if it doesn't, then you have to be able to live with that. To come back and shape up your life again."

"Yeah," Simon replied. "Sure."

The two men looked at one another in strained silence. Neither pair of eyes gave way, until finally Simon simply turned on his heel and walked out of the office.

Kimberly watched him throw shaving gear, clean underwear and socks, and an extra shirt into the overnight bag. She had both arms wrapped around her body, as if the bedroom were chilly. "I don't know why you're doing this, Simon."

"Because it might help."

"Lieutenant Troy doesn't think so, you admit that."

"I don't care very much what Troy thinks."

She moved around the room restlessly. "Do you care what I think?"

He was surprised by the question. "Well, of course," he mumbled. "You know that. But this is my job, and you can't tell me how to do it."

"How much does it cost to fly to Denver and back?"

He snapped the bag closed. "Don't worry about it."

"I have to worry about it," she said, her voice sharp. They were almost circling one another, tentative, like boxers during the first round of a match. She took a deep breath, then spoke more softly. "I'm worried about you, Simon."

He shrugged it off. "I'm all right, except that I'm running late. I don't want to miss the plane."

She grabbed his arm. "Simon, just stop for a minute and *think*. Look at yourself."

His gaze flickered past her, to the mirror on the wall. He saw himself. The jeans and shirt hung a little more loosely on his body than they had, and he needed a haircut. But that was all. "I'm all right," he repeated.

Her eyes flashed. "Shit." There was no passion in the word, only weariness. "Mike Conroy is dead. Are you trying to crawl into the grave with him?"

He froze for a moment, then jerked his arm away. "Shut up. That's a crazy thing to say."

"I'm not the one who's acting crazy; you are. I'm sick and tired of having Mike Conroy in the middle of our lives. It was bad enough when he was alive, but now it's ghoulish."

He shook his head and stepped around her, avoiding her hand, avoiding her words. "I'll call from Denver," he mumbled.

She didn't answer.

He hurried through the house and out to the car. Why couldn't she understand? Why the hell couldn't anyone understand? Mike understood. Until a bullet ended it all. Until that tall blond stranger raised his gun and blew Mike away.

Simon banged the heel of his hand against the steering wheel. Shit. Damn them all. Well, just wait. Just wait. When he had the guy, they'd all be sorry then.

-SIX-

Simon stared glumly out the small window of the plane, looking down at the early morning fog that enshrouded the city. His two days in Denver had been disappointing. To say the least. All he had been able to do was study the ballistics report on the Denver hit, and compare it to the slugs taken out of Mike and Papagallos. Even that was only a qualified success. Although he was absolutely convinced that the killings were all done with the same weapon, the Denver police would only say that it was a "probable" match.

Still, as important as that piece of information seemed to him, he had a feeling that some others would scarcely feel as though it justified the trip.

He retrieved his car from the airport parking lot and drove directly to headquarters. The first thing he did when he reached his desk was to call Kimberly. "I'm back," he said by way of greeting. "Everything okay at home?"

"Do you care?"

He leaned back in the chair, rubbing one hand over his face. "Come on, Kim. I had a long flight, and I'm tired. Could you maybe just not bitch at me quite yet?"

There was silence on the other end. "Well," she

said finally, "you haven't forgotten about tomorrow, have you?"

"Tomorrow?" he said, stalling as he reached toward the desk calendar, then tried to remember why the hell the next day was circled in red. It came to him. "Of course I haven't forgotten. The anniversary party. Eight o'clock, right?"

"It would be nice if you could get home before then."

"I'll try." He hung up before she could say anymore, and saw Troy approaching.

"Hirsch, glad to see you back. What happened in Denver?"

Simon leaned forward onto the desk. "Well, it's definitely the same gun, sir. If I can keep right on top of this, I can—"

"There's been another hooker strangled," Troy broke in. "Campbell is on his way to the scene. You meet him there." He dropped a slip of paper onto the desk. "That's the address."

"But I wanted to start going through these records," Simon said. "Maybe Campbell's fucking file clerk methods might work here. If I can—"

Troy slammed one hand down. "Inspector Hirsch, that wasn't a suggestion. It was a direct order. Get your butt out of here and find out who's killing off the hookers. Before the Chamber of Commerce gets upset."

Simon stared at him for a moment, then grabbed the paper with the address, and stalked out.

Campbell seemed surprised to see him get out of the car and walk across the street. "How was Denver?" he asked, scribbling something down in his notebook.

"High," Simon muttered. He looked grimly at the body still huddled in the alley. She looked about seventeen. "Nice to see that things are still the same around here."

"Oh, yeah. Constancy is the one thing we can count on in our line of work."

They moved a few steps away, so that the photographer could snap his grisly pictures. Simon coughed and lit a cigarette. "So what the hell is going on here?" he asked, gesturing toward the body.

Campbell shrugged, putting the notebook away. "I hate to say it, but we might have a real nut on our hands. Two dead hookers in one week begins to look suspiciously like a pattern."

"Shit. That's all I need now."

Two men from the meat wagon moved in with a plastic body bag. "So?" Campbell asked. "What happened in Denver?"

They started toward their cars. "Not much. All they had was the ballistics report. And the word on the local hotline was saying that the job was done by out-of-town talent."

"Like here."

"Yeah, like here. That boy of mine gets around." He stopped by his car and opened the door. "See you back at the office. Or should I go over to the morgue and try for an I.D.?"

"No, head in. I'll see you there."

Simon nodded and slid behind the wheel. He sat there until all the official vehicles and most of the sightseers were gone. His eyes felt gritty and tired. He stared out at the empty street, absently scratching at the slowly healing cut on his palm. San Francisco. Denver. He wondered where the guy was now. Wondered what he did when he wasn't killing people.

This damned hooker thing. It was just the kind of case that used to excite him. Something he and Mike could really go to town on. But now it was only an annoyance, because it kept him from thinking about the blond guy. Damn the bitches anyway, for getting killed.

At last, he started the car and headed back toward the office.

The rest of the day was spent trying to trace the dead hooker's movements during her last hours, and also catching up on the inevitable paperwork that had accumulated in his absence. Troy wandered through the squad room frequently, giving Simon the feeling that he was operating under a none-too-subtle surveillance. It irritated him, much like Kimberly irritated him by her watchful gaze when he was home. What the hell did they expect to see?

The shift ended finally. As the office slowly emptied of daymen and the nightshift trickled in, Simon took a pot of coffee and secreted himself in an empty cubicle with a stack of files. Campbell had offered to stay for a while, but Simon waved him out. He didn't need any interlopers poking into his investigation. Screw the department. They wanted to just forget the whole thing, so he'd do it alone.

By the time he finished reading the last report, and drank the final cup of bitter coffee, it was much too late to bother driving home, so he just crawled wearily into the by-now-familiar cot, hoping to grab at least a little sleep before his next shift began.

He lit a cigarette, watching the orange glow in the darkness, and listening to the nearby sounds of phones and voices. The past hours had been fruitless, but Simon wasn't discouraged. Relaxing in the lumpy cot, he felt confident and even a little cheerful. This reminded him a little of when he was a boy back in Boston, and the steamy summer nights when every kid on the block would be out playing hide and seek. He'd always been very good at that game, not at hiding as much as at finding the others. The same kind of adrenalin was pumping through him now.

And there was something more. It was strange, but he almost felt like they were connected, he and the killer, by some kind of weird cosmic bond. Mike would have laughed at that, of course, but then Mike had been a true believer. Simon really didn't believe in anything anymore. If he ever had, beyond himself and his friendship with Mike. Cosmic bonds and shit like that might not make much sense to anybody else, but he understood the feeling, and he knew that the other guy did, too. It was as if he could reach out in the night and if he just knew *where* exactly to reach, he could touch the man.

He wondered if the blond guy could feel that psychic hand.

At last, Simon leaned over and crushed out the cigarette. Time to sleep.

Nobody killed a hooker in San Francisco that night.

That was good news not only for the ladies plying their trade on the streets and their respective gentlemen (not to mention the Chamber of Commerce), but for one cop named Simon Hirsch, because it gave him more time to think about his case, the only case that mattered.

Campbell came in from Records, juggling a couple of files. His thoughtful face was creased in a frown. "You ever stop to think about how many crazy people are walking around out there?" he asked, sitting down opposite Simon.

"No."

"Too damned many. I don't even mean the ones we bust, but just the real ordinary-looking people, walking right out there with the rest of us. You could sit right next to one in the movies, or talk to him on the cable car, and never know that inside he's completely bonkers."

Simon was only half-listening.

Campbell tossed one of the files across the desk toward him. "The world is one big asylum," he said flatly. "And we're the keepers."

Simon stretched a little. "You sure we're not as crazy as the rest of them?" he mumbled.

Before Campbell could respond to that bit of wisdom, they both saw the old wino enter the squadroom and look around vaguely. Simon began to slide down in his chair. "Shit. Wanta bet he's on his way here?"

"Why?"

"Because all the freaks end up at my desk sooner or later. It's a legacy. Wild Mike attracted them like flies." It was easier talking about Mike now; the pain was a little less every day. The loneliness, though, was still a sharp-edged blade. He was glad that in his wallet there was a picture of his partner, because sometimes it was hard to remember exactly what he'd looked like.

Sure enough, the filthy creature in the ratty brown suit was shuffling in their direction. He cleared his throat loudly, before realizing that there was no place to spit. He swallowed. When he reached the perimeter of their territory, he paused. "One of youse named Hershey?"

"No," Hirsch said. "You've got the wrong guys."

The drunk looked even more bewildered. "The guy at the desk told me it was one of youse." He scratched his ass thoughtfully. "I'm looking for the guy what was old Mike Conroy's partner."

Simon surrendered to his fate. "Yeah, that's me. The name is Hirsch."

"Whatever," the man said. "I heared you been looking for whoever done it to Mike."

They already had several hundred "tips" shoved into the file, none of which came to a damned thing, so Simon didn't get very excited over this opportunity. "You know something, do you?" he asked, reaching with one hand for his notebook. "And, by the way, what's your name?"

"Most folks call me Red. On account of my hair."

Simon stared pointedly at the man's bald head, but the look went unnoticed. "Okay, Red, what's on your mind?"

He settled back comfortably, as if they were best buddies getting ready to have a long chat. The sour odors emanating from his body wafted across the desk, and Simon tried to listen without breathing. "I was in the Emerald Palace last night. My favorite place. You know the old Emerald?"

Simon nodded. It was a rundown bar near the wharf. Hardly a night went by without at least one squad car being forced to make a run over there.

"Well, I was sitting there minding my own business, like always, and I heard these two guys talking. Not that I was snooping or nothing, you understand?"

"Yeah, yeah, I understand," Simon said impatiently. Handling crumbs like this guy took a certain knack, and he just didn't have it. Mike used to. He glanced toward Campbell, who seemed content just to listen, not like Wild Mike, who could deal with every piece of shit that came in off the street. "Can you get to the point, Red?"

"These two guys was saying something about wasting a cop."

Simon pulled himself up in the chair a little. "Yeah?"

Red nodded solemnly. "I always liked Mr. Conroy," he said, his voice displaying an unexpected degree of sincerity. "I think whoever done him in oughta get caught."

Simon stared at the old man, feeling a sudden tightness in his chest. After a moment, he cleared his throat. "What can you tell me about the guys, Red?"

Red rubbed his bald head. "One of them was a big guy, real big. Brown hair, I think. The other guy was blond. Don't know their names, but I seen 'em in there a lot." Red got to his feet. "That's all I know. They was talking about doing in some cop."

Simon reached across the desk to shake his hand. "Thanks, Red." A thought struck him, and he pulled his wallet out.

Red shrugged. "This weren't no money tip," he said. "I done it for Mr. Conroy."

Campbell and Simon watched the old man shuffle out. "People," Campbell said finally.

Simon nodded.

* * *

The rest of the day seemed to drag endlessly, although they kept busy trying to find some link between the two hookers who'd been killed. By the end of the shift, though, it appeared that the only thing the two women had in common was the occupation. And their deaths, of course.

After checking out, Simon headed straight for the Emerald Palace. It was not a trip he took with much hope; after all, how could his boy have been in this bar, when he had just recently been in Denver? But maybe this city was his home base. Anyway, no tip was too small to follow up on.

It was still early when he arrived, and the bar was nearly empty. He took a seat in the rear booth, ordering a beer. No one paid him very much attention; it was his knack of being able to blend into the furnishings that made him a good undercover operative. They'd always done the job differently. Mike could charm the pants off an up-tight virgin —or worm his way into the affections of a bitter old hood like Papagallos. He conned people, pure and simple. But with Simon, charm wouldn't work. He did the job by watching, waiting, making people forget he was there. Or by being tough. Now was a time for waiting.

So he waited. He nursed the beer grudgingly as the bar began to fill. By shortly after nine, a goodly collection of the usual creeps and jerks had gathered. Simon checked out everybody who came through the door, but it wasn't until nine-thirty that two men entered who seemed to fit what Red had told him. The first man was large, sloppy, dressed in grimy work clothes, and had a fleshy, sullen face. The other was younger, gangly, with light-colored hair that wasn't quite blond. Simon watched as they perched at the bar. Already he

knew that this wasn't his guy. There was no way
these two idiots could plan and execute hits like his
boy did. But he had to be sure. He picked up his
beer mug and wandered over.

They ignored him, and he realized suddenly that
he must look like all the other patrons. Time to
change clothes and shave again, he thought, easing
onto a stool next to the younger man. They were
talking about baseball. He listened to their conversation for nearly thirty minutes, hearing about
the big man's fat wife, the kid's hot girlfriend, the
foreman on the dock, about the supposed sex habits of several women in the bar.

"What about the pig?" the kid asked finally.

The big man snorted.

Simon tensed over his beer.

"That pig," the slob snorted. "He gimme another fuckin' parkin' ticket last night."

The kid giggled. "How many that make, anyway?"

"Twelve. Someday, man, I'm gonna get that nig-
ger pig."

"Yeah, sure."

"Gonna run the son of a bitch down with my
car."

"He'll give you another ticket."

They both seemed to find that line unbearably
funny, and as they dissolved in laughter, Simon
gave a sigh and slid from the barstool. He walked
out without a second glance. Of course that prick
couldn't have been his boy. The guy he was looking
for had style. Class. Brains.

He decided to go home.

The block was filled with parked cars, and he
swore under his breath as he edged his way down
the street toward his own driveway. It wasn't until

he had actually parked and was pulling the key from the ignition that he remembered.

The anniversary party.

"Oh, shit," he said aloud, resting his head against the steering wheel. All the lights in the house were on, and he could hear the faint strain of music from his stereo. Well, it wasn't going to get any better, so he might as well face up to it now. Sliding out of the car, he tried to smooth some of the worst wrinkles from his clothes. It didn't help much.

Everyone turned as he opened the door and walked into the living room. They were all dressed up, holding glasses of champagne. Kimberly stood in the center of the room, looking beautiful. She looked at him, and he ached because she was so damned beautiful. "Hi," he said, painfully aware of his slept-in clothes and two-day growth of beard. "Sorry I'm late, but I had a tip, and. . . ." His voice dwindled off.

"No one cares, Simon," Kimberly said in her most regal voice. "We're having a party."

"Yeah, yeah," he said, rubbing both hands against the front of his windbreaker. "I wanted to get here on time, really, but there was this tip, you know?" He looked around the room at the faces all watching him. "It might have been him, you know? It wasn't, but it might have been."

Kimberly walked over to the stereo and turned the volume up.

Simon stood there a moment longer, then turned around and went into the bedroom. He undressed and got into bed. The noise of the party only kept him awake for about five minutes.

-SEVEN-

Campbell came into the squad room and dropped a teletyped message onto Simon's desk. "You might be interested in that," he said, sitting down.

Simon picked up the sheet and read it quickly. "I'll be damned. That boy of mine never misses, does he?" There was more than a trace of admiration in his voice.

Campbell gave him a sharp glance. "Doesn't seem to."

The details of the hit were sketchy, but Simon was sure that it was the same killer. He read and re-read the terse message, before folding the paper and slipping it thoughtfully into his pocket.

Campbell was still watching him. "I hope you're not getting any dumb ideas," he said.

"Such as?"

"Such as taking off on another wild goose chase. Like a trip to Phoenix."

Simon ran a hand through his already unruly hair. "Why is that so dumb? Hell, man, this murder is fresh. Could be my boy is still hanging around."

"Your boy, huh?" Campbell was quiet for a mo-

237

ment. "Troy would take your star and shove it up your ass," he said mildly. "And I don't think your wife would be too thrilled, either."

Simon shrugged. "I don't give a damn what Troy does. He cares more about finding out who's wasting these damned whores than about busting this killer of mine." His face twisted in a wry grin. "And my wife hasn't spoken to me in three weeks anyway."

Campbell picked up a pencil and twisted it in his fingers. "Simon, you ever stop to think that maybe everybody else is right about this and you're wrong?"

The smile disappeared. "What do you mean?"

"I mean, maybe you've gone a little overboard on this case."

Simon's face closed. "I don't think so."

"Can I ask you a question?"

"Yeah, why not?"

Campbell hesitated. "What do you think about at night, just before you go to sleep?"

Simon was bewildered by the question. "What the hell are you talking about?"

"Do you think about Wild Mike? About the old days?"

"Sometimes," Simon mumbled.

"Do you think about your family?"

"Yeah, I guess. I don't understand what you're getting at."

"Do you sometimes think about him?"

Simon studied the surface of his desk. "Him?"

"Your mysterious blond killer. Your 'boy.' I'll bet you spend a lot of time thinking about him, don't you?"

Simon decided that he didn't like the questions,

didn't like the searching expression he could see in Campbell's face, didn't like the fact that the man was nosing around in his private business. "Cut it out, Campbell," he said coldly.

"I'm only trying to help you, man."

Simon rubbed at the thin white line that zigzagged across his palm. "When I decide that I want or need your help, I'll ask for it. All right?"

Campbell sighed. "All right, Hirsch. Forget it. Come on, we're supposed to be cruising the dock area anyway, not sitting around here."

"Go on down to the car. I gotta take a leak first."

When Campbell was gone, Simon reached for the yellow pages and then the phone. He waited on hold, listening to the canned music, until the almost mechanical voice came back on the line. "Yes, sir?"

"When's the next flight to Phoenix?"

A pause. "One hour from now."

"Can I get a seat?"

He could, and with the reservation made, he left the squadroom. Avoiding the garage where Campbell waited, he went out the front door and walked around the corner to his own car.

He went directly from the airport to the Phoenix police. A couple of questions got him to Homicide, and to the detective in charge of the Tidmore investigation. Red Wing, a massive Indian wearing a lavishly embroidered Western shirt and a string tie, eyed Simon curiously, no doubt wondering if all the inspectors on the S.F.P.D. habitually ran around the country in faded Levis and sweat-patched teeshirts. "So you're from Frisco," he drawled, sounding more like John Wayne than Cochise.

"San Francisco, yeah." Simon shoved his I.D. across the desk.

Red Wing barely glanced at it before pushing it back. "I was there once. Still got that bridge?"

"Last time I looked."

"Nice place. What's your interest in Tidmore?" he asked abruptly.

Simon closed his I.D. case and tucked it away. "I don't have any interest in Tidmore at all. I'm only interested in who iced him."

"Why?"

"Because I think the same guy blew away a couple of people in my town. Including a cop."

"Yeah?" Red Wing was studying his fingers, twisting and turning a large turquoise ring. "That surprises me a little. The company usually doesn't kill outsiders. Unless the cop was on the pad and crossed them."

"This cop wasn't on the pad," Simon said sharply. "He just got in their way. He died because he was in the wrong place at the wrong time."

"Oh. Tough luck."

"Yeah, tough. About Tidmore?"

The Indian leaned back in his swivel chair precariously. "Smalltime operator. Numbers, mostly. Maybe a little pushing. Nobody around here will miss him much. A punk. The only question being asked is what on earth this insignificant being could have done to get himself killed."

Simon looked for a cigarette. "Any leads?"

"Out-of-town talent."

The same old line. "That's it?"

"Essentially. It's not easy to get hard info on

what happens inside the company."

He found a cigarette and lit it. "Can I see the ballistics report?"

Red Wing shuffled through the papers on his desk, then tossed a manila envelope toward him. "Be my guest. One bullet, right through the forehead."

The office was quiet as Simon read the brief report. He compared the photos included with his pictures of the bullet taken from Mike. Finally he looked up. "Same gun."

Red Wing looked. "Could be," he agreed.

"It is." Simon carefully replaced his pictures. "You have any idea who might have wanted Tidmore on ice?"

Red Wing leaned forward again, pushing the telephone directory toward him. "Start at 'A'," he said.

"That's not very helpful," Simon said wearily. "I really hoped. . ." His words dwindled off.

Red Wing swiveled his chair back and forth slowly. "You really came here just on the chance of finding something?"

"Yeah. Guess it was a waste of time and money." He sighed. "Shit."

The detective shoved aside the pile of folders. "Sorry." He stood, his massive body seeming to fill the room. "You a believer in gossip?"

"Man, at the moment, I'd put my faith in a frigging Ouija board, if I had one."

"Come on, then. I need lunch. We can talk."

They walked across the street, stopping at an outdoor snackbar. Red Wing inhaled four onion and cheese-laden chili dogs, washing them down with two large orange sodas. Simon toyed with a plain hot dog and gulped a cup of bitter coffee. With the edge apparently taken off his appetite, Red Wing seemed inclined to talk. "I think everyone ought to have a hobby, don't you?" he commented, apropos of nothing, as far as Simon could tell.

"I guess." Simon was hot, feeling sweat prickling his armpits and running down the backs of his legs beneath the sticky Levis.

"You have a hobby?"

"No."

"That's bad. Especially for a cop, buddy. This job'll drive you crazy real fast."

"That's the truth. I used to play softball," he offered.

"Yeah. Want to know what my hobby is?"

"What?" Simon asked without much interest.

"I keep myself informed on the local company, if you follow my drift. I like to be up on all the gossip. In fact, I have a scrapbook at home that could send about half a dozen people to prison for a very long time. If I could prove any of it." He grinned. " 'Course it could also get me very dead." He reached one large hand into his pocket and extracted a chocolate bar, which he began to eat slowly. "Unofficially, I'd be willing to bet the mortgage on my teepee that the hit on Tidmore was bought and paid for by a guy named Graven. He runs a car leasing agency in town. And he's connected."

"Why would he want Tidmore hit?"

"My guess is that it was something personal, not company business. I think Tidmore probably crossed him on some deal. Don't know any specifics, of course."

Simon could feel a stirring of excitement, like the kind he used to have when they were closing in on a case. "Have you talked to Graven?"

"No."

"Why not?"

Red Wing shrugged. "No reason to. I don't have a single piece of hard evidence linking him to Tidmore." He tapped his forehead. "But I just know he did it. Unfortunately, his lawyer would raise holy hell if I approached his client."

"Any objection to me having a few words with the gentleman?"

"No objections. But watch your step. He doesn't like people snooping around in his business. Especially cops."

"Me, a cop? Do I look like a cop?" Simon grinned. "Man, you never saw Wild Mike in action. When it comes to conning crooks, I had the best damned teacher in the world."

"Wild Mike?"

The smile faded. "My partner." He looked away. "He's dead now."

"That's why you're here?"

"Uh-huh." Simon kicked at the wall softly. "Nobody else seems to care, you know?"

Red Wing took a scrap of paper from his pocket and scribbled an address. "You can find Graven here. But be careful. I'd hate to have to ship you home on your shield, instead of with it."

Simon took the paper. "Thanks. One question— who's El Supremo in these parts?"

"Old man Antonelli. He's been in charge of things for thirty years. A real old time resident."

"How close is this Graven crumb to him?"

"Does the king talk to the peon?" Red Wing

smiled. "You know where to reach me."

"Yep." Simon watched the huge Indian move with surprising lightness back across the street. With a sigh, he leaned forward onto the counter and picked up the rest of his hot dog. He began to eat thoughtfully.

Thank God for credit cards, Simon thought, studying his image in the mirror. Gone was the gritty teeshirt-clad cop with the perpetual five o'clock shadow. Simon Hirsch was now another man. The Italian-made white suit, French cut midnight blue shirt, and glossy black shoes all proclaimed his new persona. A pimp, maybe. A numbers man on the way up. He grinned at himself.

He studied a city map briefly, before going out to his rented Caddy. When Kimberly saw the bills at the end of the month, she'd hit the roof, but it was too late to worry about that now. And too soon to worry about dealing with Troy and the repercussions of taking off like he had.

Anyway, none of that mattered. He was getting close, so close that he could almost see the face of the man he was hunting.

Graven's office was in a small, discreet building on the fringe of the downtown area. The receptionist, an auburn-haired broad who looked like she belonged in a strip show instead of behind a desk, surveyed Simon carefully and apparently approved of what she saw, favoring him with a smile.

A few moments later, she ushered him into Graven's office, leaving him with a cup of coffee and a lingering glance. He settled back in the chair and fixed Graven with what Mike used to call his Al Caponestein stare. "So, Mr. Graven," he said mildly.

The plump, greying man nodded, his face looking a little worried. "Yes, uh, Mr. Hirsch, is it?"

"Right."

Graven occupied himself with selecting and lighting a thin black cigar. "What can I do for you?"

"Nothing. This is more or less in the nature of a follow-up visit."

"Follow-up?"

"Yes. Mr. Antonelli sent me."

Some of the color faded from Graven's face. "Yes, sir?" he said, straightening a little, perhaps unconsciously. "Always a pleasure to meet one of Mr. Antonelli's representatives."

Simon reached for his cigarettes and shook one into his hand. "Oh, we've met before."

"Have we?"

His brows lifted. "You don't remember?"

Graven thought hard. "Oh," he said finally, hopefully. "At the, uh, Olympic Club, wasn't it?"

Simon allowed himself to smile. "Right. The Olympic Club."

"Sure, I remember now. Nice to see you again, uh, Hirsch."

"Uh-hmmm." He lit the cigarette, then looked for an ashtray. Graven shoved one toward him. Simon tossed the match in negligently and then sat back. "In the matter of the late Mr. Tidmore," he began.

Graven's pigmentation lost several more degrees of color. "I, uh, don't know. . ."

Simon raised a hand. "No problem. Mr. Antonelli understands perfectly. He just wanted you to know that."

"Oh, yeah?" Graven relaxed a little.

"In fact, as you know, Mr. Antonelli admires initiative. And Tidmore . . . well, frankly, Mr. Tidmore had become something of an annoyance." They were quiet for a moment, each apparently reflecting on the short-comings of the late Mr. Tidmore. Simon grinned, buddy-style, deciding it was time to plunge right in. He sent a little prayer for help. You listening, Mike? "That blond son of a bitch can really do a job, huh?" Crooks, he told himself, were usually stupid.

Graven looked puzzled. "Blond guy? Oh, you must be talking about the trigger man."

"Right."

"Yeah, he did a good job."

Simon hitched forward a little. Time for a little confidentiality. "Can I ask you something? Just between you and me?"

"Sure."

"What'd you think of the guy? Personally? Mr. Antonelli would maybe like to engage his services, but he wants to sound out some people first, people whose opinion he respects, and get a reading on him first."

Graven looked appropriately flattered, then disappointed. "Well, to tell the truth, Hirsch, I never actually talked to him."

Simon frowned. "What?"

Graven shrugged. "I never even saw the triggerman. Just this other guy, the contact. Mac."

A name. Simon kept his face blank and took a long drag on the cigarette. "So all your dealings were with Mac?"

Graven nodded.

"Good man. Haven't seen him in a couple of years. How is he?"

"Fine, I guess. Only saw him once. We met in

the park for about five minutes, and that was it. A real pro."

"He always was. Mac still fat?"

Graven looked at him curiously. "No. As a matter of fact, he was real thin. Not skinny, but lean."

"Yeah? Well, good. He used to be too damned fat." Simon crushed out the cigarette. Time to move. Never overstay your welcome was a rule they always followed carefully. At least he wasn't leaving empty-handed.

The good-byes were brief and business-like as they promised to get together for lunch at the Olympic Club real soon, and a few minutes later he was back in the Caddy. So, he thought as he fiddled with the controls of the air conditioner. It was a team, huh? The mechanic, his mysterious blond, and the other guy, the business manager. Mac.

It wasn't much, but it was something. More than anyone else had. "I'm gonna get you, boy," he said aloud, pulling into traffic. "I'm gonna get you good, kid."

Now, however, it was time to get himself out of town, before Antonelli discovered that someone was dropping his name rather freely. Simon was grinning as he drove toward the motel.

Kimberly was sitting at the kitchen table with a Bloody Mary and the new *Redbook* magazine when he came in. He dropped the car keys onto the counter and went to the refrigerator for the milk. "Hi," he said. When she didn't answer, he shrugged and took a long gulp straight from the carton.

"I've asked you a million times not to do that," Kimberly said without looking up. "It's disgusting for the rest of us who have to drink the milk."

"Sorry." He snapped the carton closed and replaced it, then came to sit at the table with her. "I
guess you know I went to Phoenix."

"Doug Campbell told me. He assumed that's
where you were anyway."

"I tried to call you last night, but there wasn't
any answer."

"I heard the phone."

"Why didn't you answer it?"

She closed the magazine carefully. "Because I
didn't want to talk to you."

He looked at her. "Well, that's clear enough."

"Good."

His hands moved restlessly on top of the table,
rearranging salt and pepper shakers, sugar bowl,
napkin holder. "Okay, you're pissed. I can understand that. I should've let you know I was going,
but it just all happened so damned fast. But, Kim,
I found something. A name. Not the actual killer,
but his upfront man. Mac." He slapped the table.
"A real name. It's just a matter of time now, honey."

"Lieutenant Troy called."

Simon grimaced. "Did he sound upset?"

"He sounded as angry as he has a right to be."
She lifted the drink and took a sip.

"Well, it'll be okay when I give him my news. It
was beautiful, Kim. What a job I did on that
damned son of a bitch."

Something like pity moved fleetingly across
Kim's face. "You really don't understand what's
going on here, do you?"

He was puzzled. "What?"

She shook her head in obvious weariness. "Never mind, Simon."

He stood, trying to smooth some of the wrinkles out of the white suit. "I better get down to the office." He pulled the blue tie out of his pocket and draped it around his neck, planning to knot it later.

"Yes, you better."

He bent toward her for a kiss, but she opened the magazine again and leaned over the page. "Kim?"

"Hmm?"

"Everything's going to be okay."

"Is it?"

"Sure, soon as I—"

"Don't," she broke in. "Don't say one damned word about finding that killer. I'm tired of hearing you talk about it." She laughed harshly. "That man, whoever he is, will never know that he really killed two cops that day."

"What are you talking about?"

Her hand gave a small wave. "Nothing, Simon. Go to work. Just. . . go."

So he picked up the car keys and left.

Campbell was the only one in the squadroom when Simon arrived. The other man's mild face was creased in a frown. "You look like a pimp on a downhill run," he said sourly.

"Thanks," Simon muttered as he dropped into his chair, realizing only then that the ends of the tie still flopped freely. "What's up?"

"Troy, mostly."

"Yeah," Simon acknowledged ruefully, "I'll just bet. Well, it won't matter. This trip was really worth it, Doug. I got a name."

"Really? I got another dead hooker."

Simon kicked the desk. "Shit. Sorry about that."

"Yeah, well, it's not your problem, is it?"

Before Simon could ask him what the hell he

meant by that, Dembroski, an eager young hustler just up from uniform, stuck his head into the room. "Ready, Doug?"

Not looking at Simon, Campbell got to his feet and gathered some papers. "Yeah, Ed, on my way." He walked to the door, then stopped and turned to face Simon. "Better go see Troy," he said, his voice suddenly kind.

Simon nodded.

Alone in the room, he picked up an empty report form and slowly bent it into a paper airplane. With a sigh, he tossed it into the air and watched it nosedive into a file cabinet. He got up and went into Troy's office.

The Lieutenant was bent over a pile of papers. When he noticed Simon standing there, he took off his glasses and pinched the bridge of his nose. "Inspector," he said.

"Lieutenant."

They looked at one another for a long time, when Troy sighed. "Maybe it's my fault. I should've taken you off the case a long time ago. Or never given it to you in the first place."

"I don't understand."

"I know you don't. Sit down, please."

Simon sat, but didn't relax. "Let me tell you what I found," he said.

"What?"

"A name, sir. Mac. He's the upfront man."

"Mac?" Troy pyramided his fingers on the desk. "That isn't much to go on, Simon."

He would not—could not—allow his enthusiasm to be quenched. "Well, I know it may not sound like much, but—"

"Inspector Hirsch," Troy said abruptly.

"Huh?"

"You're on departmental suspension, pending a hearing to determine your fitness to remain on the force."

Simon frowned, not quite understanding. "What?"

"You've disobeyed direct orders, Hirsch. Took off without telling anyone. Man, I've been breaking my ass to cooperate with you ever since Conroy was killed and. . . ." Troy broke off. "I'm sorry, but this can't go on."

"I see." Simon brushed at a scattering of ashes on the front of his jacket. "When is the hearing?"

"Two weeks from today." Troy hesitated. "I'll need your star and gun, Simon."

He nodded wordlessly, setting the requested items on the desk.

"Simon, use these two weeks to get yourself together, will you? Think about this whole mess, and then come before the board ready to return to work. If you make the effort, you'll have no problem being reinstated."

"Okay." He felt numb, like when the dentist used novocaine on his mouth, except that this was his whole body. The conversation with Troy seemed over, so Simon left, stopping only long enough to pick up a couple of things from his desk, then walking out of the building to his car.

The first thing he had to do was get another gun.

-EIGHT-

The screened-in back porch, long a neglected cubbyhole for disposing of those items with no immediate purpose apparent, but which seemed too good to just throw away, became his office. He spent the next day cleaning it, clearing out the old rake and ancient grass seed, a battered wicker picnic basket, a torn plastic swimming pool. When the room was empty, he swept the indoor-outdoor carpet thoroughly and pulled a discarded dinette table back out to use as a desk. All his notes on the case, his (unauthorized Xerox) copies of every report, he piled neatly on the table. Index cards charting the course of his investigation were taped neatly to the screen over the desk, so that he could refer to them at a glance.

Kimberly watched his activity in silence.

At last, he hooked up the electric coffee pot and set it on a corner of the desk, standing back to survey the scene with satisfaction. "Screw the department," he said to himself.

She was standing in the doorway. "What about money?"

"Huh?"

"Money, Simon."

He waved aside her words. "Oh, hell, we've got enough to get along on for a while. Don't worry so much. Now that I don't have to waste time on all that shit for Troy, I can get the case wrapped up a lot faster." He indicated the piles of folders and the index cards. "The answer is someplace there, honey. I know it is."

She waited a moment longer, then disappeared back into the house.

The day after that, he hit the streets again, wearing the new .45 strapped under his arm. He started right back at square one. Papagallos' apartment. An old man was trimming the bushes that lined the front of the building. Simon mentally shuffled through his hundreds of notecards until he hit on the right one. Ralph Ortega, handyman. Was in his basement apartment on the morning of the shooting, and didn't see or hear anything. Was probably drunk, but didn't want anyone to know it.

The grizzled figure turned, shading his eyes against the sun as Simon approached. "Help you?"

"Mr. Ortega? Remember me? Inspector Hirsch? I spoke to you after Papagallos and the police officer were killed here."

"Oh, yeah." He snipped away a couple more branches. "Didn't catch the guy yet, huh?"

"No, not yet, but we're still looking. I just came by to ask if maybe there wasn't something you might have remembered since the last time we talked."

Ortega wrinkled his face, apparently to show that he was thinking seriously about the question. Then he shook his head. "Nope, like I told you before, I was sleeping. It was Sunday, man. Who gets up early on Sunday?"

"Nobody but cops and killers, I guess," Simon muttered to himself. He twisted the worn black notebook in his hands and stared down the block. "Well," he said with a sigh, "what about the day before? Any strangers around then?"

"You asked me that before, too," Ortega grumbled.

"So I'm asking you again. Humor me."

Ortega resumed his work. "I didn't see no strangers. This is a quiet street." Another twig fell to the ground.

"There was a stranger."

The high voice came from across the lawn. Simon turned around. "What?"

The being sitting in the shadows of the porch was surely a joke perpetrated by nature upon unsuspecting humans. The boy—he might have been ten or twenty years old, there was no way of telling —had a face that was nearly classic in its beauty, but the body beneath it was an offense. The huge mound of flesh was clothed in a shapeless garment that did nothing to disguise the form beneath it.

Ortega snorted softly. "That's Billy," he said. A dirty finger tapped his forehead. "You don't want to pay him no mind. He's got nothing to tell you."

"Neither do you, apparently," Simon said. He walked over to the porch. "Hi. I'm Inspector Hirsch."

"Billy D'Angelo. You really a cop?"

"Sure."

Simon perched on the steps. "I didn't talk to you before, did I?" he asked, knowing he could not have forgotten it if he had.

"Uh-uh. I was in the hospital. The old ticker gave out."

"Yeah?"

"Fourth time," Billy said with a strange ring of pride.

"So you weren't here when the killings took place?"

"No." The mound of flesh jiggled. "Kinda funny. I hang around here year in and year out, waiting for something exciting to happen, and the first time it does, I miss it."

Simon, who had his notebook open again, slapped it shut. "So I guess there's nothing you can tell me?"

"Not about the murder itself, no. But I saw the stranger."

"Yeah? When?"

"The day before. Saturday. Before I got sick." He hesitated. "Let me tell you a fact of life, Inspector, can I?"

"Sure."

"Nobody pays much attention to freaks." There was no emotion in the voice, only naked objectivity.

Simon looked at the ground instead of the boy.

"Don't be embarrassed. I believe in calling a spade a spade. No offense intended to anyone. But when people see someone like me, they think I must be mentally deficient—like old man Ortega there thinks. Or else they pretend not to notice me at all. Quite a feat that, I would say. They just want to get away as quickly as possible." He chuckled again. "Maybe they think it's catching."

"And the stranger? Which category did he fall into?"

Billy lifted one hand in a surprisingly elegant gesture. "Now that, sir, is an amusing irony."

"Yeah?"

"He was an exception. Like you."

"What do you mean?"

"The man spoke to me as if he were talking to an ordinary person." There was a wistful note in the thin voice. "In fact, he was nice. A very kind man, I think. Maybe he didn't have anything to do with the killings."

"Maybe." Simon tried to keep his hands from shaking with excitement. "Tell me about the man, please, Billy."

"He said he was from the fire department. Inspecting for smoke alarms." A smile crossed the face. "It was a rather transparent cover, now that I think about it. I guess that even if he was nice, he didn't see me as any danger to what he was doing."

"What did you talk about?"

"Cards."

"What?"

"I was playing solitaire. An avocation of mine."

"Where were you?"

"Right here. He came around the corner. On foot. He went inside, stayed for about ten minutes, and came out. I had the cards spread on a lap board, and he stopped to look. 'Put your black eight on the red nine,' he said."

"Did he mention his name?"

"No. We just talked about cards. I explained my system of solitaire, and he told me that his game was poker." Billy shrugged. "That was all."

"Can you describe him? Was he blond?"

"No. He was tall, six three or four, I'd say. Slender. With brown hair and green eyes."

"You sound very sure."

"My memory is exceptional," Billy said simply.

"How old was he?"

"Forty or so, I guess. Good-looking."

Simon jotted down a couple of words. "Billy, if I sent a police artist over, would you work with him? Maybe we could get a sketch of the guy."

"Okay, Inspector, sure." Billy frowned. "He was a really nice guy. You think he's a killer?"

Simon shook his head. "No, Billy, not him. But I think he's involved."

The boy shrugged philosophically. "Well, he was still nice."

"Yeah?" Simon grimaced. "That's the way it goes, Billy." That old adrenalin was pumping through his body. It wasn't his boy, but it was a connection. Find Mac and he'd find the blond. He realized that Billy was watching him curiously, and he pushed himself to his feet. "I'll be in touch," he said.

As he drove away, he could see the strange figure on the porch, hovering there like an Occidental Buddha.

-NINE-

Kimberly watched him dress for the hearing before the board.

He took care with his appearance, putting on a conservative grey suit and tie. He'd even gotten a haircut the day before. "Well?" he asked, turning from the mirror. "How do I look?"

"Fine. Very handsome."

It was the first nice thing she'd said in a long time, and he grinned. "Gonna bowl 'em over, honey, don't worry. Hell, they'll probably end up offering me a promotion."

She nodded.

He walked past her, out of the bedroom, to the porch. She followed. His old briefcase, from his time in law school, lay open on the desk, and Simon began to shove stacks of index cards and folders into it. Kimberly frowned. "What are you doing?"

He took the folder with the sketch of Mac in it and tucked it in carefully. "What?" He glanced at her in surprise. "Getting ready for the hearing, of course."

She stepped out onto the porch, twisting the gold ring around her finger. "But you can't take all that

258

stuff with you. You're not, are you, Simon?"

He was confused. "Well, of course, honey. How else can I show them what I've been doing? Once they see how my investigation is going—"

Kimberly leaned against the desk suddenly. "They'll lock you up in a rubber room someplace," she broke in. "Simon, if you want your job back, don't do this. Please, for God's sake, leave it alone!"

He smiled. "Don't worry." He snapped the bulging briefcase closed. "See you later."

She didn't look at him.

He left.

They kept him waiting a little while before he was ushered into the hearing room. The Chief was there, Captain Janoski, and two civilians. Simon smiled at them all pleasantly and took his place.

"You understand the reason for this hearing, Inspector?" the Chief asked.

"Yes, sir."

"Lieutenant Troy has already spoken to us. He wants you to come back to work. How do you feel?"

"Fine, just fine. Eager to get back, sir, believe me." As Simon spoke, he began to pull things from the briefcase. The pile of cards and files grew rapidly.

The Chief glanced at the others. "Hirsch, the Lieutenant seemed to feel that the difficulties you were having stemmed from your problems accepting the death of your partner. What's your reaction to that?"

Simon paused thoughtfully for a moment, then nodded. "Yeah, that's right, I guess. Losing Mike kinda blew my mind for awhile. We were pretty close, you know?"

"I think we can all understand that." The Chief sighed suddenly. "Inspector, what *is* all of that stuff?"

Simon put the last pile of cards onto the table. "This? My records on the case, of course."

"The case?"

"Yes. I think you'll be really pleased to hear how far I've moved in the last two weeks. For example. . ." He fumbled for the right folder. "I have here a sketch of one of the two men involved —"

"Simon," one of the civilians broke in gently.

"Sir?"

"I'm Doctor Friedkin."

"Doctor?"

"I'm a psychiatrist employed by the department. Could we hold off on all that for a moment while I ask you some questions?"

"Well, if you think it's necessary," Simon said reluctantly.

"I think it might help."

He shrugged.

"Do you have any trouble sleeping, Simon?"

"No. Not much."

Two bushy brows raised. "Not much?"

Simon rested his hands on the edge of the table, feeling a thin line of sweat beginning across his upper lip. He hadn't expected this; he had figured that they'd want to talk about the case. This was almost like getting him here under false pretenses. "Not trouble, really," he said. "It's just that sometimes there's so much to think about, that it's kind of hard to settle down."

"What do you think about?"

The guy was beginning to sound like Campbell. "Everything."

"The case, mostly?"

"Yes." Sweat was running down inside his collar.

"How's your appetite?"

"Okay." Simon shifted in the chair restlessly. "Look, I want to cooperate, but this is really a waste of time."

"Why?"

"What the hell does my appetite have to do with anything? Or how well I sleep? Or my sex life?"

Friedkin smiled faintly. "I didn't ask you about your sex life, did I?"

"Not yet." Now Simon smiled, too. "But my brother is a shrink, and I know how you guys operate. It always comes down to sex sooner or later." His fingers snapped the rubber band around one pile of cards. "If you want to know—and I'm sure you do—my wife and I aren't sleeping together."

"Why not?"

"Beats the hell out of me. Maybe she just has a lot of headaches. I've been busy. A lot of reasons."

"Do you want to sleep with her?"

He snapped the rubber band again. "I don't think I have to answer these personal questions." He looked at the Chief. "Do I, sir?"

"No, Inspector, not if you don't want to."

"I don't."

"Can I ask you something else, then?" Captain Janoski said.

"Sure."

"Do you want to come back to work?"

"Yes, of course."

"Why?"

"Because I'm a cop," he said simply. "That's who I am."

The Chief leaned forward. "Are you ready to perform your duties?"

He straightened. "I have always done that, sir."

"What I mean is, are you prepared to drop this private investigation of yours? Will you leave it to the others?"

Simon frowned. "This is my case. Look, can't I just show you. . . ." He shuffled through the papers. "I have a sketch here. . . ."

"The unauthorized drawing done by the police artist?"

He found the picture. "Unauthorized?"

"As a suspended officer, you had no right to order the work done."

"Yeah, well, I needed it. This is one of the killers. His name is Mac." He held up the sketch.

"You have proof of this?"

"I *know* it." He replaced the drawing and pulled the rubber band off one pile of cards. "These are notes on other hits I believe have been committed by the same—"

"Simon," Friedkin broke in quietly, "have you considered getting professional help?"

Simon was puzzled again. "Sir?"

"I think you need some psychiatric help, Simon."

He looked at the Chief. "Sir, I want to come back. Please. I need the job. My family. . . ."

"Give up the case, Simon."

His hands pulled the pile of papers closer. "I can't. I have to find him."

"He'll be caught, Simon, sooner or later. If not

by us, then by some other department."

"He belongs to me!" Simon wasn't aware that he was shouting, until he heard his own words echoing back. "He belongs to me," he repeated in a whisper.

The room was quiet for a long time. Finally, the Chief sighed. "Would you wait outside, please, Inspector? We'll try not to be too long."

"But. . . ?" Didn't they want to hear? Didn't they care? He stared at the four men as he gathered together all the papers and shoved everything back into the briefcase.

He stopped by the door and looked at them once more. "I don't understand this," he said quietly. "I'm only trying to do what's right. If this was a movie or a TV show, I'd be the goddamned hero, don't you know that?"

He closed the door very quietly.

Kimberly was sitting on the couch, a drink in her hand. "Well?" she said.

He dropped the briefcase and sat down. "They said I couldn't come back. They said I'm not . . . emotionally stable enough to be on the force."

She didn't look surprised as she took another slow sip of the Bloody Mary. "What now, Simon?"

"I don't know." He yanked off the tie. "I don't know." He shook his head, trying to clear away some of the fog. "I just don't understand what's going on here, Kim. None of it makes any sense." He stood again, picking up the briefcase, and clutched it tightly. "I don't understand."

She only looked at him. He couldn't read anything in the flat grey eyes, and after a moment, he turned and walked out to the porch.

* * *

It was late. Simon didn't really know what time it was, but he knew that it was very late. He was stretched out on the cot he'd set up in one corner of the porch. Although he was tired as hell, he couldn't seem to fall asleep. So he smoked one cigarette after another and stared at the ceiling.

Kimberly came out to the porch, her slipper-clad feet making no sound on the carpet. "Simon," she said, "we have to talk."

He shrugged.

She pulled the chair closer and sat down, her hands clasped tightly together in her lap. "I'm going to give you a choice, Simon," she said firmly.

He rolled onto his side and looked at her. "What choice?"

"Either you give all this up and get help, or . . . or I want you to leave."

He smoked in silence for a moment. "Give what up, Kim?"

Her eyes moved around the office. "This insanity. This . . . obsession. Give it up, Simon. Talk to Manny. Get help."

"I can't do that, honey," he said gently.

"You're ruining our lives. Your daughter is ashamed to bring her friends here anymore, do you know that?"

He was genuinely bewildered. "Why?"

"Because she's afraid they'll see you out here talking to yourself, piling up some more of those damned cards."

"It's my job," he said with dignity.

"It's madness."

"You don't understand."

She gestured hopelessly. "You're right. I *don't*

understand. But, Simon, I don't *want* to understand anymore. I just don't care."

"What should I do?" His voice was soft.

"That's your decision to make."

"If you don't want me here, I'll go."

"Thank you." She stood.

He grabbed the edge of the robe. "Don't you
love me anymore?"

It was a long time before she answered. "I feel
very sorry for you," she said, staring down into his
face.

Nodding, he released her. "I'll leave tomorrow."

Without responding, she went back inside.

Simon lit another cigarette. It wouldn't be forever. This whole thing would work out sooner or later. In the meantime, it was probably all for the
best. Now he didn't have to worry about the job or
his family. It was as if his universe were getting
smaller, more manageable. All he had to think
about now was finding him. When that was done,
when he had the blond guy, then he would worry
about how to straighten out these things.

He took his daughter to lunch the next day. They
bought hamburgers at McDonald's and took them
to Golden Gate Park to eat, sitting on the grass
and watching the frisbee throwers. He unwrapped
his cheeseburger. "I'm going away for a while," he
said, not looking at her.

"Are you and Mom getting a divorce?" she
asked.

"No, what makes you ask that?"

"It's the usual next step."

He chewed thoughtfully. "Well, I don't know
what's going to happen. Whatever she wants, I

guess. Do you understand why this is happening?"

She swept blonde hair from in front of her eyes, looking just like her mother. "Sort of."

"Yeah?"

"You lost your job. You and Mom stopped sleeping together." She ate a french fry. "It's because you don't seem to care about anything but this stupid case."

"It's not stupid to me, Tammy. It means a lot."

She suddenly looked older than her years. "More than Mom and me?"

"No, but—"

"But what, Dad? If we mean more to you than the case, then why are you leaving?"

"Because I have to," he said softly, gathering the food wrappers and shoving them into the sack. "I have to do this, because I don't know what else to do. Can't you try to understand that?"

"And so what are Mom and I supposed to do while you're off playing knight-in-shining-armor?"

He plucked at the grass. "Is that how you see it? You make it sound like I'm just playing some kind of game."

She shook her head, sending golden curls tumbling. "No, Dad, it's not a game. You want to know what I think it is?"

"What, honey?"

"It's a sick joke." She jumped up. "I hate this so much. Maybe I even hate you. I'll catch a bus home." She was gone before he could speak.

Slowly he gathered the remains of their lunch and got up to throw it all into a trash bin. He walked back across the park to his car.

He went to the bank and took exactly half the

money from their joint checking account. He also cashed some bonds given to him by his grandfather. Kimberly had a little money from her family and she could probably get more. Besides, that wasn't his problem anymore; she was kicking him out, so she could just handle life on her own.

From the bank, he went back to the house. Neither Kimberly nor Tammy was there, probably by design. He packed everything from the porch into a couple of cardboard boxes, and loaded them into the car. His clothes and other things fit into two suitcases. When he stopped to think about it, there wasn't much in the house that meant a whole lot to him. The house was Kimberly's and everything in it reflected her image, not his. He wondered why he'd ever thought he belonged here anyway.

The street was strangely deserted as he packed the car, as if no one wanted to witness his departure. He went back inside for a six-pack of beer from the refrigerator and paused long enough to take a drink out of the milk carton.

He tossed the six-pack into the front seat and got behind the wheel. One small boy stood at the curb, aiming a toy six-shooter at him. "Bang, bang, you're dead," the kid said.

Simon grinned and clutched at his chest. The kid stuck out his tongue and ran off.

He started the car and drove away without looking back.

-TEN-

He lived like a gypsy, sleeping in the car to save money, eating at fast food joints, moving, always moving, either in the car or on foot. Most of his movement had no real destination; it was the motion itself that mattered.

After nearly a month of this restless existence, he called Campbell. "Doug, can we meet someplace?"

The cop hesitated. "Okay," he said finally. "Chico's for lunch?"

"Thanks, man." He hung up and walked back to the cooling Egg McMuffin that was his breakfast. The newspaper article absorbed his attention again. SUSPECTED MOBSTER SLAIN was the headline, and the article was datelined Kansas City.

> Reputed gangland boss Sam Lancinelli was shot and killed early yesterday. Lancinelli, long a powerful figure in local union dealings, was slain as he was preparing to give testimony before a grand jury investigating charges of the misuse of union funds. According to Artie Day, an aide to Lancinelli, he was in the next room preparing a breakfast tray when there was a knock at the door of the penthouse apartment. Lancinelli

himself went to answer it, and Day heard a single shot. By the time he reached the living room, the killer had vanished. Police are questioning Day further.

The story ended there.

Simon grinned to himself. Day was that close and didn't even get a glimpse of him? Hell, my boy is good, but he's not a goddamned wizard. Five'll get you ten that the son of a bitch was in on what was coming down, and that was why he just happened to be in the next room. He could only hope that the dumb cops in Kansas City knew the right questions to ask.

When breakfast was over, he drove out to Mike's house. It was a visit he'd been intending to make for a long time, but which he'd kept putting off. Today, though, he needed to go.

One of Mike's sons was playing in the front yard and he looked up curiously at Simon's approach. "Hi, kid," Simon said. "Remember me?"

After a moment, he nodded. "Yeah, sure. You're my Daddy's friend."

"Right. Is your mother home?"

"Uh-huh. In the backyard."

Simon stood there a minute longer, feeling as if there were more to be said to Mike's son, but not knowing what. Then he only smiled vaguely and walked around the corner of the house. Siobahn was bent over a small flower garden. "Hi," he said.

She jumped a little, then turned. "Oh, Simon, you startled me."

"I'm sorry. The kid said you were back here."

She stood, wiping both hands on the front of her jeans. "It's nice to see you."

He stepped forward and they embraced fleetingly. The human contact felt good, and Simon realized that he didn't touch people anymore. He wondered when he'd stopped being touched. And why. They pulled apart. "How are you, Siobahn?"

"Fine." She looked tanned and relaxed. "We're getting along. Sit down, and I'll get some iced tea."

He perched uneasily on a lawn chair and she vanished inside, returning a moment later with two glasses and a pitcher. He watched as she poured. "Thanks," he said, taking a glass.

She sipped the tea, eyeing him. "I'm glad you came by, Simon. I've been wanting to talk to you."

"Have you?" He grinned suddenly. "This old patio looks pretty good, doesn't it?"

"What?"

"Hell, how long ago did we put this in? Six years, it must be, right?"

"Yes." She was still watching him.

"Neither one of us knew what the hell we were doing, but it looks pretty damned good. Had a lot of fun that day, didn't we?"

"Uh-huh," she replied absently. "I heard about your problems with the department, Simon."

He glanced at her quickly, then away. "Yeah, well. . . ."

"And about you and Kimberly. I'm really sorry."

He played with the sprig of mint floating in the glass. "The problem," he said slowly, "is that nobody understands what I'm doing. I kept trying to explain, but I couldn't get anybody to listen."

"Explain it to me, Simon," she said gently. "I'll listen."

He looked up in surprise. "I didn't think I'd have to explain it to you. You must know already."

Siobahn poured them each more tea. "I'd like to hear what you have to say. If you'd like to tell me."

He shrugged. "All I want to do is find out who killed my partner. That isn't so damned re-markable, is it? I thought that's what I was sup-posed to do. Why does that make me so peculiar? Sometimes they all treated me like I was crazy or something."

Siobahn's finger moved up and down the side of the glass. "I know you think that you're doing the best thing, Simon, but at what cost? Your job? Your wife and child? Mike wouldn't want that sac-rifice from you."

"Yes, he would," Simon said sharply. "He'd do the same for me, if it was the other way around."

Siobahn sighed and shook her head. "I don't think so."

Simon looked at her. "Yes, he would. Mike was my partner."

"I know. And he loved you, Simon, truly he did." She was silent for a moment, watching the drops of moisture run slowly down the side of the pitcher. "He used to worry about you, did you know?"

He hadn't known. "Why?"

"Because you were always so . . . intense about everything. Sometimes he practically had to force you to let go for a little while, and remember that there was a life beyond the job. Sometimes you just wore him out, Simon."

He could feel something beginning to crumble deep inside and he wished that he hadn't come here at all. "You make it sound bad. Mike and I, we worked so hard because we liked it.

"Yes. But Mike also cared about other things." She was frowning, as if the effort of trying to say what she wanted to in just the right way was very difficult. "You could be just overwhelming sometimes, but he cared so much that he never wanted to hurt you by saying anything."

Simon couldn't quite understand what she was telling him. The words seemed like little shafts of ice cutting into him, and he wanted to tell her not to say anymore. Instead, he gulped tea and stared at the patio he and Mike had built. "Say, you remember how we—" He stopped suddenly, realizing that she didn't want to listen to any more of his memories.

"Mike always said that a good partnership was like a marriage. He could handle that, Simon. Mike had so much caring in him that he could give me and the children everything we needed, and still have enough left to offer you. Not everyone can do that." She stopped and carefully set her glass on the small table. "It hurts me to see you like this, Simon."

"I'm not any different," he mumbled.

She stared at him, then nodded slowly. "I guess that's true, really. You're too skinny, and your hair is getting too darned long. Your clothes look like you slept in them, and you need a shave. But that's all superficial, isn't it? Basically, you're still the same man. That's why Mike worried about you. He thought you ran on the edge too much. He was afraid that someday you were going to fall over."

Simon put his glass down next to hers and stood. "Don't tell me any more, okay?"

She got to her feet, putting a hand on his arm. "I'm not saying any of this to hurt you. Just please stop and think about what you're doing. For your own sake."

He stared at her coldly. "I guess you're getting

along just fine, aren't you? That's nice. You don't think about him at all, I guess."

She released his arm, stung. "That's not true. I think about him every day. Every night. But I have to live, Simon. My children have to go on. Mike is dead, but we're alive. You're alive, too, Simon. Don't let your life end because his did."

Simon walked to the end of the patio, then stopped, crouching down to look at the rocks set in concrete, rubbing a hand over the edge. "We did a damned good job on this." He sighed. "I always thought that he cared the same way I did."

"He *did* care, Simon."

"Yeah? Not as much, though, I guess."

She held out a hand as if to touch him, but stopped in midair. "No two people can care in exactly the same way."

Simon straightened, kicking lightly at the crumbling border of the patio. "We screwed this part up. It's falling apart. It's all falling apart." He looked at her. "I feel like he just died all over again. All I had left was the memory, and now you're taking that away from me."

"No," she whispered, "I didn't mean to. . . ."

"I gotta go. I gotta get out of here." He walked away quickly, his head ducked.

"Simon!"

He stopped by the corner of the house, one hand resting on the weathered wood. "Needs painting again," he said. "We did it two years ago, right?"

"Let go, Simon," she said softly. "Let go so that you can both find some peace."

He glanced around at her, smiling with half his mouth. "I can't let go, Siobahn. Because if I let go of Mike, then I won't have anything left to hold on to. And then I'll go over that edge."

He ran back to his car, not stopping even when Mike's son called out to him.

It was no good anymore. Siobahn had taken what was left and shattered it beyond repair. He could feel himself falling, slipping away, and he tried desperately to find something he could hold on to.

He started to think about the killer. Mr. X. The missing character in this fucked-up Greek tragedy. It was a strangely comforting thought that somewhere out there the deadly blond stranger was waiting for him.

He was almost smiling as he started the car.

Campbell was already waiting when Simon walked into Chico's. They both ordered tacos and beer, then carried the food to a rear booth. "Anything break on the hooker killings?" Simon asked as he sprinkled hot sauce on his order.

Campbell glanced at him in obvious surprise. "We caught the guy, Simon, three days ago. Didn't you see it in the paper?"

"No, guess I must have missed it. I was reading about the Lancinelli hit, though."

"Lancinelli? Who's that?"

"In Kansas City."

Campbell took a bite of taco and chewed. "Kansas City, huh? Missouri or Kansas?"

Simon frowned. "Gee . . . I don't know. Better find out, I guess."

Campbell sighed. "It doesn't matter. I have enough trouble keeping track of the murders here, buddy. I don't spend a whole lot of time worrying about what happened halfway across the country."

"But this was my boy again, I'm sure of it. Same M.O."

"I suppose you're going to Kansas City now?"

Simon nodded, taking a swipe at his chin with a wadded paper napkin. "That's why I wanted to see you. I don't know a damned soul in that part of the country. Aren't you from someplace around there?"

"Nebraska."

"You know anybody in Kansas City?"

"My second cousin."

Simon looked up hopefully. "He a cop?"

Campbell shook his head. "No, not a cop. He runs a flower shop. But he's a real nice guy."

Simon frowned his disappointment. "Nobody else?"

"Nope."

"Damn. Well, guess I'll just have to go in cold."

Campbell looked at his food, then shoved it away abruptly. "You're taking this all the way, aren't you?"

"I don't have any choice." Simon wadded another napkin. "And no lecture, please. I've had enough good advice for one day." It still hurt to think about what Siobahn had said. "You probably think I'm crazy, don't you?" He laughed softly, bitterly. "Well, join the club. I just found out that even Mike thought I was a little flaky."

"But you're still going after his killer?"

A little smile flickered around the corners of Simon's lips. "Of course."

"Why?"

Simon picked up a taco. "Because the killer and I, we're the only ones who still care." He took a big bite of the taco. Campbell watched him for a moment, then returned to his own lunch.

-ELEVEN-

Life quickly fell into a pattern. He went to Kansas City, as he'd told Campbell he would, arriving just in time to be there when they pulled Day's body from the river. Beyond his disappointment at being cheated out of talking to the man, Simon wasn't the slightest bit interested in that murder. His boy didn't go around blasting people with shotguns and then dumping their bodies.

He left Kansas City and went to Memphis. Then to Atlanta. Milwaukee. Cleveland. One tip led to another, and although some of the hits were several years old, he followed them all up. He sometimes wondered how many people the blond had killed.

Nearly six months after he'd left San Francisco, a hit went down in Boston that sounded good. He drove straight through from Philadelphia to follow up on it. He found a cheap motel and was all checked in, settled down to a dinner of cooling hamburgers, before he realized that he was home. He dumped the cheap meal into the wastebasket and headed for the car.

His parents still lived in the same house where he'd grown up, and the lights in the dining room told him that the old rituals were still observed.

Sabbath dinner was at seven.

The black woman who answered his knock looked at him blankly. "Yessir?"

"I'm Simon Hirsch. Can I come in?"

She moved aside. "Of course. Dinner is about to be served."

He paused in the curved doorway of the oak-lined dining room. The table was covered with a pristine white cloth. Tall ivory candles gave off tiny glows of light that danced off the polished silver and china. His parents were there, of course. Manny and his wife. A couple of teenagers who must have been Manny's. Everyone was dressed up and he realized belatedly that he probably should have changed from his jeans and windbreaker. "Hi," he said after a moment.

Everyone looked up. "Simon!" his mother said. "I don't believe it."

"Yeah, it's me." He walked into the room, his tennis shoes silent against the thick rug. "Hi, Manny. Papa." He thought for a moment. "Esther." He nodded at the kids, not even trying to remember their names.

Manny, fleshy and successful-looking, came around the table and clasped Simon by both arms. "Kid, it's good to see you. Damn, we've been worried about you, wondering where the hell you were. Kim didn't seem to have any idea."

Simon shrugged. "I move around a lot."

The maid reappeared. "Shall I set another place, sir?"

Everyone looked at the rabbi, who nodded. "My son will join us."

"Thank you, Papa."

He took the empty chair at one end of the table.

His mother was watching him. "You look bad, son."

"I'm fine, Mama, really."

"Too thin."

He made no response, and the ritual of the meal began. Simon concentrated on the food, both because he was hungry and because he hoped that would forestall any conversation.

At the end of the formalized meal, the two teenagers hurriedly excused themselves. A few moments later, the two women left. The Rabbi and his two sons stayed at the table, not talking until the dishes were cleared and each had a glass of wine in front of him.

"So," Manny said. "What's going on with you anyway?"

"Not much."

The rabbi leaned forward. "You leave your home, your family, your job, to run all over the country, and that's not much?"

"Papa, you never liked my job anyway, remember? And you weren't all that crazy about my *shiksa* wife, either."

"I should like you better as a bum?"

Simon's shoulders hunched forward. "I'm just doing what I have to do." His fingers twisted around the slender stem of the wine glass.

His father snorted. "So now you sound like John Wayne."

"With this nose?" Simon mumbled.

Manny held up a conciliatory hand, and Simon suddenly realized that his brother had spent a lot of time over the years trying to negotiate peace. "Let's just talk, shall we?" he said quietly. "Simon, we've been very worried about you. Even before you left home, Kim had called me several times.

She was afraid for your emotional health."

"She thought I was crazy," Simon said flatly. "So did a lot of people."

"She was only worried because she cared. A lot of people care."

"Right, Manny, right." He sighed and took a slow sip of wine.

"Why are you in town?" his father asked.

"The Flynn hit."

"What?"

"Robert Flynn was gunned down three days ago. He was a prime pusher, controlled almost half the city. I think my boy did the job. By this time, I can recognize his work a mile off." He gave a grin of helpless admiration. "Damn, he's good."

The rabbi shook his head. "How long will this go on?"

"Until I find him, Papa."

Manny was staring at Simon's face. "And then what?"

"Huh?"

"What happens after you catch this killer? What will you do then?"

Simon took another drink, then licked wine from his lips. "Hell, you know," he mumbled.

"You don't have any plans, do you?"

They were quiet for a moment. "Your wife is suing for divorce," his father said.

"Is she?" He thought about that for a moment. "Well, okay, if that's what she wants."

The old man stood. "I must go. Will I see you again, Simon?"

He shrugged. "Don't know, Papa. Depends."

He and Manny watched as their father slowly left the room. "He does care, kid, you know."

"Does he?" Simon smiled a little. "I upset people, Manny. I make them uncomfortable. They don't want me around."

"Even the Lone Ranger had Tonto, right?" Manny said.

"Yeah."

Manny studied him. "Don't you ever get lonely, Simon?"

He lifted a shoulder helplessly. "Sure. Don't you?"

Manny looked a little startled, then nodded. "But I have my family. My work."

"I have my work, too." He could have told Manny more. That he never really felt alone, because the guy was always with him. Funny, although he still didn't know what the killer looked like, he felt like he knew him very well. Better than he'd ever known anyone. Sometimes now if he opened his wallet and saw the picture of Mike, it took him just a moment to place the face in his memory. The blond guy . . . he was always there. But Manny wouldn't understand that. "My work is finding the man," was all he said aloud.

"An eye for an eye?"

"I guess."

"Will you kill him, Simon? Or turn him over to the authorities?"

Again he shrugged.

Manny poured them each more wine. "So much hatred hurts you far more than it hurts him."

Simon was surprised. "I don't hate him, Manny," he said. "I don't hate him at all. I just . . . want to find him." He drained the glass and got to his feet. "I gotta go. Tomorrow is going to be a busy day."

"Let us know before you leave town."

"I will," Simon said.

Manny handed him a roll of bills, which Simon shoved into his pocket.

But he forgot to let them know. He spent two days in Boston and then drove to New York. Pete Rossi, a high school classmate, was on the D.A.'s staff, and Simon went to see him. It took about twenty minutes for him to lay out what he wanted. When he was finished, Rossi frowned thoughtfully. "Look," he said finally, "I know a cop, one of the best. You go talk to him, okay?"

"Sure, Pete, I appreciate this."

The cop's name was Mazzeretti and he looked more like a successful pimp than a homicide dick. His suit was obviously tailor-made and his hairstyle probably cost more than all the clothes Simon was wearing. He tapped a gold ballpoint against the desk and listened as Simon talked. When Simon pulled out the pencil sketch of Mac, Mazzeretti leaned forward and stared at it for a long time. He finally glanced up and Simon caught something flickering through the black eyes. "You know the guy?" he asked eagerly.

"Not sure. Hell, I see so many punks. He got a name?"

"Mac."

"That's it?"

"Yeah. He works with the blond guy. No name on him yet."

Mazzeretti leaned back in the chair and closed his eyes. The room was quiet for a long time, before he sat up and nodded. "Yeah, that's the guy, all right."

Simon felt a lurching in his gut. "You know him?"

"Yeah. Hell, must be eight years ago. At least.

Had a guy in here on an attempted burglary rap."

"Him?"

"No, no. A blond guy." Mazzeretti dropped the pen and fumbled for a gold lighter. "You know how some cases just stick in your mind? A face, something that has hold of your memory, and won't let go?"

"Yeah." He knew.

"That's the way it is with this. The blond guy was a real nutcase. A Viet vet. I wanted to send him over to Bellevue, but this guy, this Mac, asked me not to. Then the owner of the store or whatever the hell it was showed up, and dropped the charges." He shrugged elegantly. "So we let the kid go."

"Kid?"

Mazzeretti frowned. "Well, he wasn't that young, really, but he was weird. Very spacey. Wouldn't even talk until this Mac showed up." He shook his head. "I knew he was strange. Didn't seem like a killer, though."

"You have a name?"

"Hold on." He made a couple of phone calls, and in a surprisingly short time, a policewoman came in and dropped a file on the desk. Mazzeretti opened it and grinned. "John Paul Griffith." He shoved the file toward Simon. "That's him."

Simon stared at the mug shot. He gripped the edge of the desk to keep his hands from shaking. The face in the picture looked scared. "John Paul Griffith," he whispered. It was almost like a greeting.

Mazzeretti was still shuffling through some handwritten notes from the file. "I did a follow-up on the other guy, too," he said. "Just to satisfy my own curiosity. One Alexander McCarthy. A known gambler, and not a very lucky one, either. Also served in Nam."

Simon was still staring at John Griffith and only half-listening, but he nodded. "Could I have a copy of this picture?"

"Well, it's not really kosher, but okay. Give me a few minutes." He left, taking the file with him.

Simon leaned back, releasing his breath in a long sigh. He didn't really need a copy of the photo. The image of that scared, childlike face was burned into his memory. Closing his eyes now, he could still see it clearly. "John Paul Griffith," he whispered again. "John." He smiled. "I'm getting close, Johnny. It's just a matter of time now. Do you know that, Johnny? Can you feel me getting close?"

Yeah, he thought, Johnny knew.

He went to the address in the police report. There had once been a pizza place on the first floor, but it was boarded up and empty now. Simon climbed to the second floor and tapped at a door.

A very tiny old lady opened the door. "Yes?" she chirped.

"Sorry to bother you, ma'm," he said, "but could I ask you a couple of questions?"

"Oh, is this one of those surveys? I'm all the time reading about them, but nobody ever asked me anything before."

Simon smiled. "Well, this isn't exactly like that. How long have you lived here?"

"Close to twenty years now."

"You wouldn't happen to remember a man who used to live here by the name of John Griffith?"

"John? Of course I remember him. A nice boy." Her face turned anxious. "I hope he's not in trouble?"

"I hope not. He lived here with another man, right?"

"Yes, that would be Mr. McCarthy. I didn't know him so well, but I think he must have been a good man."

Simon was leaning against the wall. He lit a cigarette. "Why do you think so?"

"Because John thought so highly of him. Every other word from that boy was 'Mac says this' or 'Mac says that.' " She frowned a little. "I hope John is all right. He was such a sweet boy."

Sweet?

The old lady didn't know any more than that. He thanked her and walked back down to the sidewalk.

Simon was feeling very good. He whistled a little as he got into his car. Won't be long now, Johnny, he thought cheerfully. I can almost touch you now.

Do you feel me getting close, babe?

**Book
III**

-ONE-

Waking up.

There was, as always, that first terrifying moment, that initial instant of consciousness during which the fear still held him captive. Slowly the scene and its comfortable familiarity penetrated the sleep-fogged edges of his mind. The car was barreling down the highway into the darkness; Mac was driving; everything was okay. Johnny relaxed against the seat.

"Welcome back, Sleeping Beauty," Mac said. "Christ, I thought you'd died."

"Was I sleeping a long time?"

"Couple hours."

"I'm sorry." He felt guilty, knowing that Mac liked company as he drove. "I won't sleep anymore." Reaching for a cigarette with one hand, he punched the lighter in with the other.

Mac glanced over. "Thought you were gonna quit that," he said sourly.

Johnny pulled the lighter out and touched the glowing orange filament to the end of his cigarette. "You're a fine one to talk. You smoke like a chimney."

"I have a lot of bad habits, but that doesn't

mean you should have them, too."

"I don't want the rest of them," Johnny said mildly. "Just this one."

Mac swung the car out of the lane to pass a slow-moving eighteen-wheeler. "Well, it's your life."

"Right." They smiled at one another. The next few minutes passed in silence as Mac watched the traffic and Johnny concentrated on the smoke curling up toward the roof of the car. "Where are we going anyway?" he asked after a moment of thought.

"L.A." There was a sharp edge of irritation in Mac's voice. "You know that, Johnny. I already told you twice that we're going to Los Angeles."

Johnny flinched away from the tone. "I forgot," he said in a whisper.

"Well, for chrissake try to remember things like that, will you?"

"Okay, I'm sorry. Don't be mad." Johnny felt the familiar chill begin inside. His hand reached out, but stopped before it touched Mac, resting instead on the back of the seat.

Mac rubbed the bridge of his nose. "I'm not mad, Johnny. I just wish. . . ." He broke off. "Light one of those for me, willya?"

"Sure." Pleased to be of some use, Johnny devoted his full attention to the task, and not until the cigarette was stuck between Mac's lips did he speak again. "What do you wish, Mac?"

"I don't know." Now his voice just sounded tired. "I need some coffee," he said abruptly. "There's a truck stop."

It was late and there were only a few customers in the diner. The interior was all white formica and the waitress looked like she'd been on her feet since early morning. After they'd ordered, Johnny dug some coins out of his pocket and went over to the jukebox. He punched up several selections, then came back to the booth, sliding in across from Mac. They didn't talk much until the waitress had delivered Mac's coffee and Johnny's lemon meringue pie and Coke. "I'm really sorry that I forgot where we're going," Johnny finally said, watching as his fork penetrated the stiff white meringue.

A Billy Joel song was playing in the background. "It doesn't matter, kid," Mac replied.

But Johnny wanted to explain. "I try to remember things, but they just seem to get lost in my head sometimes."

"I know, Johnny. Don't worry about it."

He ate the pie slowly, aware that Mac was watching him. After a few more moments, a new song began on the jukebox. Delighted with his surprise, Johnny grinned. "There."

"What?"

He waved the fork in the direction of the music. "I played that song for you."

Mac looked puzzled. "What is it?"

"Nat King Cole. You told me that you liked Nat King Cole."

"I did? When?"

He licked lemon pudding from the fork. "A long time ago."

Mac shrugged.

Anxiety replaced Johnny's pleasure. "That's right, isn't it? You do like him, don't you?"

"Sure," Mac said quickly. "He's one of my favorites."

Johnny relaxed again.

In a few more minutes they left the diner, but

instead of pulling back onto the highway, Mac drove around behind the building and parked again. "I want to try and get some sleep," he explained, leaning back against the seat. "Just an hour or so."

"Okay," Johnny said agreeably. He lit another cigarette.

Mac's eyes were closed. "Johnny?"

"Huh?"

"Thanks for playing the song."

A warm feeling rushed through him. "Sure, Mac. And I'll try not to forget so many things."

"Hell, you remembered about me liking Nat King Cole. Don't worry about it." He smiled, his eyes still closed, and in a minute he was asleep.

It was quiet then, except for the faint and reasuring sound of Mac's snoring. White-silver waves of light from the moon washed over the scene, enveloping them in an aura of unreality that Johnny could feel, if not define. He watched Mac, noticing with solemn wonder how sleep eased the worry lines from the craggy, familiar face.

Los Angeles. Los Angeles, California. He wouldn't forget again. Mac would be proud of how well he could remember things when he tried. Johnny wanted Mac to be proud of him. Or at least not to be mad at him. Mac's anger was an earthquake that shook the foundations of Johnny's world. He sighed, resolving yet again to be better, to do nothing that would disappoint Mac, or make the green eyes flash with lightning. Resting one hand lightly on the other man's lean arm, Johnny solemnized the promise. Mac stirred a little in his sleep, almost seeming to turn toward the touch.

Sometimes Johnny tried to remember what his

life had been like before, but it was all just a barren landscape inhabited by grey, indifferent figures hovering always just beyond his reach. No one ever touched him. His father, one of the indistinct memories, used to talk about Jesus a lot. That much Johnny remembered, and in the old man's words Christ was an incandescent being, a brightness that cut through the darkness of human existence. Johnny had never seen the Lord, though, never felt the pull, never understood what his father had been talking about.

But now he knew.

Mac was the golden light, the savior, the epicenter of Johnny's being, and his benign approval was like a long swallow of cool spring water to a parched man. Johnny sometimes yearned inside, without knowing what it was he craved, desired without knowing why. But for now he was content to sit in the bathing calm of the moonglow, watching as Mac slept, letting the night wrap around them like a blanket.

He moved a little closer and rested against Mac. The other man stirred restlessly, patting Johnny's shoulder. "S'okay, kid," Mac mumbled sleepily.

Johnny sighed. He dared a little more, draping one arm across Mac's chest. The sleeping man moved into the embrace, murmuring something that Johnny couldn't quite hear. It didn't matter. He smiled and closed his eyes.

-TWO-

He sat in the motel room, watching M⋆A⋆S⋆H, and waiting for Mac to come back with the hamburgers. It seemed to be taking a very long time. Johnny got up from the bed a couple of times and walked over to peer out the window. Sometimes, he knew, Mac got sort of distracted and ended up playing cards or something when he was supposed to be running an errand. Usually, Johnny didn't mind, but tonight he was awfully hungry. And a little lonely.

At last, Johnny heard the sound of the key in the lock and the familiar lanky figure came into the room. His relief was reflected in a wide smile. "Hi."

Mac grunted a reply and dropped a paper bag of food and a six-pack onto Johnny's bed. "Goddamned place was busy," he muttered, pulling off his windbreaker.

Johnny's smile slowly faded. "What's the matter?"

"Nothing."

"You act like there is," he insisted.

Mac finally sat down, too. "I have a headache, that's all. Don't worry about it."

Johnny nodded, accepting that, and opened the sack. "Eat something," he ordered. "You'll feel better."

"Yeah? You sure about that?"

"That's what you always tell me." Johnny smiled again and this time Mac returned it.

"Guess I'm just tense," Mac said, chewing the rubbery hamburger thoughtfully. "We've been sitting in this damned room for three days, and the contact hasn't been made. Shit, I hope this job didn't fall through."

"If it did, there'll be something else." Johnny was carefully squeezing catsup on his french fries.

"Better be. We're almost broke."

Johnny turned the volume up on the TV. "Don't worry so much," he mumbled. "You'll get an ulcer."

Mac popped open a can of beer and took a long drink. "If I don't worry, who will?"

"Want me to for a while?"

"Hah, you're too dumb to worry," Mac said, shoving the rest of the hamburger back into the sack.

Johnny shrugged and finished the meal in silence. When they were done, he gathered all the trash and shoved it into the wastebasket. "Feel better?"

"No."

Johnny frowned. "You mad at me, Mac?"

Mac shook his head.

"You sure? Because if I did something wrong, I'm sorry, really, I—"

Mac stood abruptly. "Johnny, I'm not mad." He sighed, running a hand through his hair. "I keep saying the same things, don't I?" The words seemed to be directed more at himself than at Johnny. "Year in and fucking year out. Are you as tired of it all as I am?" He stared at Johnny, who only looked back at him, having no idea what Mac wanted him to say, and long ago having learned that in such a case, it was best to keep his mouth shut. "Shit," Mac said finally.

"Yeah," Johnny agreed, not really understanding what was going on, but knowing instinctively that the worst of Mac's mood had passed. He opened a can of beer for himself and another for Mac. It was quiet again as they sat watching TV.

At last, Mac crushed out his cigarette and drained the last of the beer. "I've got a game," he said.

"Okay. Good luck."

"Oh, sure." Mac smiled a good-bye. "See you later."

"Uh-huh."

He left and the room seemed too quiet. Johnny tried to concentrate on a cop show, but the silence seemed to press in on him unbearably. After a few minutes, he grabbed his jacket and fled, leaving the loneliness behind.

The harsh vibrations of downtown Los Angeles closed around him as he moved through the crowd of night people that cluttered the sidewalks around the bars and discos. The noise and movement of the scene surrounded him, and he relaxed a little, losing himself in the safety of anonymity.

What he really wanted to do was see a movie, but he stopped in front of several rundown theatres, and they were all showing the same kind of film. The posters were of fierce-looking black men towering over frightened white men, or of Oriental martial arts experts practicing their skills on still more hapless whites. Johnny wished he could find one of the westerns he liked, the kind with lots of loud music and heroes that talked through clenched teeth.

He finally gave up on the idea of a movie, and went into a drugstore for a candy bar and a copy of *TV Guide*. As he left the store, already eating the chocolate, he got the feeling that someone was following him. It wasn't the first time lately he'd felt that way, but when he turned around, no one seemed to be paying any special attention to him, so he shrugged and walked on.

A young black kid approached him. "Hey, man."

They were standing on the corner, waiting for the light to change. "Hey," Johnny replied, wishing that the boy didn't look quite so much like one of those movie posters.

"You looking for some action?"

"What?" Johnny was staring at the pavement.

"I got what you need."

"I don't . . . uh, no. Thanks." The words were a painful whisper.

"Come on, man, everybody needs something. Girls? Boys? Uppers? Downers?"

The light changed at last, and Johnny plunged out into the street, trying to escape. He kept moving, not looking back, until finally he could duck into the safety of a coffeeshop. The booths were all filled, so he sat at the counter, giving his order in a breathless voice, trying to stop the helpless trembling of his hands.

When the waitress brought his dish of ice cream, he opened the *TV Guide* and bent over its familiar pages gratefully.

"What flavor is that?" a voice asked suddenly.

Johnny, still edgy, jumped a little. "Huh?"

"That ice cream looks good. I was just wondering what kind it is."

The man had a friendly grin, and Johnny managed a faint smile in return. "Oh. It's boysenberry ripple. It *is* good," he added.

"I'll take your word for it." The guy summoned the waitress and ordered.

Johnny glanced down at his magazine, wondering if it would be rude to start reading again. "There's a Humphrey Bogart movie on tonight," he said finally.

"Yeah? He's great. They don't make movies like that anymore."

He sounded really interested and Johnny gained a little courage. "I like westerns best, though," he said eagerly.

"Me, too." The man sampled the ice cream. "Hey, this is good." He looked at Johnny. "You live around here?"

Some of the panic returned. That was the worst part about talking to people; sooner or later, they always asked questions, and he never knew what to say. If he said the wrong thing, Mac would get very mad, so it was best not to talk at all. "I gotta go," he mumbled, slipping from the stool. "Bye."

Not waiting for an answer, he jammed the *TV Guide* into his jacket pocket and hurried away, feeling the man's eyes boring into his back as he went.

He watched the Bogart movie until Mac came in. The evening had left Johnny feeling vaguely unsettled and nervous. He watched by the glow of the TV as Mac undressed and got into bed. "How was the game?"

"Okay. I broke even."

"That's good." He sighed and turned off the television.

"Don't you want to watch the rest of the movie?"

"No." He pulled off his jeans. "I'm tired. Can I sleep with you tonight?"

As always, Mac just nodded, scooting over to make room. Johnny slipped in next to him, feeling some of the tension drain from his body at the familiar warmth of the shared bed. "You okay, kid?" Mac sounded worried.

"Uh-huh."

"Sure?"

Johnny nodded. "Yeah." He pulled the sheet up a little. "There were sure a lot of people walking around tonight."

"Did somebody bother you, babe?"

"No." He sighed. "Good night, Mac."

Mac muttered a reply. He lit a cigarette, and Johnny fell asleep watching the orange glow in the darkness.

-THREE-

His first big break came in Vegas. A rumor was circulating about a hit about to come down in Los Angeles. An intra-company squabble had been going on for months, and it was about to come to a halt. Somebody was going to play the role of sacrificial lamb.

Simon couldn't get a line on who was supposed to carry out the hit, but it sounded like the kind of thing Johnny might be involved in, so he headed for L.A.

It was the Sunset Strip hooker who put the final piece of the puzzle into place. Her name was Chrissie. Or Kristy. Something like that. The bar was filled with noise and smoke, and he wasn't really listening anyway. The meeting might have been accidental, just another of the quick encounters that took place every night in the bar. But it wasn't.

Someone pointed her out to Simon, remembering having seen her with a gambler named Mac on at least one occasion. So he picked her up, bought her a couple of drinks, left with her. They walked to her place. Once they were sitting on the couch, drinks in hand, Simon pulled out the police draw-

298

ing of Mac. It was creased and bent from the months in his wallet. "You know this guy?"

She studied it, then shrugged. "Yeah, I've seen him a couple times. "Alec. Or Alex. Something like that." As she spoke, she began to undress.

"When'd you see him last?" Simon unbuttoned his shirt.

"Couple days ago." She stood and pulled off the rest of her clothes. Wearing only bra and panties, she padded into the bedroom.

Simon followed. "You know where he's living?" he asked, piling his clothes on a chair.

"Nope." She climbed into bed. "He was playing cards with Tony DePalma, though."

He stretched out next to her, trying to remember when he'd last had sex. Not since his wife. Kimberly. A long time ago. But even so, he moved against the naked body almost absently. His hands kneaded her breasts slowly. "What was he like?" he whispered past blonde strands.

"Who?"

"Alex McCarthy."

"He was okay. Good." She squirmed. "At least he didn't talk about some other guy while we were screwing."

Simon ignored that. "He tell you anything about himself?"

"No," she said through clenched teeth.

His body continued to move against hers. If Mac was in town, Johnny had to be as well. It began to look as if the rumors he'd heard in Vegas were true.

She was wriggling beneath him, making urgent little sounds.

Simon was thinking about Johnny. Who did he screw in Los Angeles? He thought about that as his

body drove with increased urgency into
Chrissie/Kristy, the girl Mac had screwed. Ahh,
Johnny, he thought, it's almost over now. Pretty
soon, kid, pretty soon.

Johnny was somewhere in the city and Simon
wondered if he knew how close the end was.

It wasn't at all what he'd expected. His first sight
of John Paul Griffith caused a surge of bewildering
emotions inside him.

The final steps had been so simple, really. It took
only a couple of hours to track down DePalma. A
few questions and a few dollars persuaded him to
reveal the make and color of Mac's car; a few more
dollars pried loose the name of a motel where Mac
might possibly be staying.

He waited outside the motel that night, waited
until the door opened and John Paul Griffith came
out. Simon lit a cigarette, his hands trembling, and
got out of his car.

He followed the tall thin blond for almost two
hours, watching him move through the city like a
phantom. The encounter with the young black
pimp was curious, because Johnny seemed scared
by the boy. It seemed out of character for a sea-
soned hitman to be afraid of an under-age street
hustler.

Simon's confusion grew when he sat down at the
coffeeshop counter next to Johnny. Their conversation was so brief and so totally absurd—ice
cream and Humphrey Bogart—yet there was something beyond the brevity and absurdity of the con-
frontation that stayed with him. He knew fear
when he saw it, and there was a lot of it in the pale
blue eyes.

After following Johnny back to the motel and picking up his car, Simon went to his own cheap room and sat glumly over a six-pack, trying to wash away the taste of that damned ice cream, staring at the old mugshot. Johnny was a cold-blooded killer and no one knew that better than Simon, but he looked more like a scared kid who needed . . . needed what?

Simon Hirsch didn't know.

Shit, he thought, I don't even know what *I* need.

It occured to him that he should have been celebrating. For such a long time he'd been hunting this man. He'd lost track of the times he'd criss-crossed the country. No more job. No more family. No more anything, except the mugshot and his need to find John Griffith. And so this evening they met over boysenberry ice cream and talked about Bogart.

He threw an empty beer can across the room. It hit the wall and fell with a clatter to the uncarpeted floor. He opened another can. What was it his brother Manny the Wise had said? "And what then?"

"Yeah," Simon said to the mugshot. "What now, Johnny?"

He was waiting outside the motel again the next night. He saw Alex McCarthy come out first. The lean figure in the dark windbreaker paused long enough to light a cigarette, and in the sudden flare of the match, Simon could see the sharp-featured face and thin, ascetic lips. That, he thought, was the face of a killer. McCarthy tossed the match aside and got into the pale blue BMW. Simon stepped back into the shadows as the headlights swept the lot and then vanished.

It was only a few minutes later when Johnny came out. Ducking his head and shoving both hands into the pockets of his jeans, he walked toward the nearby bright lights and noise, apparently unaware that he was being followed.

The routine was much the same as it had been the night before. Johnny walked slowly along the main drags, window shopping, pausing in front of every movie theater to check out the attraction, then moving on. They might have been the only two people in the city. Simon sensed an almost unbearable loneliness in the slumped shoulders and impassive face he caught glimpses of in the windows they passed.

Loneliness, after all, was something he was sort of an expert on.

When at last Johnny went into a penny arcade, Simon followed. The blond paused in front of a U-Drive-It machine, not noticing as Simon approached. "Hi, there," he said, grinning.

Johnny spun around. "Huh?"

Christ is he strung tight, Simon thought. "Remember me? We met last night. Boysenberry ice cream?"

Johnny seemed to relax a little. "Uh, yeah, I remember. Hi."

"We seem to cover the same territory."

"I guess." He glanced around, obviously looking for an escape route.

Simon moved a little closer. "Don't take off again, man," he said.

Johnny blushed. "I only . . . I. . . ." He shrugged.

"You any good at that?" Simon asked, gesturing toward the game.

"Yeah, I am." Seeming relieved at the chance to

do something besides talk, Johnny slipped a quarter into the machine and began to manipulate the toy car skillfully through the treacherous path. He completed the game with a perfect score.

Simon grinned approvingly. "Hell, man, you're a frigging expert."

"It's easy. You try."

Simon dug for a coin and took his turn, but he sent the vehicle skidding off a mountain road and fell to a fiery death. "Oh, well," he said with a shrug. "Guess I better stay out of the mountains."

Johnny gave him an uneasy half-smile, then started edging toward the door.

Simon almost grabbed him by the arm; instead, he spoke quickly. "I'm hungry. You wanna split a pizza? Oh, by the way, my name is Simon."

After a pause, Johnny took the proferred hand and shook tentatively. "John," he whispered.

"So? How about a pizza?"

Johnny checked the time. "Well, I guess it'd be okay."

They walked about half-a-block to a small beer and pizza joint. It was crowded, but they managed to find a table near the back. Simon kept getting the feeling that Johnny was about to vanish, take off like a frightened deer might disappear into the woods, so he kept his voice calm and made no sudden moves.

Once the beers and pizza were on the table in front of them, Johnny relaxed a little. Simon pulled a slice of pizza off the tray. "This is a lonely city, isn't it?" he said. The words surprised him; he hadn't intended to say that.

Johnny looked blank.

"I mean, if you don't have any friends," Simon

added lamely. The cheese burned his tongue and he took a quick gulp of beer.

Johnny was bent over the table, concentrating on the food. "I have a friend," he said after taking a bite and swallowing. Then an anxious look appeared in his eyes, as if he'd said something wrong, and he took another bite.

"Yeah? That's nice." Simon lifted a piece of pepperoni and ate it slowly, remembering the dangerous face he'd seen in the match glow earlier. Some friend, kid, who keeps you so scared all the time. "I haven't been in L.A. very long," he offered in a moment. "I'm from back east."

Johnny looked up. "New York?"

"I've been there, yeah."

"We used to live in New York." There was an edge of nostalgia in the words.

"Too crowded." Simon poured them each more beer from the pitcher.

"I didn't mind so much," Johnny said thoughtfully. "I liked the ferry boat. We used to ride out to Staten Island and back sometimes. That was fun." He looked even younger suddenly, and Simon wondered, fleetingly, if maybe this was all a mistake. Johnny Griffith was no killer. He was just a nice, shy kid. Then the blond frowned, as if some of his memories weren't so pleasant. "There were some really terrible people there, though."

"What'd they do?"

Johnny only shrugged. He checked the time again. "I better go."

"It's early yet. Want to take in a movie or something?"

But he shook his head. "No, I hafta be there when . . . well, I better go."

They split the check evenly and walked outside. "Maybe we'll run into each other again, John."

"Maybe so," he said, not sounding like he gave a damn. He nodded, shoved both hands into his pockets and walked off quickly.

Simon waited a moment, then followed, keeping out of sight all the way back to the motel. Once there, he sat in the shadows and waited. It was nearly two hours before the BMW pulled into the lot and McCarthy got out.

Simon could tell from the studied care in the man's walk that he was drunk. He dropped the key trying to insert it into the lock, then just pounded on the door instead.

Simon could see Johnny in the doorway, helping McCarthy across the threshold, then bending to pick up the fallen key. The door closed. All he could see then were two dark shadows behind the curtains. After a few more minutes, the light went out.

Simon waited a little longer, then he crept to the window, and tried to see into the room. The only thing visible was the tiny orange glow of a cigarette. There was some soft-voiced conversation, but he couldn't make out any of the words. What could they talk about, the hawk-faced assassin and Johnny?

After a few more minutes, he got into his car and left. Instead of going back to his motel, he drove all the way down to the beach and parked. Staring out over the moon-washed water, he thought about the evening. It had been so damned long since he'd just sat and had a few beers and rapped with somebody.

He pulled his wallet out and flipped it open to

the picture of Mike Conroy. None of the old feelings were left; sometimes he'd almost forgotten why he was looking for John Paul Griffith.

Now he had Griffith.

"Then what?" said Manny the Wise.

Now what.

He reached into the glove compartment and took out the envelope with the mugshot in it. What, he wondered again, did Johnny and McCarthy talk about?

Poor Johnny. How could somebody who was really just an over-grown kid defend himself against a killer like McCarthy?

Simon stayed on the beach until dawn.

-FOUR-

The shrill, impatient ringing of the phone pulled Mac up from the heavy, hung-over sleep. He rolled over, reaching for the offending instrument, and saw Johnny sitting across the room, fully dressed. "Why'nt you answer the fuckin' thing?" he mumbled, lifting the receiver. "Yeah?"

"Mac?"

"Yeah? So?"

"Be out at the beach. Usual place. One o'clock." The man hung up.

Mac dropped the phone and closed his eyes again.

"I figured it was business," Johnny said softly. "I don't know anything about that."

"You know how to say hello, don'tcha?"

"I'm sorry."

"Yeah, yeah, can it. Shit, my head is splitting."

Johnny got up and went into the bathroom, coming back a moment later with the aspirin bottle and a glass of water. "Here," he said.

Mac took six of the aspirin and gulped them down at one time. "Thanks." He lay back to give the pills time to work. "Good thing that bastard called," he said. "I dropped it all last night."

"Run of bad luck, huh?" Johnny asked sympathetically.

Mac laughed, then grimaced as his head pounded in reaction. "Yeah, you could say that. A run of bad luck. That's what they're going to carve on my headstone. Here lies Alexander McCarthy. He had a run of fucking bad luck." He rubbed at his forehead. "Hell, the way I feel, they might be carving it today."

Johnny sat down again. "You shouldn't make jokes about dying," he said sternly.

"I wasn't joking." He sat up suddenly, staring at Johnny. "You ever think about dying, kiddo?"

"No. Not very much."

Mac hated philosophical discussions, especially with Johnny, most particularly when his head was being ripped apart from the inside. Still, maybe it was important that Johnny be forced to look cold, hard reality in the face every once in a while. Besides, he felt so goddamned rotten that it only seemed fair that Johnny should suffer a little, too. "Well, you better think about it," he muttered. " 'Cause someday we're gonna get blown away. Or else we'll get busted and sentenced to about seventeen life terms apiece."

Johnny seemed to think about that for a while. He frowned, wiping both palms on his jeans. "They won't put us in different places, will they?" he asked very quietly.

Mac sighed, already regretting that he'd ever gotten into this whole conversation. "No, Johnny," he said with bitter weariness. "I'm sure they'll give us one cozy cell."

"Well, that's okay then." Johnny's voice was placid.

The scary part was that Mac knew Johnny really meant that. After a moment, he rolled off the bed and staggered toward the bathroom. "I gotta go to the beach," he said before closing the door. "If you want, you can come."

"Okay."

Mac showered and shaved, managing to come alive a little in the process. Johnny was staring at some game show on TV, but he turned his head to watch as Mac got dressed. "Mac?" he said in a dreamy voice.

He pulled his jeans up and snapped them. "Huh?"

"If I get blown away, will you be okay?"

Mac pulled his teeshirt on with a sudden jerk and stared at Johnny's reflection in the mirror. "What?"

"I said, if I get—"

"I *heard* what you said," Mac broke in. "I'm just trying to figure out what the hell you're talking about."

Johnny's face was solemn. "I was just thinking, is all."

Mac swore under his breath and started combing his hair. "Look, man, I told you years ago to leave the thinking to me. By any chance do you remember that?"

Johnny nodded. "Yeah, I remember."

"All right then. Do it. Okay?"

In a minute, he nodded again. "Okay, Mac." A grin split his face. "Could I swim while we're at the beach?"

"Sure. Let's go now, so you'll have plenty of time."

Johnny pulled his swimming trunks on, then

donned his jeans again, and they were ready to go.
On the way out of town, Mac stopped at a drive-in
for some coffee to drink en route. Johnny had a
large orangeade.

His head felt slightly more normal by the time
they'd reached the beach, parked, and walked
down to the water's edge. He sat cross-legged on
the sand, watching idly as Johnny went to swim.
What they had to do, he decided, was just get a
fucking little ahead, and clear out. Maybe go to
Mexico and forget all this ever happened. This life
was rotten. Just a goddamned little ahead, that was
all.

Johnny was a good swimmer, and he especially
liked it when the breakers crashed over him,
submerging him completely. Everytime it happened, Mac—who disliked water in large bodies—
watched apprehensively, not even aware that he
was holding his breath, until the drenched blond
head appeared again, glistening golden under the
sun.

At last Johnny apparently had enough. He
jogged across the sand and dropped down next to
Mac. "Have fun?" Mac asked, lifting his sun-
glasses to look at him.

"Yeah, felt good." He shook his head vigorously
and drops of water hit against Mac. "I'm hungry."

"You're always hungry." Mac glanced at his
watch. "I gotta meet a guy. I'll bring you back an
ice cream."

"Okay. Chocolate, please." Johnny stretched
out on the sand, using one arm to shade his face.

Mac got to his feet, then stood still for a moment, staring down at Johnny. "See you."

Johnny smiled, but didn't say anything.

The man was standing by the boardwalk rail, reading a newspaper, which he folded when Mac appeared. "Hello, Mac. It's been a long time."

"A year," Mac replied.

"You're looking good."

Mac leaned against the rail and stared out across the crowded beach, trying to spot Johnny. He couldn't. "You have the envelope?"

"I have it, I have it. You're always in such a hurry."

"Time is money," he said absently.

"A man should never be too busy for the amenities. How is John?"

"John is fine."

"Good, good." The man took a manila envelope from his pocket. "All the usual information is in here."

Mac put the envelope away without looking at it. "And the usual money, of course?"

"Of course."

"All right." He turned to go.

"What's the rush?"

Mac paused. "John wants an ice cream."

He smiled. "Oh, well, by all means, you must go. Immediately. We want to keep John happy, don't we?"

Without answering, Mac walked away.

They both stayed in that night. Johnny stretched out on his bed watching *Charlie's Angels* and *Vegas*, as Mac studied the data on their target. It was late by the time he finished. The *Tonight Show* was on, with one guest host or another, but Johnny, his face a little red from the sun at the beach, had fallen asleep. Mac undressed slowly, turned off the TV, and got into bed.

He smoked two cigarettes, but still couldn't fall asleep. At last, he got up and crawled into bed with Johnny. Sometimes, when his own demons seemed a little too close for comfort, sharing the night helped.

Tonight, though, some vague thought kept nagging at his mind. He tossed and turned until Johnny finally stirred. "What's wrong?" he mumbled.

"Nothing. Sorry I woke you." He wasn't really sorry; he was glad for the company

"That's okay."

Mac rolled over so that he could look into the face shadowed in the half-light. "Johnny?"

The blue eyes fluttered open again. "Hmm?"

"We're gonna get out of this. Soon. Before anything bad happens. Okay?"

"Okay, Mac."

"Don't be scared."

Johnny looked at him for a long moment, then smiled a little. "Don't you be scared either, Mac."

"Okay."

Johnny rested against the pillow. "Good night," he said.

"Night, babe," Mac replied.

The blond was asleep in moments. Mac sighed, resisting the urge to light another cigarette. Instead, he closed his eyes and tried to force himself to sleep. One hand absently stroked Johnny's bare arm.

Johnny made a soft sound and sighed in his sleep.

"Shh," Mac said, his lips pressed against soft blond strands.

It was a long time before he fell asleep.

-FIVE-

The next night he followed Johnny again, approaching him outside a theatre. Johnny returned his greeting with a hesitant smile. "Hi, Simon," he said, speaking in that soft voice that was so difficult to hear over the city noises.

Simon gestured toward the marquee. "Gonna see the movie?"

Johnny shook his head. "I thought they'd be changing the bill today, but it's still the same old thing."

"Well, then, how about grabbing a beer?"

After the usual hesitation, Johnny agreed.

The bar they chose wasn't too crowded this early in the evening, so they got a booth near the front. Simon waited until the beers were served. "How much longer you gonna be around town?" he asked suddenly.

The tactic worked. Caught off-guard by the abrupt question, Johnny shrugged. "Couple days, I guess. Depends."

Simon realized that the hit must be getting close; his nights were spent following Johnny, but his days were spent on McCarthy's trail. He knew who was going to be hit and he had a pretty good idea of when. "You travel a lot, huh?"

"Uh-huh." Johnny began to doodle in the wet patches on the table. "How come they don't have very many westerns anymore, I wonder," he said.

Simon took a sip of beer. "Guess not enough people like them." He glanced around, trying to come up with another line of conversation. "You play pool?" he asked, spotting a table in the back.

"No." Johnny looked up, brightening. "I like darts, though. One time I won thirty dollars playing darts."

"Well, I'm not that good, but how about a game?"

Carrying their beers along, they went into the back room. Johnny took first turn, aiming and throwing with a concentration that was total. Each shot was better than the last. Simon shrugged, grinning. "Hell, I might as well quit now."

"No, it's easy," Johnny urged. "Just pretend like you're aiming a gun."

Simon looked at him sharply, but the blue eyes were guileless as a child's.

They played for nearly an hour, betting pennies, until Johnny had accumulated almost two dollars worth. He gathered his winnings with the air of a man who watched his money carefully. Simon wondered about that. Hell, he and his pal were damned good, and they made damned good money for what they did. How come they lived like paupers? Of course, Mac was a gambler, and not too lucky. He also drove around in a fancy car. But what the hell did Johnny do with his share of their earnings? He had no car, no bad habits as far as Simon could see, and he dressed in old blue jeans and tennis shoes. Where did his money go?

That, of course, was a question Simon couldn't ask.

They ordered a couple more beers and found seats again. Simon was trying to sort out and understand his confused emotions. The man sitting across from him was a killer. A cold-blooded assassin in a teeshirt which read "Niagara Falls." Conroy was dead because of him. Simon tried to remember Mike's face, but the image was too blurry. The only face he saw was John Griffith's. With the hesitant, soft voice; the blue eyes, foggy and unfocused even behind the glasses; his painful shyness, Griffith was not at all what Simon had expected to find. Had wanted to find.

"What then?" Manny had asked.

Simon still didn't know. He resisted the urge to run to the nearest telephone and call Manny.

Johnny seemed to realize that he was being watched, and he raised his eyes. Their gazes met, locked, held for a full minute, before Simon looked away. The blue gaze was empty.

Mac spent about twenty minutes talking to her in the bar, then they left there and went to her place. Her name was Joanie, and she worked as a file clerk in a downtown office, and she was from Kansas originally. He drank a can of beer from her meager stock, watching as she undressed and released the aureate hair from its rubber band, to fall in soft locks over her shoulders. Her clothes were carefully folded and stacked on a chair. No wonder she was a file clerk. Her glasses were set to one side and her blue eyes studied him thoughtfully.

He got up, setting the beer can aside, and undressed.

"You don't say much, do you?"

He shrugged.

She gave up then, waiting silently as he finished the beer before getting into bed. He began to stroke her body, her face, tangling his fingers in her hair. She was moving beneath his touch, making soft gasping sounds as the fervor of his stroking increased.

His mind left her, left the crummy room, left even the more fevered movements of his own body. He began to think about the hit. Sunday morning, best time. Early, before seven. Then he and Johnny could be out of town early. Maybe they would go to Frisco. Or Vegas. If he could take the cash from this job and run it up a ways, they could quit. Say good-bye to the whole fucking world. Find a beach in Mexico and drink margaritas in the sun. The image filled his mind like a picture postcard. The sun, the peace. Johnny could swim all he wanted to in the perfect blue of the water.

Blue. Her blue eyes stared up at him, into his own gaze, and she probably though they were communicating on some deep level.

Johnny's eyes were blue.

He loved swimming and he was good at it, his slender form cutting gracefully through the water, golden under the sun.

Mac was in her now, thrusting, bracing himself against the bed. He began to build, gasping a little with each forward push, building, building. Sweat poured down his face, and he closed his eyes against it.

She arched upwards toward him, her soft sounds growing louder.

As he exploded inside her writhing body, he

opened his eyes, staring down into her face, with its two vague pools and tousled blonde hair. A chill stabbed through him, because all at once it wasn't her, this nameless broad, he was screwing.

It was Johnny.

His body finished its convulsive spasms, and he threw himself from her, huddling on the far side of the bed, staring blindly at the ceiling.

"Jesus," she sighed. "That was good."

Caught up in his own swirling thoughts, he didn't answer. Johnny. No. It was just some crazy dream. Christ, he didn't want to . . . to do that with Johnny. Not *Johnny*.

She rolled toward him, giving his still-heaving chest little kisses.

He ignored her.

Think, he ordered himself. It's just nerves. The hit coming down. Johnny's dumb conversation the day before about getting iced. Yeah, that was it. Nerves. Shit, that had to be it. *Johnny,* for chrissake. Hell, the guy had never been to bed with anybody. He was like a kid when it came to sex.

And I never wanted to do that with a guy, Mac thought. Never.

She was talking to him, but he couldn't seem to understand what she was saying. Hell, he decided, enough of this bitch. I gotta get home. A pizza, he thought as, still silent, he got out of bed and started dressing. I'll find Johnny, he never wanders too far, and we'll get a pizza. Take it home and watch one of those damned old movies on TV. Johnny would like that. And once he saw the kid, the dream image would vanish. Everything would be all right again.

"Maybe we'll see each other again," she—what

the hell was her name?—said hopefully.

He looked at her blankly, already unsure of what role she had played in his life. "Yeah," he mumbled.

He drove back to the motel first, but Johnny wasn't there. That didn't surprise him much; he knew Johnny's habits well. Leaving the car, he began to walk. Johnny would be surprised to see him. It would be enough to make him grin, probably. Poor dumb Johnny. Offer him a frigging pizza and some company and, Christ, you'd think the guy had just drawn a royal flush.

Mac shook his head, smiling a little. Never would be able to understand that kid.

He read the posters outside a couple of movies, but knew that Johnny wouldn't be interested in seeing the pictures advertised. Continuing his search, he tried the penny arcade and a couple of fast food joints. It was in a small, crowded bar that he finally saw Johnny. The blond head was like a beacon in the dimly lighted room, and Mac started over, figuring to have a beer here before getting the pizza.

It was then that he spotted the other guy, a slender, sharp-eyed man with a mass of dark curls falling into his face. The man was talking, smiling, gesturing. Johnny was listening, nodding. Almost smiling.

Mac felt a stabbing pain go through him. Johnny didn't see him standing there and he turned and walked out quickly. As he walked back to the motel, he shoved the pain aside, not understanding the hurt he felt, letting anger creep in to take its place. What the hell did that stupid son of a bitch think he was doing? He was so damned stupid that if he started talking, he might say something that could get them both busted or killed. Well, that was fine if he wanted to screw up his own life, that was fine, but the son of a bitch wasn't going to do it to him. No way.

Talking to some bastard in a bar. Jesus. The guy might be a cop, for all Johnny knew. Or a pervert of some kind. Serve Johnny right if something happened to him.

By the time he got back to the motel, Mac could feel the knot of tension in his gut. It hurt like hell. He dug a bottle of whiskey from his suitcase and sat in the dark room, smoking, drinking, staring at the door.

-SIX-

Johnny saw the car in the parking lot and quick-ened his step. Mac was home. His mood lifted; the loneliness vanished instantly. He opened the door and turned on the light, feeling his happiness be-come a smile. "Hi, Mac," he said.

Mac lifted an almost empty bottle and took a long drink, flicking a cigarette butt into the waste-basket. He didn't say anything at all. He only looked at Johnny with eyes that were two chips of green ice.

Johnny's smile lost a little of its brightness. "You came back so early. I'm really glad. There's a Cagney movie on. Will you watch it with me?"

Mac stared at him. Stared through him. "What the hell do you think you're doing?" His voice was like ice water rolling over Johnny.

Johnny took off his jacket and tossed it aside. "I don't understand, Mac," he said very softly.

"Don't you? Don't you understand?" Mac's voice rose.

Johnny sank down onto the bed in front of Mac. "Are you mad at me? Did I do something wrong, Mac? Because if I did, I'm sorry—"

Mac hit him. The open-handed slap across the

face was so unexpected that it knocked Johnny half off the bed. Slowly he pushed himself back up to a sitting position. "Please, Mac," he whispered. "I'm sorry."

"Yeah? Yeah?" Mac grabbed him by both shoulders. "Don't look at me like that, you bastard, you idiot, you—"

"Mac?" Johnny tried to escape from the vise-like grip, but Mac dragged him back and hit him several more times across the face, knocking his glasses off. Johnny was crying now, making no effort to defend himself.

"I saw you talking to that bastard. Who is he?" Each word was punctuated by a slap.

"Just Simon."

"Who is he?"

"Just a guy, Mac. Just somebody I talk to. He hangs around, like me." Johnny tried to grab Mac's hand. "Please don't hit me again. I didn't do anything wrong. I never said a word I shouldn't. Don't be mad."

"How do you know what you said?" Mac formed a fist and it collided with Johnny's gut. Johnny bent over with a retching gasp. "You're so stupid you don't even know what you're saying half the time." He hit Johnny again.

"Mac, I'm sorry, I'm sorry, so sorry, please don't be mad at me." Blood gushed from his nose and ran down into his mouth.

"You want to get us killed or busted?"

Johnny shook his head. "No, no," he moaned helplessly, blood and tears mingling on his face.

"Or maybe the guy is some kind of freako; did you ever think about that?"

"I don't understand."

"No? Don't you? Jesus, how can anybody be so damned stupid? How come I put up with you all these years? He could be some kind of sex creep. Maybe he wants to fuck you. Would you like that?" Mac stopped, breathing heavily. Something terrible passed through his eyes, something that Johnny couldn't understand. "Or maybe he already has. What have you been doing, creep? Huh?" He hit Johnny across the face again.

"No, please, no, Mac. . . ." Johnny felt an utter black terror filling him, a fear so overwhelming that it even obliterated the physical pain of the attack. He trembled uncontrollably, reaching out with both hands, trying desperately to grab onto Mac. He wasn't trying to escape from the beating; he only wanted to hold onto Mac and make this nightmare end. "Oh, please," he said in a hoarse whisper. "Oh, please."

Suddenly, Mac froze. His face lost all its color as he stared down at Johnny's huddled, bloody body. "*Ohchrist,*" he said. "Oh sweet Jesus." He crouched down and again his hand reached toward Johnny's face. This time, he only touched one cheek, a fleeting caress. Then he stood and left the room, slamming the door as he went.

Johnny crawled across the floor toward the door. "Mac," he whispered brokenly. "Mac, please, don't go . . . I'm sorry . . . Mac . . ." But the door stayed closed. Johnny leaned against it, crying silently.

It was nearly dawn before Johnny finally dragged himself up from the floor. Moving like an automaton, he changed from his bloodied clothes, putting on a pale blue T-shirt that was too big, meaning it must have been Mac's, and some clean

Levis. He washed his face and combed his hair, then grabbed his jacket and left the room.

He noted dully that the car was gone.

Mac was gone.

Johnny had no plan, no idea beyond that of finding Mac, of making him know how sorry he was for being bad, of having Mac come back. He had to come back, of course. There was no other way.

He walked for hours, all day, not stopping to eat or drink or rest his aching legs, covering the area, looking anywhere he thought Mac might be.

It was almost dark when he finally started back toward the motel. A block away, he nearly bumped into Simon.

Simon stared at him, a strange light flickering through his eyes. "What the hell happened to you?"

Johnny realized for the first time that his face was swollen and sore. "Nothing," he mumbled, trying to step around Simon.

Simon grabbed his arm, then released it immediately when Johnny flinched in a new spasm of fear. "Johnny, who hit you? Was it Mac?"

Johnny forgot that Simon wasn't supposed to know, couldn't possibly know about Mac. He just shook his head. "I can't talk to you. Go away and don't come around me anymore. Please." He spoke desperately. "Please." He started to walk again. "Just leave me alone so I can find Mac."

"He can't do that to you," Simon yelled after him. "You shouldn't let that son of a bitch treat you this way."

Johnny ignored him. The blue car was parked in its usual spot and he stopped by it, resting a hand on the hood, and drawing several deep breaths.

The door was unlocked and Johnny walked in.

Mac, shirtless and barefooted, was sitting on the bed. He raised his head slowly, looking at Johnny with reddened eyes. Neither of them spoke for a long moment. Johnny took a hesitant step toward him. "I'm sorry, Mac," he said softly.

Mac shook his head. "Don't," he said. "You didn't do anything. It was me. I know you never said a word to that guy about the business. I know nothing else happened." He lowered his gaze and stared at his hands; both palms turned upwards helplessly. "All you did was talk to him. It doesn't matter."

Johnny sat down next to him. "You ran out on me. I was scared."

Mac sighed. "I won't do it again."

"But I was scared."

After a moment, Mac lifted one arm and pulled Johnny into a loose embrace. "I'm so goddamned sorry, babe. It won't happen again, I swear."

Johnny nodded, accepting that. "Thank you."

Still holding him, Mac lay back on the bed. "God, I'm tired," he said heavily.

"Me, too." Johnny was quiet for a time. "Mac?" he said finally.

"Hmm?"

"Nobody ever did . . . what you were talking about."

"I know."

"Why did you say it, then?"

"Oh, shit, Johnny. I was mad. When I get mad and drunk, I don't know what the hell I'm saying." Now Mac was quiet, one hand rubbing across Johnny's back in long strokes. "Can I tell you something, kid?"

Johnny nodded.

"It's kinda weird." Mac seemed to think before speaking again. "I was with this broad last night, you know, screwing her."

"Yeah?" Johnny's voice was soft.

"But then I looked at her and . . . it wasn't her I saw."

Johnny raised his head and looked down into Mac's face. "Who was it, Mac?"

Mac swallowed twice. "You."

"Me?" Johnny bit his lower lip. Then he shrugged and rested back on the bed again, his head on Mac's shoulder. "That's funny," he said.

Mac seemed to be waiting for him to say something else.

Johnny sighed. "Can we go to sleep now, Mac? I'm so tired."

"Sure, kid. Go to sleep."

Johnny smiled faintly and closed his eyes.

Mac stared at the ceiling, aware of Johnny's weight pressed against his side, trying not to look at the bruised and battered face. There was so much to think about and so much of it was scary. He wanted to forget what he'd done, forget his despair during the last hours sitting here waiting for the kid to come back. Wondering if he *would* come back. That was a dumb thing to worry about. Shit, he could beat Johnny regularly, and still the guy wouldn't leave.

Poor Johnny.

Poor me, he thought.

But there wasn't anything he could do for either one of them. So he reached one hand to turn off the lamp and then he fell asleep.

* * *

He stood outside the window, waiting until the light went off. Driving back to his motel, he stopped at a red light. When the hooker approached, Simon gestured her into the car. They parked in an alley. There was only one thing she could do in the front seat of a VW, so she did it and he paid her twenty bucks.

Then he went to his room and went to sleep.

-SEVEN-

He made one more preliminary visit to Frost's apartment building, fixing it all firmly in his mind so that he could tell Johnny every detail. On the way back to the motel, he stopped and picked up a pizza for supper.

Johnny was watching a Randolph Scott movie on the television, but he sat up with a smile when Mac came in. "Hi."

"Hi, yourself," Mac replied, putting the pizza box down next to him. "Haven't you seen that before?"

"Yeah, but it's not too bad."

Mac took off his jacket and opened a couple of beers, then sat down with him. "You want to go see a movie after we eat?"

"Don't you have a game or someplace to go?"

"Nope, not tonight. We have to make an early start in the morning."

"Oh." Johnny was paying more attention to the food than to him.

Mac thrust a hand-drawn map in front of him. "You study this."

"Yeah, okay, soon as the movie's over."

He dropped the paper. They finished eating just

as the news came on. Johnny had no interest in that, so he turned the volume all the way down, leaving just the flickering picture. "I don't want to go anywhere," he said. "Can we just stay here?"

Mac shrugged. "Sure, if you want."

Johnny leaned back against the wall, studying the map. Mac watched him, looking at the still-visible traces of the beating. He sighed wearily, and Johnny lifted his head. "What's wrong?"

"Nothing. I'm just tired."

"Why don't you go to bed?" Johnny always had a logical solution for every problem.

"It's not that kind of tired, kid." He leaned forward a little, trying to ease the tension in his neck. "I've got this worn-out feeling that goes all the way through me. Don't you ever get tired of this whole mess?"

"Mess?"

"This life we lead. If you can call it a life."

"Oh." Johnny seemed to consider the question briefly, then shook his head. "I don't mind very much, Mac."

Mac wanted, suddenly, to make him understand just how rotten it all was. "Johnny, I've screwed us up so good. There's no way out. We're trapped and there can't be any happy ending. Not for us."

Johnny set the map aside and folded his arms, like a man fighting off a chill. "Don't talk about things like that, please. It scares me."

"It should. You ought to be damned scared. And it's all my fault." He got up abruptly and walked over to the window. "Christ, you should have put a bullet into *my* head years ago. We'd both be better off."

"I love you, Mac," Johnny said.

Mac was watching the cars go by out front and he only half-heard the soft words. "What?"

"I love you," Johnny said again.

This time the words reached him. Love? Mac wanted to laugh at the pathetic declaration. What the hell do you know about love, he thought. Shit, you're like a baby who can't tell where he begins and his mother leaves off. You don't know what love is. You only need me.

He turned around, wanting to say all that, and found himself staring into Johnny's face, into the absurdly blue eyes shining behind the glasses. But, he thought, if you don't love me, nobody does. All these years. He lifted his hand and ran two fingers through tousled blond hair. "I love you, too, kid," he said finally. "Very much."

"I know."

"Do you?" His fingers tightened in the soft strands. "Ahh, Johnny," he said. "I tried, you know? I wanted everything to be okay for us."

"It is okay, Mac, really."

Mac grimaced and turned toward the window again. "Why do you like to sleep with me, Johnny?" he asked quietly.

Johnny was a moment answering. "Because it feels good," he said.

Mac gave a bitter laugh. "Yeah, it does that," he agreed. "Sometimes it feels too damned good."

"I don't understand."

"Don't you?" Mac looked at him. "Let me tell you a secret, baby. I don't understand either."

"Does it matter a whole lot?"

Mac was surprised by the question; he thought about it, then shrugged. "Doesn't matter a goddamned bit," he said. "If it ever starts to matter, then we might have a problem." He rubbed the back of his neck. "Go to bed, kiddo. We have to get up early."

He watched as Johnny undressed and slid between the sheets, then he turned off the television and the lights. Sitting on the edge of the bed, Mac lit a cigarette. He sat there for a long time, smoking and watching Johnny sleep.

-EIGHT-

He woke up slowly, knowing that he had to move, but putting it off until the last possible moment. Johnny was sprawled next to him, still sleeping soundly. At last, Mac slid from the bed and began to dress. He put on grey slacks, a green knit shirt, the familiar battered windbreaker, and tucked the .45 into his pocket. "Johnny," he said, as he stood in front of the mirror to comb his hair.

Johnny stirred, then sat up quickly. "Huh?"

"Rise and shine, kiddo."

"Oh, yeah, right."

As Johnny washed and dressed, Mac packed all their belongings, so they wouldn't have to come back afterwards. He was tired of this room, this city, and only wanted to leave it behind as quickly as possible. He lit a cigarette and leaned against the door as Johnny donned the holster and pulled his jacket on.

Johnny turned with a smile. "I'm ready."

Mac nodded. They each carried a suitcase to the car. "You want to get some breakfast?"

Johnny thought about it, then shook his head. "After, I guess. Could use a Coke."

Mac drove through the parking lot, stopping at the office to pay their bill. On the way back to the car, he got a Coke from the soda machine.

"Thanks," Johnny said, taking the can from him. He slumped in the seat, his legs propped against the dash, and drank thoughtfully.

"You okay?" Mac asked.

"Uh-huh."

"Want to go to Vegas after?"

"Fine. Whatever you want."

"Well, I thought we might. I figured if we could double the money from this job, we could go to Mexico. Nobody would bother us there. You could swim, whatever. How does that sound?"

"Okay. Whatever you want."

Mac sighed. "What do *you* want, kid? Why does it always have to be my decision? Don't you have an opinion?"

Johnny glanced at him. "Sure, I have an opinion."

"Terrific. What is it?"

"I want to do whatever you want. That's my opinion."

Mac looked at him for an instant before turning his eyes back to the road. "Johnny, you're crazy."

"Yeah, I guess I am."

The car turned and went into the alley behind the apartment building. Mac stopped and shifted in the seat so that he was looking at Johnny. "I was kidding," he said. "You're not crazy."

Johnny shrugged. "I don't guess it matters very much one way or the other, does it?"

Mac reached out a hand and touched Johnny's arm. "You mad at me?"

A brilliant smile crossed Johnny's face. "Of course not. I never get mad at you."

"I don't know why the hell not."

He shrugged again. "Because."

Mac snorted. "A great reason."

"Maybe it's because I'm crazy."

It took him a moment to realize that Johnny was kidding. "Shit," he said. "Get your ass out of here. Be careful."

"Sure." Johnny got out of the car and walked up the path. It took him a little longer than usual to open the door, but then he gave the familiar V-for-Victory sign and disappeared inside.

It was exactly one minute later by the clock on the dash that Mac heard the shots. For one frozen, terrible instant, he sat still. It was the first time he'd ever heard the sound of gunfire at one of their jobs, and the echoing roars paralyzed him.

At last he moved, throwing his body out of the car and running toward the building, pulling the gun from his pocket as he ran. "Johnny!" His cry rang through the quiet morning air.

He burst into the hall and ran around the corner. The door to Frost's apartment was marked by several bullet holes. He had time to notice only that one fact before the door was flung open. Frost stood there, a small machine gun in his hands. Bullets began to spray the hallway.

Mac felt the lumps of hot metal crash against his body. He fell to his knees, dropping the gun. "Johnny?" he said again, this time in a whisper.

From behind him, someone fired a single shot, and Frost crashed to the floor.

Mac tried to crawl, but his body wouldn't do what he wanted it to. "Johnny?" he said through pain-filled gasps. "Babe, where are you?" He couldn't move.

A face appeared above him, vaguely familiar. It was the man he'd seen Johnny talking to in the bar. Simon. They looked at one another for a long moment. Mac kept watching as Simon picked up his fallen gun and left another in its place. "Hey," he managed to say, feeling the blood trail from his mouth. "Johnny?"

"Yeah," the guy said. "I know. He'll be okay."

Mac tried to shake his head. This guy didn't understand. Johnny needed him. But before he could try to explain all of that, he felt a sudden absence of pain, and a grey curtain began to descend slowly over his consciousness. I'm dying, he thought, surprised to realize that the knowledge saddened him. "I'm sorry, baby," he said in a loud, clear voice. Oh, damnit, he thought. This is so fucking stupid.

Simon closed McCarthy's eyes gently. He sat there numbly, only half aware of the screams coming from inside another apartment. His plan, such as it had been, went no further, and he didn't know what to do next.

The door to the garage suddenly jerked open with a crash. A primeval roar of naked pain filled the hall. Johnny, blood streaming from the cut on his head where Simon had hit him minutes before, half-crawled and half-ran to the body. "Mac?"

He threw himself across the bloody form. "Mac? Mac? Don't be dead, please, I'm sorry, I'm sorry, it's all my fault. Please, open your eyes, Mac. I love you, please don't be dead, please, Mac, pleaseplease. . . ." His words dwindled off, becoming soft, unintelligible moans, as his hands kept up their frantic stroking of the dead man's face.

Simon could hear the squeal of sirens in the distance. "Come on, Johnny," he said urgently. "We have to go. Come on." He took Johnny's arm with one hand, while his other reached in and took the wallet from Mac's pocket. He pulled on Johnny, but the crying man didn't move. Simon got impatient. "Come *on*," he said, jerking Johnny away, dragging him across the floor toward the garage.

"Mac? Mac?" Johnny kept up the whimpering pleas all the way to the car. Simon opened the passenger door and shoved him in. He ran around to the driver's side and jumped behind the wheel. They pulled out of the garage and drove around the corner just ahead of the first squad car.

He didn't relax until they were well away, heading toward the freeway, then he eased up on the accelerator. Johnny sat huddled against the door, still crying. He cried like a child, in long helpless sobs, making no effort to wipe the tears or his running nose. "It's okay," Simon muttered. "You don't have to be scared anymore. It's all over now, Johnny."

Johnny didn't say anything.

After another couple of minutes, Simon pulled the car over to the shoulder and stopped. He reached into the glove compartment for some tissues. "Here," he said.

The only response was a blank stare from red, tear-filled eyes.

Simon used the tissues to wipe Johnny's eyes and nose. "Now stop it," he said sharply, as if to a misbehaving child. "This isn't going to help. He's dead. That's all. Now stop it."

He didn't even know if Johnny heard him. The tissues went into a wadded heap on the floor and Simon started the car again.

They drove for a long time, stopping only once for gas and food. Johnny wouldn't eat, just stared at the hamburger until Simon, angry and frustrated, tore the sandwich into small pieces and fed them to him one by one. "Say something, Johnny, willya? You don't have to be afraid anymore."

He suddenly remembered something the cop in New York had told him, about Johnny's mute act the time he got busted. Well, Mac wasn't going to show up this time, so Johnny would just have to snap out of it on his own.

Simon squeezed Johnny's shoulder and shook him a little. "I did it for you," he said. "Don't you understand?"

Johnny only looked at him.

After vaguely heading south, Simon finally stopped at a motel very near the Mexican border. Johnny sat in the car while he registered, paying in advance with some of the cash from McCarthy's wallet.

The room was small and not too clean, but it didn't matter. Johnny sat on one of the beds, both hands folded in his lap, his face blank. Simon sat on the other bed, watching him. "We'll go to Mexico," he said finally. "Stay there a while, just in case anybody's on our tail. I don't think they are, though." He waited a moment, but there was no response, so he stood. "I'll go get some food. You wait here. Understand, Johnny? Stay here."

He paused long enough to turn on the television. An old rerun of *I Love Lucy* was on, and Simon saw that Johnny's eyes shifted to the screen, although his face remained blank.

The rest of the day and evening passed slowly. They ate in the room and watched television, all in silence, except for Simon's occasional remarks.

The late news came on, and Johnny sat impassively through the lead story of the double-murder in L.A. Even when an old army photo of Alexander McCarthy was flashed on the screen, Johnny did not react.

Simon walked over and turned the TV off. "We better get some sleep."

Johnny stood and began pulling off his bloody clothes.

Simon waited until the blond was between the sheets before undressing and crawling into the other bed. Once there, he rather surprised himself by falling asleep.

He didn't know how long he'd slept or exactly what woke him, but he was jerked into complete wakefulness immediately. Moonlight streamed into the room through the window. Johnny was standing in the middle of the room, his face still empty of emotion, his gun pointed at Simon's head. Simon felt his gut tighten, but his voice was cool when he spoke. "What the fuck are you doing, Johnny?" he asked mildly. There was no answer and the gun never wavered. "You're going to kill me, is that it? Gonna blow my head off, boy? Well, you just go right ahead. What the hell; my life ain't worth shit anyway. Not anymore." He stared into the pools of blue vagueness shining in the white moonglow. "But, Johnny," he went on tenderly, "if you kill me, what happens next? You'll be all by yourself. Do you want to be all alone, Johnny? Mac is dead. If you blow my head off, who's gonna take care of you? Being with me is better than being alone, right?"

It was two full minutes before the gun slowly lowered and then dropped to the floor. Johnny stood there, hands at his sides helplessly. Another minute passed before he spoke, the faint whisper so soft that Simon could barely hear him, even in the middle-of-the-night quiet. "We didn't bring my clothes," he said. "You'll have to buy me new clothes, because those are all dirty and I can't wear them anymore."

"In the morning, Johnny."

"Blue is my favorite color."

"Okay."

Johnny took a deep breath. "Can I get into bed with you?"

Simon stared at him. "What?"

"I don't like to sleep by myself." His voice shook a little and he stopped, rubbing his eyes with the heel of one hand. "Mac always let me."

After a moment, Simon nodded. "Okay," he said. He scooted over as far as he could in the narrow bed.

Johnny stretched out, not touching him, and they both stayed very still for a long time.

"Johnny?"

He turned his head and looked at Simon, but didn't say anything.

"Were you and Mac getting it on?"

"I don't understand," Johnny murmured vaguely.

Simon opened his mouth to explain, then only shrugged. "Never mind, kid. It doesn't matter."

Johnny turned over, so that his back was to Simon. In only a few minutes, his breathing had taken on the even rhythm of sleep. Simon reached across him for cigarettes and matches. Lighting one, he lay back and stared at the ceiling.

He was tired.

-EPILOGUE-

The Mexican sun was hot.

Simon lifted the can of beer and took a long drink. "I could maybe get a job with a security firm or something," he said thoughtfully. "What do you think?"

There was no answer from Johnny. Tanned and burnished gold from their long days on the beach, he was busy reading an old copy of *TV Guide* that some previous American tourist had left in the hotel room. He didn't even look up when Simon spoke.

Another gulp of beer. "We just have to decide where we want to go. East somewheres, I guess, huh?"

Loneliness, Simon had decided during the past three weeks, was sitting in a hotel room with John Griffith.

It was getting hotter as the sun moved toward its midday peak. Simon finished the beer in a gulp. "We better go in for awhile," he said. "I don't especially feel like getting heatstroke."

Obediently, Johnny closed the magazine and got to his feet. He carefully brushed the sand from his blue jeans.

"Chicago, maybe," Simon continued. "Let's think about Chicago, huh?" When Johnny didn't even look at him, Simon felt his fingers clench into a tight fist. "Goddamnit," he said suddenly, "goddamnit, Johnny. Can't you ease up just a little? Everybody else is gone. My partner. My wife and kid. They're all gone. Mac is gone. We can't bring any of them back, kid. It's just you and me now. Doesn't that make us even?" He kept both hands at his sides, wanting to reach out and grab Johnny and shake him until there was some kind of a response. He sighed. "There aren't any good guys in this story, Johnny. There's just one dumb Jew ex-cop and one spaced-out TV junkie." He almost wanted to laugh; it was so fucking stupid.

Johnny glanced at him. "Can I get an orange juice?" he asked.

Simon flexed his fingers. "Yeah, kid, sure."

"Thank you," Johnny replied politely.

Simon kicked at the sand. "Sure." He shoved both hands into the pockets of his khaki slacks and started toward the hotel. Johnny followed, humming some private melody. Simon thought that if this damned lonely feeling inside his gut didn't disappear he would lose his mind. He stopped walking. "Hey, Johnny, you want to see what's on at the movie tonight?" The hotel ran English language films once a week for the tourists. "How's that sound? We'll eat dinner someplace, then go to the movie. Maybe it'll be a western. What about it?"

"Okay, Simon," Johnny said. "Whatever you want." He ducked his head, watching as his feet moved through the sand.

Simon tilted his head back, staring up into the

flawless blue sky. He knew exactly what the rest of the day would bring. They'd go into the hotel bar. Johnny would get a large orange juice and punch up that damned Nat King Cole song on the jukebox. He always played the same song, time after time, until Simon sometimes woke up humming Mona Lisa. He'd spend the whole afternoon there with Johnny, drinking lousy cheap beer and waiting. He wasn't even sure what it was he kept waiting for. Maybe it was just for real life to begin again.

He sighed once more and started walking again, following Johnny across the beach.

THE END

WHY WASTE YOUR PRECIOUS PENNIES ON GAS OR YOUR VALUABLE TIME ON LINE AT THE BOOKSTORE?

We will send you, FREE, our 28 page catalogue, filled with a wide range of Ace paperback titles—we've got something for every reader's pleasure.

Here's your chance to add to your personal library, with all the convenience of shopping by mail. There's no need to be without a book to enjoy—request your *free* catalogue today.